Warrior's Blood Red

S. J. Reisner

Warrior's Blood Red

Sorcerers' Twilight Book Two

S. J. Reisner

Darkerwood Publishing Group
United States of America

Discounts are available for bulk orders of this title. Contact Darkerwood Publishing Group by e-mail at:

darkerwoodpublishing@gmail.com

or visit us at

http://www.ofs-demonolatry.org/darkerwood/

Library of Congress in Publication Data:
Reisner, S. J.
      Warrior's Blood Red
      ISBN 978-0-9669788-9-6
      First Trade Paperback Edition
      I. Fiction II. Fantasy

Cover Art © 2009 by Steven Lafitte

Dedication

For Matt, who gave me the laptop and the love, support and
motivation that helped Tnasha complete a successful
second adventure.   I love you.

Acknowledgements

Special thanks to Edwina, Connie, Lisa, Terry,
and everyone else who offered input,
encouragement, and an ear.

The West Ocean Mainlands

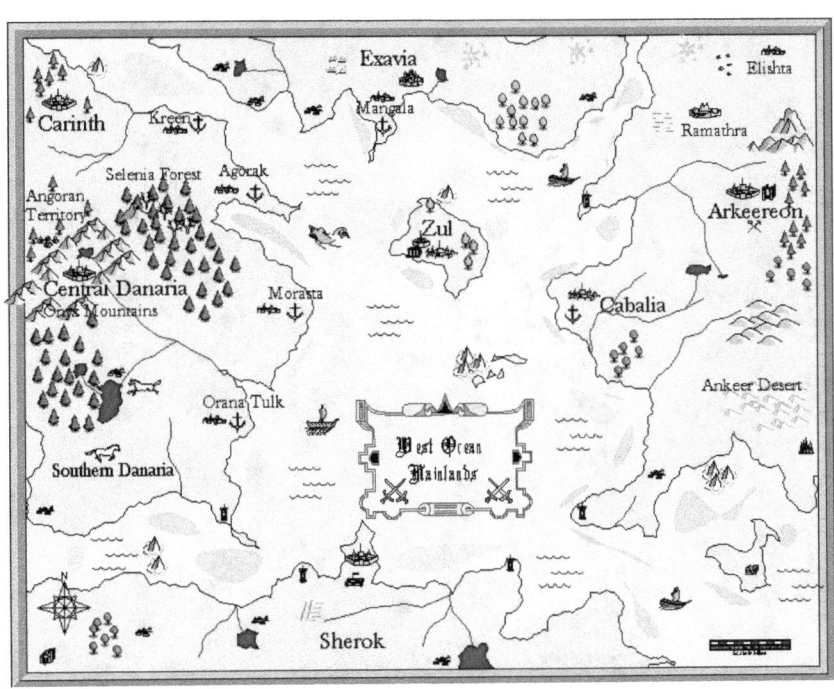

CHAPTER 1

"Sorcerer Kalath, why have you woken me?" High Priestess Caitlan pulled on a gold silken robe, the same color as the mana emanating from her skin, and crossed her arms over her chest. Her eyes bore into him expectantly.

"I apologize for the intrusion, especially at this late hour, Priestess Caitlan." Sorcerer Kalath paused, pulling the cowl hood of his robe from his head, uncovering the light blue hues of his own mana. He did not want to tell her what he had just seen amidst the black waters of his scrying bowl, but he had to. "The prophecy has begun."

The revelation stunned her to alertness and she frowned. She took a step backward. "How can we be sure?"

"I have seen the manifestation of the first prophecy with my own eyes."

"Whom is the prophecy centered around?" Priestess Caitlan ran a thin, well-manicured hand nervously through her brown hair, and picked up a glass of water from the foyer table. She took a sip.

"Tnasha fen Schoitt."

In response, the glass slipped from Caitlan's pale hand, falling to the marble floor, shattering. "But *she's* an *untrained* sorceress."

"Indeed. However, her natural abilities for sorcery surpass even yours. Trained, she will become a formidable adversary, and a sorceress to be feared. Even by us."

A low, resolute voice rang out from behind them. "Then she must be destroyed."

Kalath and Caitlan turned toward the voice. High Priest Graneck stood in the dark doorway. His silver mana moved around him in agitation.

Kalath responded first and quickly, knowing Graneck had always feared Tnasha's anomalous mana. "We cannot destroy her, Graneck. She's the one who can save us. In destroying her, we would be killing ourselves. Besides, I was only speaking figuratively when I said we should fear her. She will never sway her allegiance against Danaria and her own family."

"The question is whether or not she can complete the tasks prescribed by the prophecy and bring us peace." Caitlan stared off into the darkness.

"Surely there are others of our kind more qualified." Graneck leaned against the doorframe. "She's a young and inexperienced neophyte sorceress and a poor warrior at best."

Kalath tipped his head in thought, searching for the words that would put Graneck's fears at ease. "Perhaps she is. Even so, she has proven her resolve and fortitude. Her bravery is admirable."

Graneck rolled his eyes. "She was kidnapped by Kersians during what *should* have been a simple rescue mission."

"Ah, but she escaped the clutches of two adept Kersian sorcerers," Kalath said in defense.

"Who got away." Graneck shook his head and stepped into the hallway next to Caitlan, who looked small and frail next to her husband's tall, sturdy frame.

"Only because one of the Kersian sorcerers has the ability to appear and disappear as he pleases." Kalath found himself half tempted to turn and leave, but the situation was too important to allow a man like Graneck to deter him.

Graneck grunted disapprovingly. "What, exactly, happened on Zul?"

High Priestess Caitlan said nothing. She bent down and began picking up the shards of broken glass. With shaking hands, she tossed the shards into a silver bowl on the foyer table.

"It looks as though you've picked it all up, Caitlan. Let the servants finish it. Come. We should retreat to one of the sitting rooms where no one can overhear." Kalath outstretched a hand, helping Caitlan to her feet. Together, the three sorcerers slipped down the slumbering dark halls of the Temple Dagon, to a quiet sitting room near the kitchens.

Once inside, Caitlan closed the heavy door behind them. She took the chair across from Kalath, motioning Graneck to sit. "She was captured by the Kersians and then?"

Graneck sat down with a heavy sigh, shoving both shoulders into the thick cushions behind him. "Yes, then what happened?"

"She escaped, along with the Warlord Kyran's daughter, losing her amulet in the process."

Caitlan gasped. Graneck snorted.

Kalath pulled a pipe from his robes and began filling it with a sweet smelling tobacco from a small leather pouch he carried. "Somehow the first Kersian sorcerer did not realize Tnasha was a sorceress until she escaped. She hides her mana well. But she had assistance from her friends."

"She needed assistance. Need I say more?" Graneck was obviously displeased.

Kalath ignored him and continued. "They decided not to come back to Danaria, and came to me instead. Tnasha was injured from the fall that led to her capture in the first place."

The high priest and priestess remained silent with their eyes fixed on him. Kalath lit his pipe. "For brevity I'll tell you that while she healed and rested I made her read several magical texts those few days she and her friends stayed with me." He paused and stared into the flames of the hearth remembering. It seemed like it just happened yesterday and the memory of it sent a shiver down his spine. "I also discovered the Sorcerer Morvack had her amulet, and it healed the deadly wound given to him by the human soldier Kolgern, one of Tnasha's friends. I was the one who told Tnasha that she had to go to Zul to retrieve the amulet."

Graneck snorted again. "Stupid girl."

"Hold your tongue, Graneck. Perhaps you should place yourself in her position. What would *you* have done?" Caitlan raised a thin eyebrow in warning, waiting for her husband's answer.

He smiled. "I would have *never* been caught to begin with."

"Nonsense, Graneck. This entire situation, this war, has thrust Tnasha into its grasp without her consent. Don't you see?" Kalath took another puff from his pipe and leaned forward, catching both their eyes with his own. "She had very little control over the events that have transpired. While she and two of her friends, Kolgern and Alena, left for Zul, *I* was escorting the Warlord Kyran's daughter, Rassia, back to Danaria where she belonged. We had the misfortune of running into the Kersians, and being taken captive by the Kersian sorcerer Morvack. Were I younger I may have given Morvack a stronger fight. But I am old, and my mana is degenerating even as we speak..."

"I assume the rumors that you have been to Zul are true then?" Caitlan asked.

"Yes. They wanted to employ my scrying abilities in hopes they could defeat her. They wanted to use Rassia as a sacrifice. Kolgern and Alena were the ones who freed Rassia and me from our prison inside the manor of Gavgal. I don't know the specifics of what happened in the Kersian temple. Tnasha conjured something that terrified Gavgal and Morvack, enough that they retreated, giving us all time to escape. Mostly unscathed."

Caitlan trembled. Kalath could tell she did not want to ask, but he knew Caitlan and knew how the priestess' mind worked. She would ask about it for years if he didn't tell her.

She asked like he knew she would. "What did she conjure?"

Kalath took another puff from his pipe and watched the thick white smoke rise. He knew when he told them, Caitlan and Graneck would be even more frightened. "It came naturally, I assure you. As natural as the prophetic dreams she has begun having. The dreams, except for the last, have come true."

"That's not what I asked, Kalath. What was it she conjured?" Caitlan's voice threatened anger, her long nails bit into the arm of the chair and her brow furrowed in expectation.

"It was a serpent conjured by invoking Dagon in Aithian's name." Kalath's eyes traveled from the priest to the priestess, wondering what their reaction would be.

Caitlan's face went white. "By Natyis, it's happening. The first prophecy has come to pass."

"It seems so." Graneck stared into the hearth's flames, as if searching for something. He swallowed – hard. "We should prepare for the second prophecy."

Caitlan nodded. "Tnasha must retrieve the Raven's Claw. It's the only way."

Kalath stood. "Gavgal and Morvack already have plans to retrieve the staff. As do others. I have seen this in my visions, and so it shall come to pass. The journey will be dangerous for everyone involved."

High Priestess Caitlan's brown eyes turned gold, with mere slits for pupils. Her gaze fixed on Kalath's. "She will take four companions with her. A protector, a guide, a warrior, and a scout. But first, she will require additional training."

Kalath nodded. "I shall see to that myself."

"Where is she now?"

"For obvious reasons King Aragel of Sherok became involved in this last engagement. The Kersians convinced Exavia to usurp Sherok's throne. I trust you've heard about this?"

Graneck nodded. "I heard something about that, but I was not given a detailed account."

Kalath continued. "Tnasha is currently with the Danarian troops who accompanied Prince Aragel back to Sherok. They should be on their way back by now, along with Warlord O'Schoitt." Kalath knocked the dottle from his pipe into the hearth and tucked the pipe away.

Caitlan turned to Graneck. "Summon Tnasha fen Schoitt to the temple immediately. Inform her family, the members of the sorcerers' council, and the high command. The four must be summoned as well. You know who they are…"

"But Caitlan she and the others are still days away." The annoyance in his voice made it clear that Graneck did not like how his wife hurried him.

"And yet the warrior's blood still runs red." Her eyes went distant again. "We must make haste. There is little time."

In the mid of night Priestess Caitlan made her way to the ritual chambers to pray while the sorcerers Kalath and Graneck left the temple Dagon behind them in preparation for the arrival of the neophyte sorceress and her companions.

CHAPTER 2

Tnasha leaned forward in her saddle and snatched the note from her father's hands. "It's mine."

"I just wanted to see who it was from." Warlord Termark O'Schoitt tossed up his hands in defeat.

She bit her lower lip, turned the parchment seal side up, and pointed at the imprint. "Temple Dagon. It's probably one of the priests or priestesses trying to convince me to join the temple again."

Termark laughed. "Probably."

The horses they rode ambled along the main road leading directly to Central Danaria. The air was thick with the dust kicked up from the horses ahead of them. They were in no hurry to arrive. After riding for several hours, Tnasha's ankle hurt. It seemed reasonable it would be sore after all she had been through. Her friend Kolgern rode behind her with several of the other soldiers. Occasionally the soldiers' voices rose above a whisper, but for the most part, they kept their conversation to themselves.

Once they reached a break in the canopy of trees above them, she lifted the note skyward, hoping the sunlight would reveal the note's contents. It didn't. With a sigh of resignation, she cracked the wax seal and unfolded the parchment. Half grinning she read it aloud in a boisterous voice. "Sorceress Tnasha fen Schoitt, You have been summoned by the High Priestess Caitlan to the Temple Dagon in Central Danaria *immediately*. The matter is of *utmost* urgency. Please respond *promptly*. Sincerely Yours, High Priest Graneck, Scribe of Temple Dagon."

Kolgern grinned and looked around as if making sure Alena was not there to smack his good arm. Tnasha smiled. He was safe, for Alena had ridden ahead with Warlord Kyran and Rassia. She watched him as he cradled his sore, but mostly healed arm and rubbed around the bandages. She wondered if he would ever admit to loving Alena.

He looked at her, his eyes lost in thought. "I wonder why this is suddenly so urgent?"

Tnasha shook her auburn head of hair. "It can't be that serious. Last time I received a note like this Priestess Areia was trying to get me to join the clergy. It was urgent as well."

Termark cleared his throat. "They have probably heard by now that you were on Zul and managed to get away from two adept sorcerers. They're wondering how you did it."

"They probably know now that you're one of the greatest sorceresses that ever lived." Kolgern burst into laughter and added, "By default perhaps."

"Thank you." Tnasha leaned forward in her saddle in a mock bow. Behind them almost a hundred soldiers took up the rear. Fifty more, or so, rode ahead. Tnasha turned to her father, wondering what he was thinking behind the mask of reserve he always wore. The question blurted from her lips before she could stop it. "Do you think I'm defective?"

With wide brown eyes, Termark gave his daughter a startled look. "By Natyis, no! Why would you ask such a question?"

"Just making sure," she said, frowning.

"Shouldn't we *hurry* back to Danaria?" Kolgern asked.

Tnasha rolled her eyes. "Hurry for what purpose? So they can try to recruit me into the temple faster? That's pointless."

Just then, another messenger riding at a full gallop past the front company of soldiers came to a halt in front of the warlord. Termark O'Schoitt allowed an annoyed sigh to emerge from his lips. "What now?"

"Maybe they want to recruit you into the temple, too, Lord Termark." Kolgern tried to keep a straight face.

Termark took two notes from the messenger. He kept one and passed one back to Kolgern. Termark wasted no time opening his. "It's from the High Command. General Daxin." Termark smiled and chuckled. "It seems the temple has gotten to Daxin as well. This is an order for the legion to return to Central Danaria to deliver you immediately to the temple for debriefing with High Priestess Caitlan. The order is countersigned by approval of the High Council, and the Sorcerer's Council."

"By Natyis, Tnasha. They must really want you. I wonder what mine says." Kolgern warily looked at the envelope. Afraid to open it, he held it at arms length.

"Just open it," Tnasha said. She ran a hand through her long mess of tangled hair and nodded at him. "Well? Open it!"

With the seal cracked and the parchment unfolded, he begrudgingly read the contents. A look of confusion passed over his face. After refolding the note he looked up to find questioning eyes on him. "I've been summoned to the temple as well."

Tnasha wrinkled her nose. "Hmm. That's *very* strange."

Termark agreed. "Perhaps it is more important than we initially believed. You did, after all, have contact with Kersian sorcerers. As did he. It seems reasonable they would want to know any details that may provide a future tactical advantage." Termark looked at her expectantly.

Tnasha noticed her father's eyes on her. She had not ventured to discuss, at any great length, the details of what had happened on Zul. Her friends, too, had remained silent about the incident. "Perhaps they would be interested in knowing that Gavgal has the ability to disappear and reappear in another place? At his own will. He can also take other people with him when he disappears."

"How do you know?" Kolgern asked.

"How do you think he and Morvack got away from me? If it weren't for that bit of sorcery I would have had them both." She frowned and clenched the reins in her fists.

Termark turned to her. "That information, Gavgal's disappearing trick, would be an important detail they would need to know. That would mean he could come into Danaria as he wished and take any woman or child he pleased."

"He wouldn't do that," Tnasha said matter-of-fact.

"You can't be certain of that, unless you know something?" Termark asked. He looked into her eyes.

Her father often said she remained a mystery, even to him. She shrugged. "It would be too soon for him to retaliate by abducting people. If I get exhausted after a simple incantation, I can imagine if he used his ability for such feats of magick, he would be so exhausted he might go into a death-like sleep until his mana could regenerate. He might even require elemental balancing."

"Rassia told me Morvack can do wind magick. That's how she and Kalath arrived on Zul before we did. He can also send lightening from his hands, and he reads minds. I don't think he has as much ability as his brother though," Kolgern said thoughtfully.

"He's probably not as well trained, but it sounds to me as though he has plenty of ability," said Termark.

Tnasha inhaled the fragrant, warm spring air. It was moist and sweet, smelling of flowers and damp earth. Summer would be here soon. The dense forests of the Danarian terrain surrounded them in a tunnel of blue and green foliage. The sunlight broke through in spots, bringing a cascade of light onto the road every hundred foot lengths or so. "We can't really hurry back. The horses need to be rested."

Her father nodded. "The High Priestess and the councils will have to be patient and wait. We will get there quickly, just not as quickly as they would like."

Kolgern exchanged glances with Tnasha. "How quickly, General, Lord Termark?"

Termark turned to Tnasha's thin blond friend, who looked more like a ruffian rather than a trained Sirus soldier. "We will resort to short breaks to rest and water the horses, but we will ride through the night. We should be home by morning."

"I can barely contain my excitement," Tnasha said, annoyed. "I thought we weren't going to hurry?"

"We are certainly not going to race home to Danaria and put over one hundred horses in danger of exhaustion. There are two things to remember, Tnasha. The first is to follow orders, so long as they are reasonable and do not put a legion in danger. In that case, you must make modifications to keep your losses to a minimum. In this instance we must worry about the horses. The second is to realize that orders are not given without good reason. Especially in concurrence with the High Council. Perhaps something bad has happened."

Tnasha's stomach turned sour. Her imagination began to race. What could have happened for the High Command, the High Council, and the High Priestess to collaboratively request their immediate return? With this in mind, she voiced her thoughts aloud. "I doubt they're so interested in how we escaped the Kersian sorcerers." Then the thought hit her like a giant stone in the chest. She turned to her father. The hair on her neck stood on end. "What if the Kersian sorcerer, Gavgal, has already retaliated?"

Everyone nearby shifted his attention toward her, astonished. An uncomfortable silence befell them.

CHAPTER 3

The Temple to the no-name god on Zul lay in ruins. Gavgal stared at the heaps of fallen stone, shaking his head in defeat. He let out a deep sigh of resignation.

Morvack stood behind him, his eyes cast to the ground. The untrained sorceress had defeated them and he felt responsible. In his own guilt, a tear escaped the corner of his eye, but he wiped it away quickly. "Gavgal, I am sorry."

Gavgal turned to his brother with an uncharacteristically soft expression. "Why do you apologize?"

"It is my fault this has happened. I underestimated the power of the sorceress."

The Kersian Sorcerer, Gavgal, forced a weak smile and put a reassuring hand on his brother's shoulder. "There was no way we could have known."

"We have lost everything."

"We have lost nothing."

"What do you mean?" Morvack looked up, forcing himself to meet his brother's eyes. "The seer escaped, the sorceress escaped, Exavia did not succeed in taking Sherok. We have failed!"

A sneer spread over Gavgal's thin, pale lips. "That was but one plan, dear brother. Do you think our god would allow us to fail? He has merely thrown an obstacle in front of us. He is testing our resolve. Come. Walk with me."

Gavgal started toward the grand palace, thankful little else in the city was damaged during the serpent's attack aside from several dwellings and shops. The Kersian people, his people, were already removing the rubble so they could rebuild. Gavgal kept walking and Morvack followed, still sulking.

"During my prayer in the private holy temple the Unnamed told me what we must do."

Morvack perked up and quickened his pace to match his brother's. "Go on."

Gavgal's eyes narrowed and he turned to Morvack. "You can relinquish your guilt because I have a very important task for you. If you succeed, we will not be stopped upon our next attack. We will have the advantage. The beauty of it, really, is that no one will anticipate our next move." He paused and pursed his lips. "Except, perhaps, the Seer Kalath. He should be destroyed immediately. Come. I have something to show you."

Gavgal led him into the palace, through the halls and into the library. Inside, he closed the door and strode across the room to an open book that sat upon a small mahogany table. He motioned Morvack to stand beside him. "Look here."

Morvack's eyes fell where Gavgal directed. The ancient grimoire upon the table read, *Mana Weapons*. His gaze slid over the drawing of a staff. "What is it?"

"The Raven's Claw. A magical weapon of great power. It directs a sorcerer's mana through the staff, which then emanates from the orb hundreds of times stronger than a sorcerer can naturally project. An entire castle could be obliterated with one blate of mana cast through the staff." Gavgal smiled appreciatively.

Morvack's chest tightened and he felt himself take a gasp for air. He coughed and tipped his head toward his brother. "Who would create such a thing?"

"Ancient sorcerers." The smile fell from his lips and his expression turned somber. "First, the seer must be eliminated. I will send our brother, Seth, to deal with that task. You will acquire the staff. But first, you must spend five days in the holy temple in prayer. You will need all the strength of the Unnamed for this task. The journey will be long and tedious. I am putting a great deal of trust in you, Morvack."

"I understand, brother. I will not fail you." His stomach twisted in nausea.

S. J. Reisner

"No, you won't." Gavgal's tone changed quickly then. "The staff is in Northern Arkeereon in the wastelands where the city of Ramathra once stood. I will have the scribes prepare you a map."

"About the seer." Morvack paused, almost afraid to share his thoughts. "What if he has already foreseen this?"

"This is precisely why you must gather your strength before leaving. I want you to be well rested. If he has foreseen it, the Danarians will have a legion close behind you. It will be up to you to find the staff, avoid capture, and bring the staff back to me. Once you have the weapon, you have my permission to use it against any Danarian troops who stand in your way. Then we shall start over. We will test the staff on the holding in Exavia. The king has become somewhat disagreeable since the failure in Sherok and the death of his son. The true test, however, will be Arkeereon."

"Arkeereon?"

"There are nine dying sorcerer bloodlines living in Aratia, Arkeereon. It sits close to the mountains and Southeast of Ramathra. There are perhaps eighty sorcerers in all living there. They will be the weapon's first test against other sorcerers. Of course, we should take their women first. No sense in destroying perfectly healthy breeding stock." Gavgal smiled. "Then, if the test is successful we shall move on to Danaria. Undoubtedly they will attempt to remove the women and children from their cities before we strike. We'll be waiting."

Morvack shuddered not knowing if he was sickened or excited with his brother's plan. But he knew what his brother expected him to say, so he said it. "It is a brilliant plan, Gavgal."

"Yes, it is," Gavgal said, his face smug. "Well, let us get started. I shall send orders to our brother about the Sorcerer Kalath."

"I must rest." Morvack turned and left his brother behind him, retreating to his room where he could think more clearly.

Morvack sat on the edge of the feathered mattress bed and rubbed his eyes. Finally, he held his hands in prayer and looked toward the ceiling. "Oh great Unnamed One. I pray you grant me strength and wisdom. Though I fear my brother's plans, I know that You are watching over us. I seek Your truth and wisdom. I seek…" he paused, uncomfortable with the word that almost emerged from his lips. "I seek love," he finally whispered. His gaze fell to the floor, and a deep aching, yearning washed over him.

"You will receive everything you seek," a woman's voice whispered through the darkness.

Morvack looked around, searching his chambers for the source of the voice. "Who's there?"

"Look into your heart and you shall find what you seek." This time the voice came clearly from behind him. He turned toward it. Nothing.

"Who are you?"

"Ashtar."

"Demon?"

"Goddess."

"By the Unnamed I cast you out!"

"Do not be so quick to exile me. I know you." These last words drifted from the room, leaving deaf silence in their wake.

Morvack looked around. Suddenly, he felt more alone and empty than he ever had before. The anger swelled within him. He felt his fists tighten and his head begin to pound. The blood surged through his veins in a torrent of aggression, and then – the feeling suddenly vanished. A cold calm washed over him and he lay down on the bed, closing his eyes. As he lay there, he felt the blankets cover him. The scent of a woman's perfume, heavy with lavender, wafted to his nose then subsided just as quickly. The world faded black around him. That night he dreamt dreams of the family he so desperately wanted.

CHAPTER 4

Temple Dagon rose high above them. Granite snakes wound their way up and around the towers and spires to rear their heads high above the streets of Central Danaria. The only other buildings matching the temple's awesome height were the castle holdings and keeps of warlords and sorcerers. Tnasha tipped her head back and looked up at the main spire, vaguely able to make out the snake's head nestled close to the stone. The temple brought back bad memories. When she was a child her grandmother often brought her to the temple, making her sit through well-rehearsed rituals and classes meant to teach children the ancient religion. Religion in its practiced form, however, meant very little to her. She had her own relationship with her gods, however non-traditional it was.

Kolgern and her father came with her. It was her father's voice that broke the silence. "Are we going in?"

Tnasha frowned. "Yes."

Kolgern's worrisome expression bothered her. He started up the stairs first, only pausing to look back.

"I'm coming," she reassured him. She made her way up the steady incline of stairs with her father by her side and Kolgern ahead of her. The temple doors stood wide open and welcoming. The scent of temple incense, sandalwood and patchouli, poured over them in a wall of invisible smoke, carrying a feeling of magick and mystery with it. She could sense them. The Sorcerer's Council, the members of the priesthood and the humans of the High Council. The heavy blend of mana touched hers in recognition.

They paused in the foyer. Tnasha knew exactly where to go. She stepped past Kolgern, leading the way into the main temple. As they stepped into the large ritual chamber all eyes focused on them, and Tnasha felt anxiety rise in her chest. With each breath, the altar seemed further and further away. The frown on her lips remained solid. She searched the faces of those present and stopped when her eyes met Kalath's. He stood next to the altar with her cousin Margore nearby. Her brow furrowed with confusion. What was Margore doing here?

High Priestess Caitlan stepped away from the altar. "Tnasha, thank you for coming. We are still waiting."

Tnasha exchanged a mutual glance of confusion with Kolgern. "Waiting for what?"

"For whom," Caitlan corrected.

"All right. Waiting for whom?" Tnasha asked, annoyed.

"Approach the altar."

With a sigh, Tnasha stepped forward. She hated the vague, archaic and cryptic nature of the priesthood. "Should Kolgern come, too?"

Caitlan nodded. "Yes."

They approached with caution, attempting to shake the wondering stares of the Council members and other onlookers.

"Is it necessary to have all of these people here?" Tnasha finally asked, looking down on Caitlan, who was several inches shorter.

"This matter concerns all of us." The priestess gazed up at her with brown, distant eyes. She took Tnasha by the hand and led her to altar. Atop it sat a scrying bowl. "I have been told you can see the images Sorcerer Kalath invokes."

"Yes."

"Stand with him and see for yourself what has happened."

Tnasha's blood went cold. Without question, she stepped up beside Kalath and forced herself to gaze into the clear water of the black scrying bowl.

Kalath conjured the images. The water clouded then cleared and there within the clear liquid the vision came forth.

Two staves. Morvack. A barren wasteland. The ruins of a castle still burning and glowing a deep red from the blate that destroyed it.

She pulled her eyes away and looked down at Priestess Caitlan. "I know what I saw, but how is it my affair?"

A sad smile appeared on the High Priestess' lips. "You must make sure this weapon does not fall into the hands of the Kersians. Otherwise, everything you have just seen will come to pass."

The dream came back to Tnasha then. Gavgal and his mounted soldiers, at the cliffs. Strangely, she had not fallen prey to the dreams since Zul. They simply stopped. She returned her attention to Caitlan and the people surrounding her. "Why must *I* do it?"

"Because you have been chosen by the gods to fulfill the prophesies of this generation."

"And Kolgern?"

"He is your protector. He will accompany you along with your cousin Margore, the warrior. As will Shadon Longbowe, the scout. Lastly, there will be one other. A guide who knows Arkeereon well. That guide is Commander Kauf of Carinth. King Farnaginn has been informed you will be taking Commander Kauf with you. The king has offered Carinth's full cooperation. Do you understand the full weight of this situation?" Caitlan was serious.

"Yes. Of course I do," she said, even though she was not sure she did.

"Very well. You have several days to rest and spend with your family. But you must leave as soon as possible. You will go to Kalath's where you will gain additional training."

Tnasha looked at Margore and Kolgern. "Is that all?"

"Isn't it enough?" Caitlan smiled, reassuring like a mother.

Kolgern kept looking at his feet, visibly uncomfortable in the presence of so many. "Can we leave?"

"If you wish."

He reached his hand out and took Tnasha by the elbow. Together, Tnasha, Kolgern and Margore left the temple behind them in search of bathing, food, and the comforts of home.

•

When they reached the castle holding of the O'Schoitt family, Tnasha led the way. The three darted past open doors, on Tnasha's command, to avoid too much contact with her family. Tnasha knew they would only want to question her and she was not in the mood to discuss her recent adventures. They finally reached her private quarters. Once in the room, she closed the door behind them, making sure it was locked. "By Natyis, I swear."

"How did I become involved?" Kolgern's face boasted a genuine look of shock. He paced back and forth in front of the silent hearth, rubbing the seam of his black tunic between his thumb and forefinger.

"It seems you were involved from the beginning," Tnasha said, mimicking the deep, reserved voice of Kalath.

Margore snickered.

Tnasha's tone turned serious. "They probably decided Shadon was the brains, you were the sneaky one, and Margore was the brawn."

"Then where does that leave you?" Margore, her favorite cousin looked at her thoughtfully through golden brown eyes. His mana was light green, though it did not emanate as far from his body like most sorcerers. His was internal and not as pronounced. Whether or not he would ever be able to throw blates or work sorcery had yet to be established.

"I'm the magical warfare." She sat down heavily on the bed with a groan. "That's what I'm worst at."

A light knock on the door silenced them. "Your bath has been drawn, Lady Tnasha," said the muffled voice from beyond the door.

"Thank you."

A playful spark lit up Kolgern's eyes. "What about me?"

Tnasha laughed. "I'm taking my bath alone."

"It seems to me a bath is where all of this started." Kolgern smiled.

Margore looked on, confused, and ran one thick, square hand through his shoulder length brown hair. Today he was absent of the threadbare garb Tnasha was accustomed to seeing him in. Instead, he wore a clean, pressed tunic in deep green, enhancing his mana. He had probably dressed for the temple.

"Bath?" Kolgern asked, prompting her thoughts back to his previous comment.

Tnasha grinned, remembering. He was right. She had just finished her bath when Kolgern came to fetch her after the Kersians kidnapped Warlord Kyran's daughter, Rassia. "Well, perhaps a bath signifies a new beginning."

Kolgern shrugged. He and Margore stood to leave. But before he opened the door he said, "I'm going home for awhile. I might come back for the mid day and evening meal."

"That's fine. I'll see you both later."

Margore nodded, remaining quiet as usual. Both men left and for the first time in a month, Tnasha finally had some time to herself.

CHAPTER 5

"The Kersians have their eyes on what our ancestors left hidden in the ruins of the temple at Ramathra." Lord Natyis kept himself hidden behind the black, cowl hooded robe he wore.

Lord Eury leaned forward. His pale skin contrasted his black hair, and seemed to glow in the dim light of the room. "What is it they seek, Lord Natyis?"

Natyis' voice rang cold in the cavernous room. "The Raven's Claw."

"Should we worry? After all, not all can wield the Raven's Claw. You know as well as I that only those sorcerers who possess benign mana or mana with the fire element can use such a weapon." Eury took a sip of tea from the cup next to him. "Even then, you know how rare benign mana is. And if they send a fire element, he must be trained how to use it. Projecting one's mana through a staff such as the Claw takes great focus."

Natyis remained silent for a few moments, contemplating the possibility. The image came to him then. In the vision he saw the sorcerer Morvack. "They *will* send a fire element to retrieve it. You do have a point that the sorcerer must have the proper focus and the one who will come for it is not as adept as he could be, which is in our favor."

"What about the Danarians?"

"What about them?"

"They will undoubtedly know of this plan as well, and will send one of their own."

"Ah, yes, they have a seer of great power. Sorcerer Kalath. *He* is in grave danger. But that is no concern of ours. Though you are probably right. They will know and they will send their own."

"What shall we do? We have no fight with them." A look of concern passed over Eury's face. His white eyes stayed focused on the Dark figure of Natyis.

"We will send Aithian and Lucas to Ramathra."

Eury was not convinced. A feeling of dread swept over him. "This will start a war unlike any we have seen."

Natyis' gaze went distant. "Aithian and Lucas will keep themselves well hidden. They will be observers only."

"They will be discovered." The dread refused to subside. He could feel it and wished he possessed Natyis' sight to see exactly what was causing the feeling.

"No. They will not. You are the last person I would expect such skepticism from. I expect it from Lord Luithian more than I do you."

"This is going to start a battle," Eury repeated.

"The war you are so worried about starting has already begun, my friend. We have been at war for centuries." Natyis shifted his gaze to the fire. "The war began ages ago when Delepitore was taken from my great, great, grandfather."

Eury knew the story well, as all of the Arkeeronish sorcerers did. Thousands of years ago, Natyis' great, great grandfather's daughter was taken from him. Now, centuries later, nine families descendant of ancient sorcerers still hoped for Delepitore's mana rebirth begotten from their own bloodlines. Natyis saw things. He was more than a seer and adept sorcerer. As elder of the ancient bloodlines he looked no older than a fifty-year-old man even though he was almost eighty. To this day, the humans of Arkeereon saw the sorcerers as gods, an imperial hierarchy to be revered. Even the younger sorcerer bloodlines still worshipped the ancient sorcerers, or more properly, their mana. And that mana flowed freely still, reborn generation after generation in the ancient family lines. Eury wondered then about the Danarians. They still followed the ancient religion. "Who will the Danarian's send?"

Natyis did not answer.

"Are you all right, Lord Natyis?"

"I'm fine." Natyis cleared his throat and rubbed his eyes.

"Why do you not answer?" Eury pressed on, knowing that if he pried long enough Natyis would eventually give in. It required less prodding than he expected.

"That is the question confounding me." Natyis pulled the cloak from his head revealing his own long black hair streaked with gray, and looked at Eury through black, all-seeing eyes. "When I look to Danaria I can see numerous sorcerers. But there is one that eludes me. The one they will send appears as no more than a mist. I cannot see past it no matter how hard I try."

Eury sat back, mouth agape. "I wonder why. I wonder if the seer Kalath can see this sorcerer."

"I imagine the sorcerer chooses who sees him and who does not. I can see those he travels with clearly. They are human."

The fire crackled in the hearth, shooting short bursts of flame spitting upward. Flaming ash sparkled and died as it drifted on the air, settling into a fine powder on the stone tiles in front of the hearth.

Eury cleared his throat and took another sip of tea. "How much time do we have?"

"We have time. Nonetheless, we should inform Aithian and Lucas soon. There is no room for mistakes."

"Perhaps we should send them to Ramathra to take the claw before anyone comes to retrieve it." Eury tipped his head, wondering why they would allow the staff to fall into the hands of the Kersians at all.

"I have considered that."

"Then why aren't we sending them to take it?"

"All things happen for a reason, Eury. I cannot tell you why. Some things are best left as they are."

"May I ask a question of a personal nature then?"

Natyis looked at him hard, then his expression softened. "Yes."

"Do you ever feel cursed knowing what will happen?"

Natyis smiled, amused. "A curse, a blessing. I do not judge the gifts bestowed upon me. They simply are. I have grown to accept them. When I was younger I tried to change what I knew would happen. It happened anyway."

"You have given up?"

"No, my friend. I have merely resigned our fate to the whole of creation where it belongs. Please summon Aithian and my son. They should be given time to prepare as they should leave before the next new moon."

Nodding, Eury stood. "I will return with them shortly."

Eury, Natyis' closest advisor, left the room and retreated to the dark, hollow halls of the castle holding of the Imperial Hierarchy of Arkeereon. Once, these halls were filled with the laughter of children and the soft voices of women. Now it reminded him of a tomb. Their bloodlines, much like the Kersian sorcerers', were dying out. Without enough sorceresses and the high mortality of mother and child during childbirth they were left with few females and even fewer children with every passing generation. His own wife died giving birth to his youngest son, Baba'al.

He hurried on, shoving the gloom thoughts to the back of his mind, and made his way to the common room where many of the sorcerers spent their time. When he reached the room he did not hesitate in opening the door and entering unannounced. "Aithian, Lucas, Lord Natyis has requested both of you in his chamber."

Lord Aithian, son of Luithian, lay sprawled on a cushioned bench staring at the ceiling absentmindedly tapping a dagger on his knee. Natyis' second to youngest son, Lord Lucas, sat sharpening a sword. The Sorceress, Lady Tezryan, wife of Natyis' middle son, Agalia, played a harp at the far end of the room. The announcement did not interrupt the chords emanating forth as her fingers tread expertly across the harp's strings.

Lord Aithian looked up, bored. "At this hour?"

Lucas put down the stone and wiped his sword with a rag. He sheathed it and stood. "C'mon Aithian."

With a grunt, Aithian stood, sheathing the knife at his side. They followed Eury back to Lord Natyis' chamber in silence.

●

"Please sit." Lord Natyis had since pulled the hood back up over his head. His eyes, which were always dilated from his ability to see, found the bright light too painful.

The young male sorcerers did as instructed.

"I have a task to assign both of you."

They met his statement with an expectant silence that beckoned him to continue.

"Before the end of this moon cycle, the Kersians will be on their way to Ramathra. They seek the Raven's Claw, an ancient magical weapon fashioned by the hands of our ancestors. The weapon may only be wielded by fire sorcerers, and the Kersian sorcerer who is coming for it is that."

Eury broke in. "The Danarians will also be sending their own sorcerer after the weapon."

Natyis nodded. "Yes. I want you both to go to Ramathra quietly. It is important that neither the Kersian sorcerer, nor the Danarian sees either of you. I want you to find out which side acquires it."

Lucas bit his lip. "Father, can you not see already who will acquire it?"

Natyis took a measured breath. "No. I cannot see because the sorcerer the Danarians will send blocks my vision. Anything he is involved in, I cannot see clearly."

Eury gasped. "I did not realize the Danarian sorcerer had affected your vision so greatly. You failed to tell me this."

Natyis sighed with more resignation. He had not intended to divulge his new handicap. "He has impaired my vision so greatly these past few weeks that I was unable to see what the Kersians were doing until yesterday. The Danarian sorcerers have been elusive for much longer. It has been almost fifteen years now that I have been unable to see them."

Aithian spoke up then. "This Danarian sorcerer could be dangerous then?"

"Possibly. Or perhaps he is out of my reach due to a mana conflict. I am unsure as to why this is." Natyis frowned and reached into the hood of his cloak to tug at his hidden graying black beard.

"Or as you suggested earlier, perhaps he chooses not to let you see him," said Eury.

Nodding with some reluctance, Natyis agreed. "Yes."

Lucas rested his head in one hand. "Why don't we take the weapon and bring it back here? Flereous could use it, or Amducius..."

Natyis shook his head with vigor; terrified his son would suggest such a thing. "Because they will come for it and our surviving women and children... We will put them in unnecessary danger."

"You have said many times there will come a day when the Kersians will come for them anyway. Now, later, what difference does it make? They will come regardless, and when they do, the war will return in full force. We have a chance to use it against them and we should take it!" Lucas did not hide his disapproval for his father's plan.

"It is not the time. If the conflict starts again, now, we will lose. All things in their own time, my son. I'm asking you to do this my way for a reason. Good reason."

"Hmmph." Lucas sat back heavily, folding his arms across his chest. He narrowed his gray eyes and looked over at Aithian.

Aithian turned to him. "Your father's right. It would be prudent to gather our allies before we start a war."

Lucas did not spare his sharp tongue. "So you've said before. We need allies. Human allies will do us little good in a sorcerer's war."

"Who said we needed human allies?" Aithian half smiled.

"Do you hear this? Aithian believes sorcerers are not a dying race." Lucas laughed, shaking his head.

Aithian lifted a dark eyebrow, and scratched his thin, angular nose. "If the Kersians are constantly at war with Danaria we can logically conclude that Danaria must have more than a few sorcerers. And," he added, nodding for emphasis, "Sorceresses as well. I believe the Danarian bloodlines are thriving while we hide ourselves in a remote part of the world allowing our family lines to quietly die."

A broad smile slid across Natyis' lips though the others could not see it. "Aithian is correct."

Lucas jumped from the chair. He could not mask the hurt and anger in his voice. "You have never told us this. Why?"

"All things in their own time, Lucas."

He threw up his hands in anger, and glared at his father, then he turned to Aithian and Eury. "We could have had families and children by now. Instead, our bloodlines die all because everything *happens in its own time*." He paused and turned from them. "I've heard enough."

Aithian stood and followed Lucas from the room.

"That went well." Eury forced a smile.

Natyis eased further back into the chair and closed his eyes. "They both reacted as I expected them to."

Eury looked at him in question. "As you expected it?"

Natyis chuckled. "A man who has want for nothing is motivated to do nothing. A man who wants is a motivated man. Motivation spurs action. And with action, my friend, comes change. Very soon, our lives will change. I just wish I knew how. The Danarian sorcerer is preventing me from seeing our own future."

A dead silence filled the room, but Natyis heard Eury's thoughts as if he had spoken them aloud. *What if we have no future?*

CHAPTER 6

"Tnasha?"

Tnasha bolted upright with her heart in her throat. Her eyes darted around her room wild and frantic, and finally settled on High Priestess Caitlan's face. "Don't do that!"

"I'm sorry. I did not realize you were sleeping."

"You could have knocked. You're as bad as Anetta and the triplets! This is the reason I should lock my chamber door!" She pressed her hand to her chest as if that would slow her heart's violent rhythm.

"I did knock and when you didn't answer I got worried. You were sleeping heavily."

"I'm exhausted."

"Of course you are. I would expect as much with everything you have been through." Caitlan sat down on the edge of the bed. "Kalath told me about your dreams. Have you had recent ones?"

Tnasha rubbed the sleep from her eyes. "No."

"He cannot usually see beyond a few days at a time."

Tnasha cocked her head, rubbing her neck. "Kalath?"

"Yes."

"That's not unusual for a seer is it?"

Caitlan smiled. "I suppose not."

"Then why mention it?" Tnasha gave her a puzzled look.

"No reason in particular."

Tnasha pursed her lips, knowing she was trapped in another cryptic conversation. "Why are you here?"

"I must talk to you." The priestess paused, stood, and went to the window. She peered outside to the gardens below. "How did you defeat the Kersian Sorcerers?"

Tnasha shrugged. "I conjured a serpent."

"How?"

"With an incantation? I improvised as I went along. How else?" She swung her legs over the side of the bed and leaned back, stretching out her arms. "My shoulders hurt."

Caitlan turned to her, and came back to the bed. She sat down. "Turn around. Let me rub your shoulders. I imagine you are very tense."

Tnasha did as she was told and let her head fall forward. Caitlan's small thin hands were firm. She pushed Tnasha's long auburn hair aside and kneaded her shoulders vigorously.

Wincing, Tnasha turned her head back toward Caitlan ever so slightly. "Ow. I can't really explain it. I remember thinking about what Kalath told me. He said that everything I would ever need for sorcery was all around me. I just let it flow like the blood in my veins. I felt it come out of me like a natural river of mana. The more I tried to control it the less powerful it was." She whirled around with a sudden surge of excitement, startling the priestess. "But when I let it go, the mana floods out of me like a raging mountain river."

Caitlan folded her hands in her lap and crinkled her forehead. She swallowed. "That seems almost…"

"Too easy?" Tnasha jumped up and bent over to touch her toes then whirled about on her heel, and leaned in facing Caitlan again. "It was invigorating. I had this sense of power, like I needed no ritual, nothing. You want to know something?"

Caitlan did not respond. Instead her attention lay focused on Tnasha's violet mana as it jumped and rose and emanated even further from her body than normal. Its violet color had become more pure and opaque.

"I think it would have worked whether I used an incantation or not." Tnasha shrugged. It was something she had not considered until now. She smiled, remembering her special ritual. She would have to remind herself to do another. But not until Caitlan left. "That's all rituals and incantations are for anyway."

Caitlan lifted an eyebrow. "What?"

"Focus."

The priestess smiled and nodded. "Just promise me you will always remember one thing, Tnasha. It is very important."

Tnasha gave the priestess her full attention knowing another cryptic response so typical of the priesthood was coming.

"When cut, the warrior's blood still runs red regardless if that warrior wields a sword or sorcery." Caitlan paused, searching Tnasha's face for understanding. "Do you understand?"

Tnasha sat down and fought the urge to roll her eyes. "I know I'm not immortal."

Caitlan smiled at her again. "Of course you do. Come. Let's eat. I heard your grandmother has been working all day to prepare a large meal to celebrate your return. You need to eat and keep up your strength."

With a sigh, as if a huge burden had been lifted from her shoulders, Tnasha stood and followed Caitlan to the dining hall. At least she had survived the lecture condensed into a single sentence.

When they arrived, it seemed half of Danaria stood present in the dining hall. Tnasha sat to the left of her father as she usually did. She looked down the long table and smiled at Kolgern and Margore at the far end. Across from her sat the priests and priestesses including high priest Morvack. When her gaze met his, a warning went off in the back of her mind. He sucked in his left cheek and glared at her. She looked away and turned her attention to the feast of food in front of her, not really looking at it. For the entire meal she sat, uncomfortable in her own thoughts, and painfully aware of the eyes on her. Particularly Graneck's. He watched her the entire time, and as she left, she felt his gaze follow.

With the mid day meal thankfully over, Tnasha, Kolgern, and Margore made their way to the gardens. "Did you see that?" Tnasha asked them once they were alone.

"What?" Kolgern busied himself pulling blades of grass, one by one, from the patch of turf he sat on.

"Graneck was scowling at me the entire time I was eating." She buried her head in her hands. She could not even remember what she had eaten. Instead, she recalled hurrying through the meal, fighting the urge to bolt from the dining hall. "I have a terrible feeling."

Margore looked at her thoughtfully. "I noticed that he was staring at you. Kind of creepy if you ask me."

"I didn't notice him glaring." Kolgern's gaze shifted beyond the garden to a window above him. He quickly turned away and said through clenched teeth, "By Natyis, he's watching us right now."

Tnasha turned slightly, trying to look upward from the corner of her eye. She caught a shadow move away from the window.

"Don't look."

Margore followed Tnasha's example and peered out the corner of his eye. "There's no one there."

Kolgern looked up. "He was there. Just a moment ago."

She turned around and looked up at the window then turned back to her friends. "I have a bad feeling."

"I'll go take a look." Margore stood.

Tnasha nodded, watching him disappear through a nearby doorway.

"It doesn't make any sense," Kolgern said, picking up a twig. He placed it on the bridge of his nose, attempted to balance it, and caught it in his hand as it fell. "Why would he scowl at you? He's a temple priest. Is he angry that you wouldn't join the temple?"

Tnasha wrinkled her nose. "Yes, I'm sure that's why he's watching me *and* glaring at me."

"Now you're being sarcastic."

"That would be an inane reason for him to be acting so strangely, wouldn't it?"

"Then what do you think it is?" Kolgern snapped the twig in his hand in two, and he examined it.

She allowed her imagination to form its own conclusions. "Maybe he's in league with the Kersians."

Kolgern snorted. "He's married to Caitlan. She has to be the most devoted sorceress I've ever met. It's the reason she's the high priestess."

"Now you're being sarcastic."

He tossed the broken twig to the ground and sat back, leaning on his hands. "No, I'm being serious. He's not in league with Kersians. Traitors and treasoness behavior are easy to spot. Caitlan is an intelligent woman. She would have spotted any strange behavior on his part immediately."

Tnasha lifted a finger in defiance. "Not if she was too busy to notice."

"You're being paranoid."

"Fine. Then you tell me what's going on." She leaned forward.

A wicked grin slid over his lips. "He secretly wants you and is angry that he's married." A chuckle tumbled from his throat.

She smacked his leg. "You're a swine, Kolgern."

He burst into laughter. "That sounds more plausible."

"No, it doesn't." The mere thought of Graneck lusting after her made her stomach turn.

"All right, fine. Maybe he just doesn't like you. Have you ever considered that? Why does everything have to be a plot against you?"

She smiled at her own paranoia. "Maybe you're right. A lot of males hate having women in their military, because war is not a woman's work."

The same grin reappeared on his lips. "No, it's not."

"Shut up." She shook her finger at him, grabbed a dirt clod and hurled it at him, catching him in the chest.

"Ha. Wench." He brushed himself off and looked up as Margore once again emerged from the doorway.

Tnasha turned to him. "Was he up there?"

Margore shook his head. "He was up there. But he was talking to Lord O'Joshan. They got quiet when I entered and stared at me until I left. I pretended I left something in the room."

She turned to Kolgern with a raised eyebrow. "You have to admit *that* is strange."

Kolgern shrugged and looked to Margore for validation of his lack of suspicion.

Margore offered none. "I thought I heard them say something about you being dangerous."

Kolgern nodded with vigor. "She is."

She hit him again, harder this time. "Thank you. You are such an ass, Kolgern."

"Well! You almost killed us!"

"Not on purpose." She turned to Margore with narrowed eyes. "He said I was dangerous?"

"That's what I thought I heard. I could be wrong." Margore sat down next to her.

"See, I was right, he just doesn't like you." Kolgern forced a grin.

Tnasha thought about it for a moment and shrugged the anxious feeling off. She decided to change the subject. "I'm not looking forward to this trip."

Kolgern began picking grass blades again. "I'm not either. I just want to go back to my normal routine."

"I thought it would be fun." Margore gave them both a puzzled look.

She groaned with exaggeration. "Margore, it is not going to be fun. We're going to be sleeping on the ground, going for days, even weeks without bathing. Eating dry bread, dried meat, dried fruit. We're going to be cold and miserable. Always having to watch for the Kersians. I'm with Kolgern. I want things to go back to normal."

He shrugged and looked down at his hands in his lap like a small child who had just been disciplined.

"Will things ever go back to normal?" Kolgern's expression turned sober.

"Probably not."

Kolgern looked over at her then. "What did you see in the bowl anyway?"

"The bowl?"

"The scrying thing. You know: the bowl."

"Oh." She almost did not want to tell them, but since they were involved they had a right to know. "I saw what would happen if we failed."

Margore looked up. "What?"

Her voice emerged nervous and sharp. "A sorcerer's war."

•

High Priest Graneck looked through the window into the gardens below. She was down there, the beast. No, he corrected himself, not a beast but rather an abomination. The young woman was unlike any sorcerers he had ever seen. The blazing violet mana that stood more than a foots length from her body terrified him. Ever since she was a small child he had wanted to voice his concern to the council. Had wanted tell them to put her down gently, like one might a horse with a broken leg. He had once suggested to Lord O'Brunweh that she could be dangerous. As a result he received a verbal lashing from the elder. Clearly, her bloodline prevented his opposition.

The O'Schoitt family, along with the O'Sheadahl, O'Brunweh, and O'Frean were the original four tribes of Dranar. They founded and built Central Danaria with their human sympathizers. The other sorcerer families, composed of wandering sorcerers mostly of the clerical cast, had merely found themselves a place where they were accepted and decided to call it home. But even before then, the four tribes of Dranar, all of them warrior cast, had usurped this land from their oppressors and declared themselves a free human and sorcerer nation. Danaria.

There was only one option now. That option stood before him, looming in the dark recesses of his mind. It was almost too horrible to think, but he had no choice. It was the only way he could save them all from her destructive abilities. With her mana, she could easily take over the council of elders, declare herself ruler, and force all of Danaria, or even the world, into submission. Only one thing scared him more. If Caitlan discovered his plan, she would have his head. Their marriage had been arranged in the elders' plan to selectively breed Danarian sorcerers into a society the sorcerers dominated. He was the last of his line, and *that* was a problem. By that standard alone, he was an insignificant amidst a society of sorcerers attempting to repopulate their race. And as long as no children existed between himself and Caitlan, he remained unimportant and could not make a name in the bloodline records for his family line, just as she could easily have him put to death if she even suspected him of such thoughts. Furthermore, the family lines like the O'Alanht, O'Caughnacht, O'Brokhan, and O'Friedahl were close supporters of the original tribes of Dranar. Caitlan was of the O'Alanht family, and her father was a close friend of Warlord Termark, Tnasha's father, and Lord Drazen, her uncle. To make matters worse, Caitlan saw herself as Tnasha's elder sister and held Tnasha's spiritual confidence. This was a predicament, but he was used to being in difficult situations and felt sure he could find a way to solve the problem of Tnasha.

When Tnasha's friend noticed him, he turned from the window and found himself face to face with Lord Bradran O'Joshan.

"High Priest Graneck, it's good to see you." O'Joshan extended his hand.

"Bradran, I haven't seen you at the temple." Graneck forced a smile and offered his hand in return.

Bradran leaned over toward the window and looked out. "I've been busy. You, uh, keeping an eye on them?"

Graneck lifted an eyebrow, feeling a surge of fear run through him. He took a deep breath. "I'm hoping Tnasha comes through for us."

He nodded. "Yes. With the destructive force of that mana…"

"She could be a danger to herself and her companions, and possibly all of us," Graneck finished with a nod. Just as he said it, he wished he could take it back. Standing in the doorway, attempting nonchalance, stood Tnasha's cousin, Margore.

"Umm, have either of you seen a…" the young man paused uncomfortably. "Never mind, I think I left it in the other room." He turned and left in haste.

Graneck wondered then what Margore had overheard. He turned back to Bradran with a shrug. "You are worried, too, then?"

Much to Graneck's relief, Lord Bradran, who raised and trained some of the finest warhorses in Danaria, nodded. "I've always wondered about her. And I assure you it has nothing to do with her father and me. I may not like the man, but I do respect him. His daughter, however, has a knack for causing calamity wherever she goes, it seems. Stories like what happened on Zul travel fast."

A genuine smile came to Graneck's lips when he realized he might have an ally. "I only wish I could convince the council to be more selective, to watch her more closely. But when I try, I am met with resistance."

"I wish they would watch her more closely, too. Of course they see her as quality breeding stock, so suggesting she is anything but is almost impossible." Bradran put on a malicious grin. "But if she were to have an accident…"

Graneck felt his eyes widen. Not completely trusting Bradran, he leaned in. "What are you suggesting?"

"Only what you have been thinking. You know…" Bradran folded his hands behind his back. "It could be arranged."

Feigning shock, Graneck pulled back and looked around to make sure no one was listening. "Now you're talking assassination," he whispered. "If anyone found out, we'd be hung in front of the temple, and my wife would pull the lever."

"No one has to find out," Bradran said with a wink.

"How so? That cannot be guaranteed. There are eyes and ears everywhere. Even speaking of such things…" Graneck looked around warily.

"Not if the Kersians do it. Even then, we would need to be sure. Have an alternative plan."

With another glance toward the doorway, Graneck lowered his voice. "What makes you think I want to be involved?"

"The way you look at her, with contempt. With fear. It's obvious. I'm surprised one of the elders hasn't confronted you about it."

"Nonsense. I'm sure several of them know, they simply don't agree. I do see her as a threat to the survival of our race. With that kind of power…" Graneck found himself at a loss for words and sighed.

"Not all of us think she's harmless. There are some of us who believe she was not the proper choice to retrieve the staff weapon. If she had it, what would she do with it?" Bradran leaned in toward him. "She should not be allowed the chance."

"We don't even know how the weapon works, or if she'll succeed." Graneck suddenly felt like sitting.

"No. But can we take that chance at all?" Bradran sighed. "I should go before someone overhears this conversation. But I trust you can, and will handle this, Priest Graneck?"

Graneck nodded. "I will see what I can arrange."

"If you need help from those who support you, send for me. You know where I am." Bradran nodded respectfully and left the room wordlessly, leaving Graneck to his thoughts.

He wondered then if his fear of her was strong enough to go through with such a plan. All the same, he did not trust Bradran. After all, Bradran could very well be working for the elders. No. If he was going to do this, he decided, he would do it alone without the interference of anyone else. The fewer people who knew, the better. Even if someone, like Bradran perhaps, accused him, they would have to prove it. Though Bradran had a good point. If the Kersians did it, it would be easier. Though that could not be guaranteed. An assassin assured a more predictable outcome. Either way, he would have to be very careful to make sure the attempt *never* came back to implicate him.

•

Lord Bradran O'Joshan entered the private council chambers of the sorcerer's council unannounced. He looked around, pleased to see only the eldest two of the council were present. Both gray haired men sat at a table with a deck of wooden cards between them. Bradran closed the door behind him then spoke. "It is done."

The eldest, thinnest, and palest of the two men, Lord O'Frean, gave him a brief nod. "Good. He'll fail, of course. But it is the only way to know for sure what his intentions are, and catch him."

Bradran scratched his neck and took a step forward, fully aware that his expression implied the final question because both of the elders leaned forward expectantly. He needed reassurance. "I have only one question. I have done everything you asked, but I am not sure why you asked me to go the temple on Zul and pretend to be an invisible god."

O'Brunweh laughed, O'Frean smiled. Lord O'Frean beckoned Bradran forward with a wave of his thin, frail old hand. "I thought it would be obvious. With that, Lord Bradran, we satisfy the priesthood and their prophecy, and ensure the Kersian's demise as well. A sorceress like Tnasha fen'Schoitt is anything but a curse. Many of the priesthood believe she will save us all by fulfilling the prophecy. But it seems the prophecy needed a small push in the proper direction."

Bradran's eyes widened in surprise. *That* was a reason he had not considered.

CHAPTER 7

The private temple within the palace had no heat. Morvack sat shivering in the front pew. He closed his eyes, trying to ignore the cold and concentrate on staring into the eyes of the Unnamed. A soft breeze blew by his ear. His eyes shot open and he searched the darkness for a sign of the invisible wind. "Who is there?" he called out into the blackness.

He almost laughed at himself. On the Danarian mainland he felt surer of himself. But here, in his brother's domain, he felt nervous and anxious. Insecure even.

Then a noise, like air seeping through a small hole, resounded to his left. He stood, approaching the wall, searching for a hole.

"What do you seek?" came the voice in a whisper from behind him.

He whirled around. "Where are you?"

"I am everywhere. I am within you and all around you," said the voice. It came from all sides.

Morvack spun around on his heel seeing nothing but the dim, vacant room surrounding him. Candlelight flickered on the walls casting dancing shadows in every corner, behind the altar and around each pew. He set his jaw. "What do you want from me?"

"It is you who have summoned me."

"Are you a demon?" His voice rose and fell. Then there was silence.

"Are you a demon?" returned the soft, female voice.

"I serve the Unnamed," he said with forced pride. "I cast you out! No demons shall dwell here in this holy place!"

"Then I am your guardian angel."

Morvack felt light headed then. Stumbling, he returned to the pew and sat down. "Why are you tormenting me so?"

"I am here to help you."

"Where are you?"

"I cannot take form unless you will it. Though I am afraid you do not possess the ability for such a task."

He sniffed and coughed, feeling his breath catch in his throat. Zul's humidity proved much more than his body was used to. Leaning forward, he rested his head on the partition in front of him. "I must focus on my task," he said aloud to himself. He took a deep breath.

"Why do you deny my help? You have asked for it, and yet you will not take it."

Fear welled within his stomach, bursting forth in a rush of instinctive defense. "Leave me alone!"

"I cannot leave."

"You will leave." He felt his face contort into a mask of rage.

"Your anger comes from your pain. Your loneliness."

"You know nothing of me."

The voice drifted on the air, directly in front of him. "I may know you better than you know yourself."

He sat, unmoving, paralyzed by fear.

"Look inside yourself and see…"

When he closed his eyes, a white light appeared. Inside it, the images loomed forth. A beautiful woman, a sorceress, stood there looking back at him. She carried an infant child in her arms. Then the vision changed. Blackness and fire spewed forth, devouring the skeletons of charred building frames. Shouting filtered to his ears, chaos. He lifted his hands and covered them. The heat overwhelmed him. Forcing his eyes open, he gasped for air. Sweat poured down his face, and soaked through his tunic. "What did I just see?"

"There are two paths, Morvack. You must find what you seek. Choose with wisdom." The voice faded into the silence.

His eyes darted around the temple. He was alone again. The heat subsided and the chill returned. He shivered, stood, and half running, left the temple. The door slammed shut behind him. He recoiled, turned, and found himself face to face with Gavgal. Gasping, he jumped back. "I did not expect you to be there."

Gavgal looked his brother over, noting his sweat soaked tunic. He put a hand on Morvack's shoulder with a genuine look of concern. "Are you unwell?"

He avoided his brother's gaze, and decided to lie. "I was in the temple. I fell asleep and was awoken by a nightmare. I am very tired."

"You are freezing cold, yet look as though you are wrought with fever."

He forced himself to meet his brother's gaze. "The temple has no heat."

"I will see to it that the hearth is tended to." Gavgal searched his eyes. "You seem frightened. It must have been a terrible dream."

"I remember it vaguely."

"Perhaps you would like to discuss it over hot tea?"

Morvack shook his head, knowing his brother's compassion was falsely put on to make sure Morvack went along with *the plan*. "Perhaps in the morning. I must sleep."

"You should take the tea. Perhaps a blend that will help you sleep. I will have one of the servants bring it to you in your room." Gavgal squeezed his shoulder.

Morvack fought the urge to pull away. "Yes, thank you brother. I would like that."

He hurried from the hallway to his room and shut the door firmly behind him, leaning against it once he was inside. He took a deep breath. The warmth radiating from the nearby hearth comforted him.

"Why do you not read his mind?" the voice whispered. It was faint, but he heard it clearly.

"I cannot," he whispered. "He would know."

"He would not. He does not have that ability."

He squeezed his eyes shut. "Gavgal knows everything."

"Does he?"

41

"Yes, yes – he will know." Soft sobs emerged from his throat. He fought them back and slid to the floor, burying his head in his hands.

Another voice came to him then. But this time it came from his memories. "Do you worship your brother?" They were the words of the Sorcerer Kalath, the seer. He had asked Morvack that.

"Do you?" asked the melodious female voice.

He balled his fists and shoved them hard into his cheeks. "No."

"Delve into his mind then."

His breathing became laborious. The light-headed feeling surfaced again. "No."

"You have to know."

"Leave me be. I beg you."

A knock pulled him from the fearsome frenzy. He drew in a deep breath and stood, wiping his eyes. "Who is it?"

Gavgal's voice emerged from the other side of the door. "I have brought you tea."

With a look of confusion, Morvack opened the door pale-faced. "I was expecting one of the serving girls."

His brother carried the tray into the room and set it on the small table near a chair, then turned to Morvack with a concerned look. "You look terrible. Perhaps I should call the physician."

"Yes. Perhaps that is prudent. I feel worse now." He sat down in the chair and poured himself a cup of tea with shaking hands.

Gavgal bent down and looked Morvack over. "You are pale."

"I am nauseated and light headed." Bile rose in his throat and he fought it back. He tried to stand, but fell forward. The last thing Morvack remembered was falling into the darkness.

Gavgal stood, raced from the room and found a lone serving girl dusting a side table standing in the corridor. "Summon the physician. My brother has fallen ill. Hurry, girl."

After a short time, Morvack came to. He opened his eyes to find Gavgal and the gray haired physician standing over him.

"I will give him a tea that will allow him to sleep soundly." The physician helped Morvack into a sitting position and handed him a cup. "Drink."

He took the cup and drank as instructed.

"How long must he rest?" Gavgal impatiently tapped his finger on the armrest of the chair.

"Another day or two." The old man picked up his bag full of medicinal herbs and tonics. "Until he feels strong enough."

After the physician left, Gavgal pulled the chair to his brother's bedside. "The Unnamed is testing your strength."

The impression of Gavgal's true feelings made its way through Morvack's mana. He knew then that even Gavgal was unsure of his own words. Without believing himself, Morvack said, "Perhaps I am not strong enough to undertake this task. I have failed the test of strength."

Gavgal's eyes lit up. "Nonsense. You have *passed* the test."

Fear. Morvack sensed fear in him. His mind reached out, drawing his brother's mind into full view. He did not like what he found. Lies. Lies and self-righteousness. Gavgal saw his brothers as personal servants to his whim. Morvack shook off his newfound knowledge in denial. It could not be right. The disembodied voice of the demon was playing tricks on him. "I am very tired."

Gavgal nodded and stood. "I will see you in the morning." He paused at the door. "Sleep well."

Once the door clicked shut, Morvack breathed a sigh of relief.

"He uses you." The voice whispered from afar.

Morvack thought about it for a moment. "Perhaps. But he is my brother and whatever happens, my loyalty lies with him."

The voice whispered back, "That will change very soon, Morvack. Give it time. Then you will know I am right."

CHAPTER 8

Aithian found Lucas lounging on the banks of the Angor River. "It's too cold to be sitting here. What are you doing?"

Lucas stretched his arms out and yawned. "Thinking."

"Are you still upset with your father?"

An angry grunt emerged from his throat. "He dictates all our lives. He stands between us and everything that can save our bloodlines. Do I sound upset?"

Aithian sat next to him. His eyes went distant into reflection. "Well, yes, you *do* sound upset." He sighed. "How are we to know if our kind was meant to live on? Perhaps this is our fate."

"Do *not* get philosophical." Lucas furrowed his dark brow and shoved a wisp of black hair from his eyes.

"Why not? Is it implausible that maybe the gods have different plans for us?"

"To the humans, we *are* the gods. To other sorcerers our bloodlines descend from the gods. There are no overseers living in the clouds watching down on us. We are our own gods. Our family lines are ancient. We boast stronger mana than any sorcerers alive."

Aithian snickered. "If we do not know what sorcerers exist beyond Arkeereon, how can we boast our mana superiority?"

"You think too much." Lucas stood and brushed the dirt from his legs. His tall, thin frame towered over Aithian.

"I have nothing better to do. But then I'm not the one sitting next to the river thinking, either." He lifted a knowing eyebrow and stood, then followed Lucas up the embankment.

Lucas headed upstream.

"Where are we going?"

"Just walking." He bent down and picked up a rock only to toss it into the water. It struck the water's slow flowing surface with a splash.

"Are you going to sulk all afternoon? I thought we were going to have a pint of ale later with Atan."

"I'm not sulking. I'm planning."

"Planning what?" Aithian put on a wide grin. "Retaliation?"

"No. We are going to go to Ramathra and we are going to take that cursed staff." His voice toned determination.

Aithian stopped walking. "All right. Then what?"

"Tell me now, are you with me or not?" Lucas turned to him, his black eyes meeting Aithian's in question.

"That depends on what you plan to do with the staff. If you think we are bringing it back..."

He shrugged. "I don't know. Bury it somewhere?"

His tone made Aithian's stomach jump. "I do not like the sound of *somewhere*."

Lucas shook his head. "I don't know. I haven't planned that far."

"You mean to tell me you have been sitting here by this river half the day and that is as far as your plan goes?"

"That's not all I was thinking about. I just got to that part."

Aithian laughed. "You're serious?"

"Yes."

"What if your father is right and regardless of what we do, the staff will still be taken?"

Lucas rolled his eyes. "If he can't see into our future then he does not know that."

"He probably knows what we're talking about right now."

"Probably. But he will not stop me."

Aithian raised an eyebrow. "How do you know?"

"Whatever will happen will happen, Aithian. Didn't you know that?" Lucas smiled. "Ha! He knew I would take the cursed thing the very second he told us what he wanted us to do."

"I hadn't thought of that."

"When I was a child my mother made some sweet bread. She told us not to take any because it was for the midday meal." He paused and grinned, remembering. "I already had it in my mind that I was going to take some. So, my father pulled me aside and cautioned me against it. He told me I would get into trouble with my mother. I didn't listen and did it anyway. You know what?"

Aithian smiled. "Let me guess, you were caught?"

Lucas nodded. "I've never seen my mother that angry."

"I cannot even begin to imagine." Aithian laughed, trying to imagine a refined and dainty woman, like Lady Unsere, flying into a rage. He shook the image from his mind. "So what are we going to do?"

"We need to plan this carefully. So no one except you and I know where to find it. Some place where it will not be disturbed and no one would think to look."

"Since you are planning to take the staff and there is nothing I can do to stop you..." Aithian stopped, just in case Lucas wanted to offer an alternative. Lucas remained silent. "I cannot believe I'm going along with this."

"You are with me then?" He held out his hand.

"Do I have a choice? I mean, I am thinking of the consequences of hiding it."

He dropped his hand to his side. "Such as?"

"Well, what if it merely spurs the Kersians to overthrow us and interrogate us one by one until they find it? What if the Danarians have hordes of sorcerers they send over to find it? We could start a war and may never be safe again."

Lucas snorted. "They would not know we have it."

"It would be the logical conclusion that we had it. This would be the first place they would think to look. They have seers, also, remember that."

"Well I don't plan on bringing it back here."

"I would certainly hope not." Aithian's expression turned sour. "I'm worried."

"Don't be. This will be the most exciting thing you have done in years. I promise you that."

"Then why do I feel queasy?"

"Because you worry too much."

"I'm not the one who thinks my father is out to destroy us all."

Lucas shook his head. "I never said that. I said he was leading us to extinction because of his caution. The longer we remain isolated from the rest of the world, the more danger we put ourselves in."

Deep down, Aithian knew he was right. "So we hide the staff. How does this help us? Why don't we just destroy it?"

"We can't destroy it. It's an artifact."

Aithian could see Lucas' point. It would be like destroying an ancient grimoire just so no one else could have it. He also knew that Natyis would have thought of that and for whatever reason, had chosen not to. Lord Natyis was a seer, after all. "Okay, so we hide it. I ask again, how does this help us?"

"I don't know. I would feel better if it was hidden, that's all. I don't know what to do about the rest. Maybe we could take a trip to Danaria."

"Your father would never allow it. Especially if the Danarians are hostile."

"Maybe, some day, we'll find out. Come on. Let's go home. I'm hungry."

Aithian nodded. They turned back down-river, toward home, with the hope of a future within their grasp.

S. J. Reisner

CHAPTER 9

The Kersian Sorcerer Seth crumpled the piece of rough parchment in his fist. It was a letter from his brother on Zul. Scowling, he looked over his weary troops. Their eyes told of sleepless nights and many hours enduring the cool spring weather of the Northern continent. "We will be at the Northern entrance of Central Danaria by afternoon."

His first officer met his statement with a questioning glare. "To what end?"

"You question me?!" Seth fought his initial reaction to knock the man from his horse.

"These men are tired and need rest, sir. We are not in proper condition to meet their soldiers in battle," the first officer said in a plain voice. He looked upon Seth without fear.

Seth gave the aging human officer a menacing smile. "You question the Unnamed? You question *my* orders? You question Gavgal?"

"No sir." The man began to fidget beneath the sorcerer's gaze. He looked down at the ground in forced humility.

Seth's smile faded, changing back into an angry scowl. With an outstretched hand, a deep orange blate of mana pulsed forth from his palm, striking the man square in the chest, knocking him from his horse. There the man died. None of the other soldiers made move to help him. "Would anyone else like to challenge the Unnamed?"

A strange silence overtook the Kersian troops, and not a single eye lifted in challenge.

Seth could feel their fear. Their obedience. "Very well, let us keep moving." He turned his horse back toward Central Danaria. The Kersian soldiers followed. Two scouts hurried ahead of them, disappearing deeper into the forested expanse of the Northern Danarian countryside. They avoided more heavily traveled roadways, carving their own path through the thick foliage of the blue and green hued forest. The orders were clear. Gavgal entrusted the assassination of the seer to his brother, Seth. And Seth had every intention of succeeding where his younger brother, Morvack, had failed. He smiled at the thought, shaking his head. Morvack was by far one of the best priests of all his brothers next to Gavgal. His abilities as a warrior, however, were quaint at best.

The best distraction to keep the seer from invoking the heathen sorcerers of Danaria remained putting one hundred soldiers at their gates. With ease, Seth knew he would be able to approach the old sorcerer's reclusive home and destroy him without fear of interruption. He wondered how Morvack managed to miss such a simple opportunity. His second officer urged his horse alongside Seth's.

Seth felt his presence but made no move to look at him. His voice emerged cold and lifeless. "Do you disagree with me?"

"No sir. I serve the Unnamed." The man's voice trembled so slightly that Seth smiled.

He forced the smile to subside, even though he relished in the power the soldier's fear gave him. "Then why do you approach me?"

"I mean to ask about the battle plan, sir."

"Hmm." Seth stared straight ahead, his deep orange eyes dead and unmoved. "When we reach a feasible location you will go ahead with the troops and distract the Danarians. I have other business. I will leave you to hold your ground."

"Yes sir. How shall we distract them?"

"Your presence alone will be a distraction."

"Umm. Indeed. But what I meant was should we aggressively engage the enemy?"

Seth thought on the question for a brief moment, and ran a thick, calloused hand through his greasy light brown hair. "No. Hide amidst the forest. Let them know you are there. Defend yourselves. Shoot arrows at them if you have to."

"Yes sir."

From the corner of his eye he caught his second officer biting his lip. He turned his head slightly. "I merely need a distraction commander."

"Yes sir."

"I have private business to attend to without Danarian interference." He added the further explanation to curb the confusion and apprehension he could feel from his subordinate. His jaw visibly relaxed when he noticed the explanation seemed to calm the man.

"Yes sir." Seth's second officer reined his horse to a pause, falling behind Seth's bay gelding.

Seth narrowed his eyes then. His thoughts drifted to the appropriate method by which to rid the world of a heathen seer. Above them, the sky darkened belching forth the first growls of thunder threatening rain.

After what seemed hours, Seth reined his horse to a stop and lifted his hand. "Here. You must go on foot here." He turned to his second officer. "I will leave my horse here as well as I will not accompany you to the gates. We can set up a rope corral and ground-tie the horses between the trees."

The petty commander relayed the orders to the soldiers. "The men are working on it."

Seth pursed his thin, chapped lips. "I *can see* that." He shook his head in disbelief at the human's stupidity.

"May I ask why we are leaving the horses here?"

"I have changed my plans. I have decided that perhaps you should not make the Danarians aware of your presence unless they attempt to send soldiers through the gates." He looked over his troops. Many of them bore unshaven faces and torn, dirty clothing. The stench from their unwashed bodies wafted to his nose. "They will either discover our troops on their own, or they will not realize we are there at all. I simply need the gate watched and defended until morning. At daybreak, we will all meet back here and turn around. We will ride for Carinth. The horses will be rested by then."

"Yes sir."

"Good, tend to my gelding." He handed the reins over, gathering his supplies from his saddle packs. He looked over his troops one last time and called out, "Commander Durig is in charge. You will follow his orders until morning."

The Kersian soldiers exchanged glances. Seth turned from them. Just before he disappeared from view, he felt a strange presence. He turned around and looked about. The forest seemed desolate. Stretching his mana out, he felt around. Someone was watching. A spy. He narrowed his eyes and continued on. He knew then that by morning he would be traveling alone to Carinth.

CHAPTER 10

High Priest Graneck, Scribe of Temple Dagon, tapped his fingers on the desk in irritation. His eyes remained cast outside into the emerging growth of green, lost in thought. Danaria could not afford the inept sorceress' failure with the staff weapon, nor could they afford the staff weapon in her possession. The idea to destroy her before she made it to Arkeereon had presented itself earlier that day. Graneck did not make it a point to spy on others. Sometimes, however, the opportunity presented itself and Graneck believed that everything that happened, happened for good reason. It was in the corridor outside the council audience chamber that he had overheard them speaking.

"The Kersians have set up camp outside the Northern gates. One of them broke off from the troop and headed East into the Selenia Forest," a man said.

"For what purpose?" The question came from General Daxin.

"To meet someone? Another legion perhaps?" the man replied.

It was then that Graneck had devised his new plan. Now, in the silence and privacy of his temple chambers he wondered if he could truly get rid of the sorceress before she was sent to Arkeereon. "But what reason would require her to leave the city through the Northern gates with the enemy camped outside?" he muttered aloud.

The sound of footfalls echoed from the corridor beyond his closed chamber door, pulling him from his thoughts. Once the sound faded in the distance he leaned back in the chair and closed his eyes. *Charasis.* That was the answer. The plan began falling into place and he jumped from his chair and went to the books lining the wall, pulling an alchemical grimoire from a high shelf. "Goloxia. An alchemical preparation of wormwood and pythorian will wear off in several days, but will cause the person who ingested it to exhibit symptoms of Goloxia," he whispered aloud, aware of the excitement in his voice. "The only cure for both is Charasis, which only grows in the Selenia forest! Graneck, you are so brilliant." He chuckled, realizing he had complimented himself out loud.

The plan was flawless really. The only question that remained was who he would give the preparation to. Tnasha's father? Her mother perhaps? *No,* he decided quickly, giving it to either of them was too risky. It would have to be given to someone close, but not that close. *Someone naïve and unsuspecting.* The name of his victim came to him unbidden. "Malarissa, one of the triplet cousins to the sorceress and daughter of Lord Drazen O'Schoitt," he whispered. "Yes." After all, the preparation would not hurt Malarissa, it would only appear to hurt her.

This also invited the question as to how he would convince the O'Schoitt family to send Tnasha after the charasis rather than sending a legion to deal with the Kersians outside the gate. He knew he could manage it by using the excuse that as a sorceress, she had magick to deal with situations like this. Plus, utilizing that magick would make her stronger, more prepared for her coming task. But as with questions, each new question brought on another.

What if she manages to avoid the Kersians? he wondered. An alternate plan would be in order. He would have no choice but to go to the South section of Central Danaria, a veritable stomping ground for Danaria's less than desirable citizens. Harlots, thieves, assassins and criminals of every ilk could be easily bought there. On the off chance the girl avoided the Kersians, the assassins would be lying in wait to kill her. Order would be restored, Tnasha would be out of the way, and sorcerer soldiers, real sorcerers and soldiers, males, could be sent to retrieve the staff weapon. He resolved to go to the South section that afternoon.

With a satisfied sigh and a sense of nervous excitement, Graneck took the grimoire to the worktable and pulled a mortar and pestle from a drawer. He then took the jars of necessary herbs from the shelves and began mixing the concoction that would set his plan into motion.

It did not take him long to find Malarissa. The girl was so predictable in habit that he knew he would find her in the sitting room off the main hall. Alone. She sat quietly doing her needlework, a flowered pattern in red, green, and gold thread.

"Lady Malarissa, I noticed you sitting here by yourself and thought I would bring you tea," he announced, setting the silver platter in front of her. "And," he admitted, "I do not like taking my tea alone."

Malarissa smiled, showing a set of perfect, white teeth. "How kind of you, High Priest Graneck. I would be delighted to have tea with you."

He smiled back at her and sat down across from her, leaning over to hand her the already filled cup specially prepared for her consumption and hers alone. "I must admit I am surprised your sisters are not here with you."

She took the porcelain cup from him, careful not to spill anything on her perfect silk dress. "We may be triplets, but we are not joined at the hip. I enjoy my quiet time."

He poured himself a cup from the steaming kettle. "Me, too."

"The weather has been warm this year," she said.

He nodded, having known he would have to engage in pointless banter to pacify her. To get her to drink the tea. "Hopefully we're not in for a drought."

She pushed aside a wayward brown strand that had fallen from her perfectly coiffed hair. "Hopefully not," she agreed.

He fought back the urge to frown. She wasn't giving him much to go on. If he wanted her to drink it, he would have to work harder. Just as he was about to open his mouth, she took a delicate sip of the brew. "Do you like it? It's my own recipe. There is honey on the tray," he pointed out.

"Oh, no, it's lovely. What's in it?" She leaned forward seeming genuinely interested.

"Hibiscus, some mint," *to kill the taste of the other ingredients*, he added silently.

"Ah. A guarded secret."

Graneck nodded. "Perhaps." He took a long sip from his cup and sat back in the cushions of the chair, then looked on as she drained the cup of its contents and poured herself a second cup.

•

A feeling of dread embraced her. After what little time she had taken for herself that day, Tnasha set her book down, got up and strode to the main hall. There, her father and uncle stood huddled with one of the physicians and High Priest Graneck. Her aunt and grandmother stood off to the side speaking in hushed voices.

"What's wrong?" Her stomach twisted and turned violently.

All eyes turned toward her. Her father was the only one to offer an answer. "Your cousin Malarissa has fallen ill."

"Yeah. Well I hope it's not catching." Tnasha turned to leave.

"Wait. Tnasha, your assistance may be needed."

She groaned. "Fine."

"Malarissa has Goloxia."

"And I am supposed to help by...?" The minute she said it she regretted it. Goloxia was rare and sometimes deadly if not treated in time. She stood, waiting for an unkind response to her own selfish indifference.

High Priest Graneck forced a grin. "Charasis is the only known cure. But it must be quite fresh. It only grows in the Selenia Forest."

Outside, a crack of thunder vibrated the walls of the castle and a steady drizzle of rain poured from the sky. Tnasha felt goose pimples on her arms and she rubbed them away. "I know, and? Our herbalists don't keep it in stock?"

Her uncle Drazen spoke up then. "It must be fresh and doesn't tolerate domestication, let alone pots. There is a Kersian legion camped at the Northern entrance to the city. We cannot send anyone out to get the charasis. They would have to go through the encampment."

It was suddenly apparent to Tnasha what they were hinting at.

"Frightful weather. Why haven't they gone?" Tnasha's grandmother asked irritably. The crimson sky gave way to night in a loud rumble of defiance. Through the window, white lightning ripped through the clouds gleaning a red tint, and through the rain, a sliver of the moon stood stark white against the blackness.

Tnasha began pacing the length of the main hall. "Grandmother, the Kersians don't intend on leaving and they won't until we fight and chase them off. Why haven't we done that already?" She tipped her head and looked out a high window. "So you know I'm not climbing that mountain for a sprig of Charasis. By the time I've gotten over the peak the Kersians will be gone, the rain will have stopped, and Malarissa will have died."

Her father chuckled. "No one expects you to climb the mountain. There are other ways."

She hated weather like this. It made her uneasy, and that uneasiness reminded her of the Kersian island of Zul. Another crack of thunder brought jagged rods of silver lightning running in all directions.

Drazen cleared his throat "This time, the Kersians stormed through the Selenia Forest and headed straight to the Northern entrance without so much as a battle cry. Right now I suppose they are taking advantage of the low visibility and are hiding in the dense brush. We haven't sent anyone out because we can't tell how many there are, or where they are for that matter."

"Just how far into the Selenia Forest will I have to go?" Her eyes went wide in protest. Why they decided to send her when there were others just as capable for such a task, she did not know.

The physician spoke up then. "It grows deep in the forest closest to the Northern salt marshes."

She gasped. "That's almost all the way to Kalath's cave. How am I suppose to get past a legion of Kersians and travel, on foot, what would normally take at least an hour by horseback?"

"We figured you are the most resourceful." Graneck smiled with narrowed eyes. "You have sorcery on your side."

"Maybe you need to find someone well versed in espionage. I'm not sure how to go about this, Uncle Drazen. I cannot help you." She paced quickly, back and forth, her deep blue gown swirling about her ankles. She stopped suddenly and nervously ran her hand through her long, auburn hair.

"But you have to get the Charasis." Her aunt's blue eyes plead with her.

Her uncle let out a mournful sigh. "Use sorcery, Tnasha. You're a sorceress. Use sorcery."

"And what? Work more weather magick? You know how terrible a sorceress I am. Undoubtedly I'll conjure something by mere accident. That aside, I could cause a flood throughout Danaria. You have no idea what kind of sorcery I do. What destruction I'm capable of." Tnasha clamped her jaw shut, feeling her breath catch in her throat. There was a difference between saving herself and having someone else depend on her for their saving. Her family had more faith in her than she did. Where was the sorcerer Kalath when she needed him? She knew better. He had already gone home to the Northern salt marshes. *Exactly* where *she* was expected to go. "Can't one of you send a telepathic message to Kalath and have him bring it?"

Graneck shook his head. "There is no one with that ability in all Danaria. We were thinking perhaps you could create a distraction of some sort."

"All the sorcerers who live here and not one can communicate over long distances with another?" She crossed her arms over her chest. "I wouldn't even know where to begin to create a distraction without drawing attention to myself. So you're sending me in hopes my flawed sorcery will get me out the gate? Maybe I can *fly* to the Charasis. I wonder if there's a spell for that."

Everyone seemed to ignore her sarcasm.

"What if your sorcery works this time? Practice makes one better, Tnasha. If you practiced your sorcery half as much as you practiced your swordsmanship you'd be an adept sorceress," her uncle Drazen said casually. His pretended stoicism was wearing thin. She could hear it in the edge of his voice; see it in the creases of his weathered face. His unkempt gray hair was knotted and tangled. He was tired, and worried and much too old to help obtain the cure for his eldest daughter. He favored his bad left leg, and limped to the doorway that led through the long main corridors of the castle. The others turned to follow.

"You're all leaving me? Here Tnasha, here's what you have to do, goodbye? I would like some ideas, sage advice," she called after them.

Drazen waved a hand at her. "I'm going to Malarissa. I know you won't fail us Tnasha. You're resourceful." With that, he left. The others followed.

Tnasha's father paused, leaned in toward her and lowered his voice. "You have been acting arrogant, even invincible, ever since you returned from Zul."

She looked down at her feet, unsure how to respond. Her cheeks burned crimson. "But…" she started in protest.

"You need to stop it." Her father's tone was stern. "I did not raise you to behave like a spoiled child, or to throw tantrums, or to be disrespectful to your elders. You act as though you are untouchable because of this great power you were born with."

She felt her mouth contort into and angry frown. "I am not behaving like a spoiled…" Stopping mid-sentence, she realized his gaze had shifted into a disappointed glare. The same glare she had worked so hard to avoid. "I'm doing it right now, aren't I?"

He nodded once. "Your mana may be strong and you could probably move mountains with it. But that is all the more reason you should practice some humility. You are responsible for that power in how you use it. Especially when you are dealing with others. Have I made myself clear?"

With a gulp, Tnasha choked back her pride. "Yes, sir."

"Good. Now either you will help your cousin or you won't. The reason you were chosen is because of the power at your disposal. I'm sure they could find others to help, but Graneck and your uncle have more faith in you than any thief, sorcerer, or soldier in this entire city. She is your cousin, your own flesh and blood, after all. Whether you decide to help or not is entirely your own decision, but you should also know that your family is depending on you." He turned from her and left the room.

At that moment she knew she could never turn her cousin away, even if she and her cousin weren't that close.

She finally looked up, noticing Graneck had been standing in the doorway, and had probably overheard. He gave her what seemed a forced reassuring smile. "You can do this. We have faith in you. More faith than you have in yourself," he said before he left.

For that brief second, Tnasha thought she saw a look of satisfaction cross Graneck's face.

•

Changing into attire more befitting did not take long. Now dressed in breeches and a heavy tunic Tnasha pulled a light cloak over her shoulders, tucked the book of sorcery Kalath had given her beneath her arm, and ran out into the now drizzling rain. The streets stood empty of people save for the occasional passing of night patrol soldiers. Undoubtedly there would be plenty of soldiers at the Northern gate. Two legions in the very least.

She now knew that the Kersians wanted Danaria's sorceresses, and would resort to murder, subterfuge, and hundreds of years of war in order to obtain them. Knowing this, she smiled at her own disbelief in what she was about to do. Her uncle was right. Sorcery was Malarissa's only hope. Hacking and slashing her way through an army of Kersian
Soldiers with little chance of surviving, was not an option.

She inhaled the cool damp air and walked briskly toward the Northern gates, pulling the book tightly to her chest. It was in there. Page seventy-three. *How to turn oneself invisible.* She inhaled another deep breath. Faith, that is what she needed, she decided. But she had never had faith in her magick before, and she was not planning to start now. However, under the circumstances she had no choice but to try anything.

She reached the gates to find exactly what she had expected. Several hundred soldiers adorned in their armor and bearing weapons, waited. The gate stood barred to the hidden army outside. "Petty Officer fen Schoitt," came a voice from somewhere in front of her.

Her eyes searched the sea of soldiers for the owner of the summoning voice. She found him walking toward her through the drizzling rain. He was human. "Commander Girk. My father has sent me here on business," she said with a hearty smile.

Girk nodded to her. "What are you doing here? Horrid weather, eh?"

Tnasha gripped the book with all her might, feeling her knuckles go white. She was soaked and cold. "Commander, I need to get through the gate."

Commander Girk laughed. "Nonsense. No one is getting through *that* gate tonight, not even on order of the Council. Not unless visibility improves. Then there's the small problem of the Kersian army." He paused and peered through the rain at the gates. "If you don't mind me asking, why do you need to get out?"

"I need to go into the Selenia Forest for some Charasis. My cousin has fallen ill." Her eyes traveled to the Danarian archers peering through the slits of the wall, high on the towers of the fortification. "My father sent me," she repeated, then asked, "Why aren't they shooting?"

"The Kersians are hard to see in this rain. They've made themselves barriers and hidden themselves among the trees. We can't see them so we don't know how many are out there. It could be a handful, or maybe a few hundred. We've dispatched an army from Carinth to take up the rear. But it could be morning before they arrive."

Tnasha shook her head. "You don't seem to understand my dilemma. I need to get through the gate *tonight*. If I wanted to wait until morning, I would have climbed the mountain. Tonight - or my cousin will die. And my family will hate me."

Commander Girk wiped a bit of rain from his gaunt face and scratched his balding head. "Uh, no. Can't let you do it. This fortification is under my command. I'd be decommissioned if I let you walk straight into the hands of the enemy again. You are not even armed."

Tnasha stepped beneath a nearby overhang to keep the water off and pulled the book into view. "See this? There's a spell in here that will make me invisible."

Commander Girk stifled a chuckle. "Indeed?"

"Look. I know it sounds silly to you being that you're human and that you've only seen parlor trick sorcery rather than grand displays such as invisibility, but you have to trust me. You can send someone to ask my father or Sorcerer Graneck. They are the ones who sent me."

"Well then, you'd better have a spell in there that can help you walk through a steel door. I could let you out the passage next to the gate, but there is a dense thicket on the other side. You would make so much noise going through it they would hear you. Do you see *my* dilemma? Warlord General O'Schoitt may be angry, but General Daxin will kill me." he challenged.

Tnasha took a deep breath. Commander Girk was proving to be difficult. She realized then she should have arrived with a written order, but she had left quickly, not stopping to think anyone would question her. Girk was agitated as it was. Guarding the walls of the city with Kersians outside was a big responsibility. But with or without his approval, and with no time to find a general or get a written order, she intended to get over the fortification and through the Kersian camp at any cost. Even if it meant her life, at least she tried. That was all that really mattered. She stepped past Girk wordlessly, and walked toward the wall.

"As a commanding officer I forbid you. You cannot do this. It's insane. You'll die out there," he called after her. "Someone grab her!"

Yet no one stood in her way. The soldiers simply watched her pass. They were more interested in watching the city gates and the wall. She could feel Commander Girk behind her; hear his heavy boots squishing into the sodden ground. She turned suddenly to face him. "Once I become invisible, I'll slip over the wall. I'll use a rope to get down half the way, then I'll drop to the ground." With a fake smile she opened the book.

She went beneath another awning and stood against the inside wall close to the gate. Commander Girk followed angrily. There was a torch there, fastened with heavy steel drilled directly into the stone of the fortification. She opened the book, keeping it out of the rain, and began reading the words to herself, feeling the power in each of them. The wind and rain picked up pulling page seventy-three from her grasp. She wiped the rain from the page, thankful it had not smudged the ink and fumbled to find her place. She said the words aloud, picking up where she had left off.

"Denash Orac Yanna," she said softly. Suddenly, her body began to feel extremely light.

Commander Girk gasped. "You're really disappearing," he whispered in disbelief.

With the incantation complete, Tnasha put the book under her arm and started toward the stairs leading to the top of the battlement. Commander Girk followed hesitantly, seemingly unsure as to where she was. "Find me a rope, please," she said, mildly amused in knowing that Girk had never seen such sorcery.

The commander frantically searched for one. Upon spotting a rope over the arm of a lone soldier, he dashed over and took it from the surprised man. He ran back to where Tnasha had been standing. "Here," he said, holding the rope out.

Tnasha took it from him with invisible hands and threw it over her shoulder. "Thank you." She started up the stairs. When she reached the top, she secured the rope, took up the slack, and slowly descended the wall. Ten feet down the other side she positioned herself over what looked like the softest spot of ground, took a deep breath, and let go.

She dropped the remaining six feet, feeling her ankle twist beneath her. Her legs buckled under her and she fell on her side with a dull thud. The sharp side of a stone tore at her side. Standing, she felt her ankle ache beneath her wait, she then brushed herself off and attempted to inspect the invisible wound from the stone. She looked up to see the soldiers above pulling the rope back over the wall.

Once satisfied she was in one piece she stepped away from the wall into the wide clearing. Her body ached from head to toe. On this side of the wall the forest was cut back fifty yards or more.

She could see several placid Kersians hiding in the forest watching the wall. Their faces remained blank and stolid, their feet unmoved by the muddy ground encompassing them. Tnasha slid by them, painfully aware that her own boots squished clamorously through the mud. That is when she felt it; the sudden bulge as if her stomach had expanded. Her feet felt heavy. The squishing of her steps became louder. So loud in fact, that the Kersians began searching for the source of the noise. With labored breathing, she pulled the extra weight, and looked around to see if she was caught on something.

What, in the name of Natyis, she thought. She wondered then if her spell was wearing off. She quickened her steps. If she wanted to get through the camp before the spell dissipated, she would have to run. But she could not. Each step proved more weighted than the last and the book began to feel like a slab of stone.

A startled scream pierced the black night. Tnasha turned to her left, and noted quickly that they saw her. Startled at first, she stopped short and looked straight into the eyes of the panicked man. They were wide with terror.

"What is it?" he cried loudly. He backed up, reaching for a halberd standing against the tree behind him.

Ten soldiers advanced quickly, each keeping his distance out of fear. With spears, axes, and swords in hand they surrounded her. "Oh now, come on. I'm an unarmed woman," she told them. But that's not what she, nor they, heard. Instead, the words that emerged from her lips sounded more like garbled gibberish. Tnasha panicked, and looked down at herself. It was then she realized that something was not right.

Her body, instead of being invisible, was contorted into something of a beast-like nature. Heavy, solid, and dripping wet. There was fur on her ankles. She could feel it rubbing against the inside of her boots. It itched something horrible. Her hands emerged from the transformation into hideous, clawed appendages covered in thick, black, matted fur. "Oh no," she wailed. *Flowing from my fingers like a river indeed, cursed mana*, she thought.

Once again, her sorcery had not worked as planned. Now, she had to find a way to keep herself from falling prey to the Kersians.

Growling, she stepped forward. The Kersians stepped back. A mob of soldiers came at her from the rear and Tnasha did what anyone would have done. She ran forward as fast as her legs would carry her, knocking two soldiers out of her way as she went. The path in front of her stood clear. If she could only reach the forest... Crack! A flail hit her square between the shoulders, and she stumbled with a cry. Regaining her footing, she kept running.

With each step, her body began to feel a bit lighter. *The spell is wearing off*, she thought. She threw her full weight into each step, increasing her speed until finally she disappeared into the shadows of the forest. Without armor, or weapons, or weight she was faster. She did not stop running until the shouts of her pursuers became mere echoes in the night.

CHAPTER 11

Tnasha paused to catch her breath. She looked down at herself. Her body turned invisible again. It did not diminish the fact that she felt every scratch, scrape and bruise from the fall and from running through the forest. Every muscle ached with pain and fatigue. The rain finally subsided, leaving the now uncovered moon to light her way.

Sighing with relief, she continued deeper into the Selenia Forest, searching for the Charasis along the path. She found she could move faster, though she could still feel the burning pain in her side and back. Farther into the forest she thought she heard horses coming from the North. Undoubtedly, the Carinthian legion Commander Girk dispatched earlier that day would arrive soon. She pressed on in hopes the Kersians would be gone by the time she returned. Otherwise, she would have no choice but to try the spell again unless it held out.

By the time she found the Charasis with its blue leaves that looked gray in the moonlight, and now closed flowers that were bright yellow by day, she began to feel heavy again. This time, her legs tingled and sharp pains darted through her side and back. After uprooting several large charasis plants and putting them in her satchel, she sat down on a rock and pulled out the book, turning to page seventy-three. She brought forth the soft glow of her mana so she could see better and glanced over the incantation a second time. But something was wrong. The first half seemed right and yet she did not recall the second half of the incantation at all. "Yumac, Lara, Catre? That's not what I read," she whispered to herself.

As if in answer, the wind picked up and lifted page seventy-three from her grasp, turning the page to page seventy-five. There, on the same part of the page, an incantation for another spell stared at her. *How to turn oneself into a vile creature.* "Oh great. Isn't this my luck," Tnasha yelled into the night. With Malarissa's condition being grave as it was, Tnasha had not taken the time to look over the spell more thoroughly before leaving. Now she wished she had. With a resigned sigh she browsed past the incantation to the spell's specifics. She read on. *In order to break this spell, the castor must eat one Rolick Berry with one grain of pure salt. This spell will not wear off on its own.*

"Hmm. It figures. What is a Rolick Berry? I've never heard of that," she said aloud to no one.

"Someone's there." came a male voice from further down the path.

Tnasha closed the book, shoved one last sprig of Charasis into her satchel, and made haste to the nearest tree. She crouched low to the ground and watched the path as horses approached. Just then, she felt the familiar bloating and heaviness. She was turning into *it* again.

A woman's hushed voice answered. "There's no one there. Probably an animal. Our scouts have been by here already."

"But it sounded like talking," came the man's voice again.

The sounds of horses erupted from the darkness into full view. It was indeed the army of Carinthian soldiers come to help drive the Kersians back to Zul. The scent of wet chain mail, and drenched horses drifted on the air. Tnasha peered from behind the tree and recognized their golden colored, horned helms. The urgency to get away overwhelmed her.

With this in mind, Tnasha crouched closer to the tree, wanting to become one with it. She held her breath. The Carinthian General and his soldiers took to arming themselves with the weapons they carried.

His eyes went wide as he peered at the tree. "There is someone behind that tree there."

"There is no one there. It is probably an animal," a woman's voice said.

Tnasha tilted her head back and looked to the sky. It was getting late and Malarissa's condition was undoubtedly worse. But she could not allow herself to be seen by the Carinthian soldiers, nor could she go home without resolving her current problem either. If she entered Danaria looking as she did, they would kill her instantly and ask questions later. That was the nature of Danaria's military.

The Carinthian General finally spoke after what seemed like a long span of time. "You're probably right. Let's move out."

With a silent hand signal and a few whispers, the message to move out was relayed back to the soldiers behind. The Carinth army of no more than two hundred men and women moved off toward Danaria. Tnasha breathed a deep sigh of relief. Once they were gone, she headed deeper into the forest toward the salt marshes.

She forced her mana to shine brightly, like a beacon in the darkness, helping to light her way through more dense underbrush. She hurried along, ignoring her pain. With each step, her body began to feel lighter. She knew it was happening again. Soon, she would disappear. Her eyes searched the darkness for something familiar. Instead, she found nothing but shadows and strange sounds. Luckily, Kalath's cave was not far off. She would be there soon. She began moving faster until finally, the unmistakable tingle of energy swept her weight away and she was able to float like the wind. Her mana, too, faded into the blackness.

A twig snapped somewhere in the distance. She stopped short and looked around, feeling the invisible hair on her arm stand on end. Shivering, she started down the path again. Her pace quickened and she broke into a run. The sound of voices brought her to a halt.

"This is horse crap," a man's voice said. "We won't get paid now."

"It is not our fault she didn't turn up. Graneck assured us she would be there. Maybe we didn't wait long enough."

Tnasha saw a small campfire between several trees. She knelt down behind some underbrush and looked on. Two men with light white and gray mana sat near the fire.

"So you're saying we should be paid either way?"

"We delivered our part of the bargain to the extent we were able to. The sorceress never turned up. That was Graneck's part. He did not uphold his part of the bargain. Besides, we had to sneak past those stupid Kersians who were heading to the Northern gates. Luckily we got out before they arrived. That feat alone means we should get paid."

"Yes, and Graneck could lie. He's well respected and they would believe him. All he would have to say is he knew of our plot to kill Termark O'Schoitt's daughter. We are not getting paid."

Obviously the assassins were inexperienced. Tnasha rolled her eyes, it figured Graneck would try to kill her inexpensively. She gasped when a twig beneath her snapped loudly, not realizing they could hear her.

The men jumped up, drawing their swords. "Who's there?"

She turned and ran, not caring if they heard her footfalls or not. It was clear now that Graneck really was out to get her. She kept running, still invisible, toward the salt marshes.

When she felt it was safe, she stopped to catch her breath, looking back to see if she was being followed. The forest seemed empty. She looked around, taking in the surroundings. The ever growing salt marshes had long since rendered the trees in this part of the region barren of the green leaves and the fruits they once bore. Their trunks stood crusted in salt; their bark dried and cracked. Gnarled branches twisted and rose into the night sky like giant, burned talons. Finally, something familiar greeted her. As she approached the wooden bridge that led to Kalath's cave Tnasha felt her heart skip a beat. The heavy feeling overwhelmed her. She stepped forward, paused, and looked around. Somewhere in the distance, she felt eyes watching her.

She hurried forward, feeling the fatigue deep in her muscles. Once she reached the other side of the small bridge, she bolted toward the entrance of the cave, through the thick mud the flood from her last visit, and the recent rain had left. The leaves rustling against the wind in the one living tree, the tree she brought back to life in her first attempts at sorcery, flooded her ears. The flicker of torchlight flooded the entrance of the cave and out into the night. Within the cave, Kalath played his flute, and the music drifted outside to her ears, echoing on the night air.

Her normal body was coming back. She could feel it. But she knew it would not be long before the creature came out again. It was getting tiresome, really. And Tnasha was not sure she could handle another transformation. Not tonight. Not ever. She could feel fatigue settling into her bones, and her wounds burned with intense pain. It was then she vowed she would get even with Graneck.

Looking down at herself, she noted her thighs seemed bloated. "I feel like I'm going to heave," she whispered to no one. Her stomach twisted violently. "Kalath!"

The flute stopped. "Who's there?"

"It's Tnasha," she called back. "I've got a really big problem."

Just then, she began her transformation. Her stomach went into spasms and her abdomen heaved. Each breath resulted in another transformation. Her calves widened and her thighs thickened, and the hair on her ankles began rubbing against the inside of her boots. "I need a Rolick Berry and salt!" she cried. The transformation seemed painful this time.

The tall, frail frame of the Sorcerer Kalath emerged from the mouth of the cave. And when he saw her, he stopped short and gasped. "Tnasha? What have you done?"

"The book." Tnasha handed it to him, wiping the sweat from her palms. "I made a mistake. It was supposed to be page seventy-three, but seventy-five got in the way!"

Kalath nodded. "I see," he said. "I was not expecting you for another day at least, but I suppose this did warrant your early arrival. Let me see if I can find a remedy."

He led Tnasha into the cave. Kalath's rustic home was warm and inviting as usual. Crude wooden shelves lined the stone walls and the flames from the hearth and numerous lighted candles filled the cavern with a soft light. Sparsely furnished, an old chair sat next the hearth while another sat next to a small wooden table. On the floor, which was still damp from the flood, lining the East wall, were many small bottles and earthen jars filled with herbs and salves; their scents lingered in the air, spicy and sweet.

"Sit down next to the fire, Tnasha," the graying sorcerer ordered. He went over to his collection of herbs and rummaged through it.

"I mixed two of the incantations up because I had to get charassis for Malarissa. She fell ill and will die without it. There was a Kersian legion outside the gate so the only way I could get out was to use a spell for invisibility."

Kalath looked over his shoulder. "Why am I not surprised?" he asked playfully. He went back to his herbs, glancing at the spell book, which was open to page seventy-five. "Elder Berries. Juniper Berries. Hmm. Rolick Berries. I have never heard of those."

Tnasha put her head in her grotesque hands. Her heart sank even deeper into her chest.

With a clap of his hands, Kalath strode across the room to a pile of books on a shelf. "Where is my Alchemist's Handbook?" He shook his head in dismay and addressed her. "Sometimes these odd plants are not odd at all. Sometimes they are just given fancy pseudo-names for mystery's sake."

Tnasha nodded and said nothing.

"Hmm. Here it is," Kalath said in triumph. He pulled the thick, leather bound book from the middle of the stack and wiped the dust from it. "I believe it is alphabetical, but maybe there is an index..."

He paused and peered deep into the book with squinted eyes as if searching for some impenetrable mystery. He flipped through the pages with a long, bony hand. "There is not an index, but it is alphabetical. Ah ha! Here it is. How fortunate! Page seventy-five."

Tnasha rolled her eyes. It was her luck that there was something to the page seventy-five phenomena. "Whart sis itch?" she asked.

He looked at her, confused then waved a hand at her. "Do not try to talk, child. Rosehips are also called Rolick Berries by tribes in Srean. I had rosehips. But I am afraid I am out. They are wonderful in teas you know..."

Tnasha closed her eyes. *Wonderful in teas, great. Can he be any more relaxed about this?* her mind screamed. "So wha no?" she asked, disappointed.

"Patches of rosehips grow along Danaria's Northern fortification wall. They should be in bloom this time of year." Kalath smiled at her.

Tnasha threw her arms into the air. "Itch figrr!" which meant *it figures*.

"Well, I suppose you had better get that charassis back to Central Danaria. Along the way you can get the rosehips, and take the spell off," Kalath said.

"Wha ab te invisb spe?" she asked.

Kalath wrinkled his nose, bringing out the creases in his forehead. His eyes suddenly went wide with understanding. "Oh, that should wear off on its own. Now I would love to sit and talk, but you should really be on your way. If this spell is not taken off soon, your body may end up as the creature permanently. I will see you in a few days."

Tnasha's eyes widened in horror and her stomach churned with anxiety.

Kalath went over and picked up the spell book. He handed it back to her. "Malarissa's illness was no accident."

Tnasha felt her jaw drop open as a thin line of drool slid down the side of her mouth. "Grnk. Assen. I saw the in forst."

"The serpent wise deals death to lies. Be wary. This will not be Graneck's last attempt. Stay away from him," Kalath said without hesitation. He took the grimoire from her and opened it with a sly grin. "This is it."

She took it back from him.

"Page twenty. Make no mistake Tnasha," he paused and looked into her eyes as if waiting to know if she understood.

Tnasha nodded for him to continue. The light feeling, as if she was turning into air, started again.

"Page twenty," he repeated. "On this page there is a spell to enchant with the power of stealth. When you reach the outskirts of the Kersian encampment outside the gates, read the incantation and cast the spell. This should get you past the Kersians, to the rosehips. It will wear off on its own."

Tnasha nodded and pulled the book to her bloated torso. *I won't fail this time,* she told herself.

"Do not forget the salt." Kalath handed her a small vial with several large grains inside. "This is pure sea salt. Only one."

She nodded again and turned from the cave, tightly grasping the vial in her deformed hand. Kalath followed her to the cave's entrance, and stayed there until she disappeared into the blackness.

Tnasha turned invisible midway back to where the Carinth army sat awaiting their orders. And she remained invisible until she was a short distance from the Northern gates. Then she began changing into the creature again. Twice now, her stomach convulsed with dry heaves and she wanted nothing more than to get the Charasis back to Danaria and then fall into her warm and waiting bed. But there was, as her luck would have it, the matter of the spell to be dealt with first.

She was hesitant about the new incantation Kalath proposed. She did not want to attract attention to herself. It was no use. No matter how hard she tried, she always seemed to end up creating chaos. A heavy sigh escaped her lips. If she was anyone else but herself, she knew she would not want a sorceress notorious for her flawed magick to be reciting incantations anywhere near civilization. She did not have much of a choice, of course. If anyone saw her, she would be killed for sure. Least of all, she did not want to disappoint Kalath. After all, he took his time to help tutor her in the ways of sorcery before her trip to Zul. Not that it had done any good. But he had never turned her away. He was like a second father to her. She sighed with sadness. *So much for being born a sorceress with natural talent, whatever that means,* she thought.

She approached the rear of the Carinth army and hid behind a tree, wondering if their horses would sense her.

"How many?" asked the Carinthian General.

"Approximately one hundred maybe more," a soldier said, pointing at the ground. "They're scattered here, and here.

Hiding behind trees and rocks. There are a few over there to the left, too."

"Time to get into position. Leave the horses," the General told his second in command. The blonde woman nodded and gave the signal to dismount.

Tnasha waited as they dismounted and armed themselves. She stood patiently wishing she had brought her own weapons. Then she thought how much harder that may have been.

"Okay, let's go. Ready?" he asked dryly.

The blond woman nodded again.

Tnasha's body was becoming lighter again. The Carinthian soldiers slinked wordlessly toward the Kersian camp. She waited until she could feel her voice before she whispered to herself, "I promise not to mess up."

She was not sure she could keep that promise to herself. However, she intended to try. She directed her focus. "I'll hold the pages tightly with both hands and will not avert my eyes from the text. I swear it."

Tnasha opened the book to page twenty like Kalath had told her. Holding her palm over the page for light from her mana, she found the spell to enchant with the power of stealth easily. Meanwhile, her mind screamed at her to do it right while her body began to disappear, once again, into the translucent air. She concentrated, reading every word as if it were sacred, pronouncing every syllable under her breath. "Ganic Tasa Herac," she finished triumphantly. She looked up and gasped. Around the Carinth soldiers appeared a soft blue light that glowed brightly in the tenebrous night. It surrounded each soldier and faded into the presence of something, but it wasn't stealth. In fact it seemed to get the Kersian's attention.

The Carinthians exchanged puzzled glances. Their eyes searched around them for the source. Tnasha winced.

The General made several gestures to his waiting soldiers, pulled his sword from its scabbard, and led the Carinth army into the Kersian camp with a battle cry.

Tnasha lingered behind, gauging whether or not she was about to turn into the beast again. She crept from the forest and into the clearing as the roar of battle rose high into the oncoming horizon. It would be morning soon. She saw her chance between the fighting soldiers and the wounded littering the ground, and she ran. Halfway to the fortification wall she could see the rosehips. Hundreds of them. Their plump red bodies though gray in the moonlight stood out from the deep dark leaves of their parent plants. Her mouth watered in anticipation for that which could cure her.

She started to change. "Not again," she moaned. As if answering once again, the sky suddenly opened to a downpour of rain that slid to the ground like sharp shards of crystal. Tnasha glanced at the cloud-covered sky and pushed on, moving to the wall in haste. As she ran a sharp, stinging pain shot up her calf, through her thigh, and into her lower back. She cried out, but kept moving.

When she finally reached the wall, she put her back against it and slid to the ground. A lone arrow protruded from her calf. She breathed a deep sigh of relief and let her now solid hand drift to one of the plants beside her. After pulling one of the berries from its mother plant, she removed the vial of salt from her satchel. Her hand now malformed into the hideous shape it had taken on several times that night. Quickly, she slipped one berry and one grain of salt into her mouth; letting both slide to the back of her tongue and down her throat.

Looking up from her hands to the battle before her, she realized what a vulnerable position she was in. With what little strength she had left, she lifted herself to her feet noticing she was not changing back. But it did not seem to matter. No one noticed her, in all of her beastly form, standing there. Her body suddenly began to vanish. She had the Charasis and needed to get it to Malarissa. Just then, the Northern gates opened to an onrush of Danarian soldiers.

Dreading it might already be too late, Tnasha sprung to the gate and slipped into the city. She hurried past the fighting, and dodged the mounted horsemen who could not see her. Once the danger passed, she limped toward home clutching the satchel. Behind her, she heard the faint echo of blades ripping into one another with sheer force. By the time she reached the castle the sounds of battle seemed a mere faded memory, while the sun emerged from behind the Eastern mountains.

CHAPTER 12

Seth saw the beam of violet light approach from a distance. It looked like a thin line moving toward the cave of the seer. As it came closer, it began to take form. It was not human or sorcerer. Or was it? He squinted, trying to bring the thing into focus. A woman. A sorceress. His eyes watched her in wonder. Just as he could begin to make out the details, her shape began to change. In horror, he watched as the sorceress shape shifted into a creature. He recoiled and hid in the underbrush, stifling his own mana. The impression he read from her was that of fear and exhaustion.

His mind raced. A shape-shifting sorceress was unheard of. Then he heard it speak. He could not make out what she said except one word, "Kalath!"

He peered over the thick tangle of underbrush a second time. The seer emerged, said something inaudible, and both the sorceress and the seer retreated into the cave. Seth bit his lower lip and ducked into the underbrush again. "What abominations are the heathen's breeding?" he asked himself.

After a short time, whatever it was left as a hideous beast creature, with mana the strength of three fifth generation sorceresses. Its mana stood from its body five foot-lengths or more. Perhaps the seer summoned it. He shuddered. He did not have time to think about it. More important tasks were at hand. He waited until he could no longer see the violet mana of the creature, then stood from his hiding place and made his way into the clearing in front of the cave. He looked around, still horrified, and forced himself toward the cave's entrance.

Without hesitation, he entered unannounced to find the seer kneeling near the hearth. The old man examined the drying herbs hanging there.

Seth sneered. "Stand seer."

The seer whirled around and gasped, wide eyed. "What is it you want?"

Seth approached him, pulling the old, gray haired man to his feet. "My brothers should have destroyed you when they had the chance. But since they did not, I have come to do what they could not."

The old sorcerer squeezed his eyes shut and began reciting an incantation beneath his breath.

"You will not invoke your shape shifting whore! Nor will you summon the Danarian heathens!" With one swift motion, Seth struck the old man with the back of his hand, square on the jaw, knocking him easily to the floor. He laughed, enjoying himself.

Kalath cried out in pain. "I am an old man. I cannot harm you. Leave me be."

Seth growled. "You are an interference, old man. It is by Gavgal's order, in the name of the Unnamed, that you will be destroyed."

Kalath backed away from him, dragging himself on the dirt floor. "You will fail."

"Will I?" His eyes turned an even deeper, glowing orange. He lifted Kalath to his feet, dragging him from the cave. Once outside, he shoved the old man to the ground, neutralizing Kalath's light blue mana. It stopped moving around Kalath's body, solid, and started to fall in on itself. Kalath gasped for air.

Seth drew his sword. "Your ability to see is too great. That is something we can no longer risk."

Before Kalath could respond, the Kersian sorcerer plunged his sword deep into Kalath's chest again and again until the old sorcerer stopped struggling and his now unmoving light blue mana faded into nothing. Satisfied, Seth retrieved his blade and wiped it clean with his own tunic. Once he replaced his sword in the sheath at his side, he reached into his mana and pulled a second sword with a gold colored pommel, guard, and grip. After dragging the sorcerer's body outside, he turned him over onto his stomach and thrust the clean, never used blade deep into Kalath's back. He wanted to send a message.

The Kersian sorcerer turned then and fled into the surrounding darkness. The dawn this day, for him, would signal a new beginning. If all went as planned, Gavgal, his annoying impotent brother, and Morvack, the foolish one, would hand over what he needed. Then, and only then, he could usurp power and rule the new world. A hearty chuckle escaped his lips and he grinned with smug satisfaction.

S. J. Reisner

CHAPTER 13

$\mathbf{A}$ young sorcerer with gray mana entered Graneck's private study unannounced.

Graneck sat at a desk near a window. "I have been waiting for you."

The man lifted an eyebrow, but said nothing.

"I see the sorceress still lives." Graneck looked up from his writing and stood, leaning over the desk. He knew he shouldn't have hired inexperienced assassins, but they wanted less than the others and Graneck's resources were somewhat limited if he did not want Caitlan to find out. "What happened? Why does she still live?"

The red haired sorcerer responded. "She was not there like you told us she would be!"

"Or maybe you were in the wrong place."

"I came here to tell you we are not working for you anymore. This is too risky. We had to slip by those Kersian soldiers and could have gotten killed. Aside from which my friend and I have decided it would be too easy for you to lie about us."

Graneck smiled. He would not make the same mistake twice. This time he would hire more experienced brethren. "That's fine. I have employed someone else."

"Good."

"If you tell anyone..." The threatening tone of Graneck's voice was clear. "And I am not paying."

The young sorcerer nodded. "Yes, I know. I have only one question."

Graneck met his gaze with expectation. "Yes?"

"Why do you want to kill her?"

Graneck scowled. "Let us just say she is dangerous."

The young sorcerer shook his head, turned, and left. Graneck stared after him. He looked to the sundial outside his window, then grabbed his cloak and hurried from the room. He did not want to be late. The Angorans were prompt people, and their proposition was too good for him to ignore.

He met them in a nearby common house. The bustle of hurried people signaled the midday meal, and a low rumble of voices filled the air. In the far back they sat. They wore the black woolen cloaks and the clothing of commoners. Their hoods hid their faces and features. The space around them stood empty, a likely sign the Angoran sorcerers were hiding their mana from any Danarian sorcerer who might cross their paths.

Graneck approached the table. "I hope I have not kept you waiting."

"You made a pivotal mistake," one of the men said.

"Did I?"

The second man spoke. "You hired two of your own to kill her. They were obviously inexperienced and did not succeed. Even now, they may feel…" the man drained the flagon of ale in front of him. "…guilty for even trying."

"They will say nothing."

"You sound confident," said the first.

"I am. If they say anything, I merely claim no knowledge. It is hearsay."

"And if they warn her?" the second asked.

"That is now your problem. I have told you how dangerous the sorceress is. I should not have hired inept boys to do an adept's job."

The first leaned in to the table, still hidden behind the cowl hood of his cloak. "What is her element?"

Graneck thought about this for a moment. As far as he knew she had no definitive element, but Kalath had mentioned her ability with water sorcery. "It is benign, but strong with water," he finally said.

"With the strength of an elemental?" The Angoran's voice remained emotionless.

"Yes."

"We are raising our price."

Graneck's calm expression turned sour. "That was not the deal."

The second Angoran drew a deep breath, exhaling with a growl. "That was the deal before we discovered she has no element."

"I told you from the beginning she was anomalous," he said, fighting the urge to raise his voice.

The first pointed at him with a rough, square finger. "We expected her to have elemental mana, but not without an element."

Graneck cleared his throat, straightened his tunic, and frowned. "How much of an increase?"

"Five thousand shinder, fifty-five keldin," said the second without pausing. He looked toward his associate who nodded approvingly. That was more than enough money to keep a single tribe properly fed and clothed for several winters in the harsh wilds of the Onyx Mountains.

"That is ridiculous!" People at nearby tables fell silent turning toward Graneck. He looked around and calmed himself. "Fine. What else will you need?"

"The route she plans to use in order to reach Ramathra. We will make it look like a Kersian attack."

For the first time that morning, Graneck smiled a genuine smile. "I will have it to you by morning. They will be leaving then."

"Good." The first lifted his hand, summoning a serving maid. "More ale."

Graneck reached into his purse and pulled several shinder, handing them to the young woman. "It is the least I can do. I must go. I have business to attend to. The information will be sent to your room at the inn."

Both men nodded. They did not turn to watch him leave. Deep down, Graneck felt a slight pang of anxiety. It subsided quickly as he realized he would be ridding the world of a hidden danger. The sorcerers' council would thank him some day.

CHAPTER 14

The late morning beamed bright through the window. Tnasha looked outside. It was sunny without any trace of the rain save for several puddles still lingering in the streets. She dressed as quickly as she could manage and emerged from her chambers bandaged, sore and not quite rested. Despite the pain, she was awake with the anticipation of knowing how Malarissa was. She limped slowly through the corridors to the main hall, and finally found her uncle in the library with, of all people, the Carinthian General.

"Feeling better, Tnasha?" Drazen greeted.

She eyed her uncle and the General with suspicion. "I'll live."

Her uncle smiled in understanding. "Tnasha, I would like to introduce General Kauf of Carinth."

Tnasha nodded at him. "Pleasure to make your acquaintance. How is Malarissa?"

Drazen smiled. "The charassis is working. The physician believes she will be well enough to get out of bed by the end of the week. The physician also expressed concern that you should rest today."

Tnasha rolled her eyes and turned to Kauf. "Thank you for your help last night, General Kauf."

The General looked at her, confused. "Pardon me?"

"Your army's arrival unexpectedly coincided with mine. You not only helped drive the Kersians off, but your soldiers kept the Kersians distracted, which enabled me to get back into the city with the charasis to save my cousin's life. I am very grateful."

"Oh. Umm, you're very welcome." He smiled, a bit uneasy.

Drazen shoved a strand of brown hair from his face. "General Kauf was just telling me he is going to be the guide for your undertaking."

She raised an eyebrow. "That's right, Priestess Caitlan mentioned him. She has faith in him."

Kauf smiled. "I am looking forward to working with Danaria to procure the item."

Drazen looked on expectantly.

"You have been briefed already?" she asked. "You know Arkeereon well I've been told. I'm glad you will be going with us. Though I have to know, have you been given details?"

"Yes."

Tnasha put on a pout. "You probably know more than I do. I hate surprises."

"I have been put in charge of this mission so it would stand to reason I would know more than you, but I will share what I know when the time comes."

She sighed. "I guess I thought that since I'm the magickal warfare Caitlan would at least have let me be in charge to some extent."

"Tnasha..." Drazen looked at her with kind brown eyes. "Someone with experience needs to be in charge of this assignment. Its success could mean the life and death of thousands of humans, and all our kind. Kauf here knows Arkeereon better than any of you so it would stand to reason that he would be leading. Not to mention his many years of experience."

Tnasha nodded with a shrug. "Oh, I know. That's fine. But when it comes to sorcery and sorcerers you might want to stand back," she told the General. "As far as I am concerned, this is not a military issue, nor a human issue. It's a sorcerer's issue. I am the only sorceress going and therefore, I am the only protection you have against other sorcerers."

"And from what I've heard you are somewhat haphazard at that," Kauf offered with a grin.

Tnasha gave him a weak smile. "You and Kolgern. You'll both be lucky if I haven't turned you into toads by the time this is over with."

"So we leave in the morning then?" Kauf asked.

"I don't know. You're leading this mission, so I suppose it's up to you." She gave him an angelic smile, turned and started toward the door.

"Uh, yes. We leave in the morning," he called after her.

Tnasha snorted in response and turned around in the doorway. "I look forward to it, General." She nodded at her uncle. "Thanks Uncle Drazen."

"Thank you, Tnasha. I knew you were resourceful." Drazen smiled and nodded approvingly.

Tnasha returned the smile. She tipped her head and stretched her sore arms with a yawn. "I'll tell you one thing. When Malarissa is better, and when I get back from finding the Raven's Claw, she owes me a cup of Sherokean coffee."

Drazen chuckled. "I'll make sure I tell her."

Tnasha retreated to her room, examining the now non existent injuries she had gotten the night before. Healed and faded, all that remained as a reminder were her aching muscles. She yawned again. Someone knocked on her door.

She sighed and climbed back into bed, pulling the quilts up around her neck. She rubbed her shoulder. "Come in."

Priestess Caitlan entered with a warm, concerned smile. "How are you feeling?"

"Not well."

"You have healed nicely thanks to Physician Roderick. He does good work repairing flesh wounds using one's own mana. He was here early this morning."

Tnasha let out a light laugh. "Here I thought my amulet healed them. Or that maybe my mana decided to give it a go."

"Well, had you focused on healing yourself, your mana or amulet could have healed you. In time you'll learn how to make that happen. Once you become more adept. Self healing is something you should concentrate on next time you have an injury." Caitlan sat down on the side of the bed. "You must rest.

Feel your own internal sense of strength envelope you. By tomorrow morning, you should be well rested."

Tnasha ignored Caitlan's comments about healing. She had heard the same from Kalath after she escaped the Kersians the first time. She knew they were right, but she didn't have time to think about healing. Graneck and the assassins weighed heavy on her mind. "Something isn't right. I learned something disturbing last night, in the forest."

Caitlan cocked her head. "What is it?" She put a comforting hand on Tnasha's shoulder.

"I ran across two men who meant to kill me."

"What?" Caitlan's eyes grew wide with genuine surprise.

"They were talking about how they were supposed to kill me, but because I never showed up as I was supposed to, they would not be paid."

The priestess gasped. "Who would hire assassins to kill you?"

Tnasha took a moment's pause, fearing that if she said it, Caitlan's actions would be unpredictable. She said it anyway. "Graneck."

Caitlan jumped from where she sat. "By Natyis, he will have my wrath to deal with. Now you rest and don't worry about that. *I* will deal with my husband." The high priestess turned on her heel and hurried from the room.

Tnasha stared after her in surprise. She had not expected Caitlan's reaction. The reaction she was looking for was denial, shock, or anger at Tnasha and the priestess offered none of these. Which meant only one thing: Caitlan suspected Graneck's actions already and knew it was true.

Tnasha closed her eyes. She pulled strength and resolve from the core of her center, allowing it to wash over her in deep blue shades of mana to heal her aching muscles.

●

Kolgern's shoulder had healed quite nicely. The wound left by the Kersian High Priest Morvack's dagger only a month before was now a scar. Kolgern put his tunic back on, watching the physician's expression closely for signs of concern. "Is it healed completely then?"

The man nodded. "Can you move it without pain now?"

"Yes."

"Then it's fine. Although you should be careful for a few more weeks. Freshly healed wounds are susceptible to strain. Light exercise, however, could be helpful."

Kolgern stood, thanked the man, and strode from the building. Outside, a familiar face greeted him. Shadon, dressed in his usual black garb, looked up at the sign then at Kolgern. "Getting a check up?"

"I had to make sure my arm was all right."

Shadon smiled. "Or were you looking for excuses to not go?"

Kolgern ignored the question. "Did you speak with Priestess Caitlan yet?"

"Yes. It sounds interesting."

"Hmm." Kolgern walked alongside him. "I was not expecting to see you until after we'd arrived at Kalath's."

"I make good time trading off horses at each stop and riding long hours."

Kolgern gave him a sideways glance. "Does it ever bother you?"

Shadon raised a dark eyebrow. "What?"

"That you are never home for more than a few days at a time?"

He shrugged. "I'm used to it. It's the nature of the job."

"Yeah, well I would have liked a few months break between traveling. I like stability."

Shadon's lips spread into a wide grin. "There is nothing wrong with that. Let's get a drink. I'm thirsty." He led the way to a small tavern on the adjacent street corner, immediately finding his way to a corner table in the far back of the room.

Kolgern followed and sat across from him. "Do you always take the chair next to the wall?"

"When I can. You never know who's behind you." He lifted his hand to the young man serving tables. The man immediately responded, bringing two flasks of ale to the table. Shadon leaned on his elbows and yawned. "Where is Tnasha?"

Kolgern shook his blond head of hair. "Trust me; you do not want to know."

"More trouble?"

"Her cousin mysteriously ended up with a rare illness and she was sent to find charasis in the forest last night. Through a legion of Kersians and back again."

"Is she all right?"

"Yeah, she had some minor injuries, but she's fine."

"This must be her year for misadventures."

"She thinks Graneck wants to kill her." Kolgern laughed.

Shadon grinned back. "That's probably not too far from the truth."

"What do you mean? He just doesn't like her, that's all." Kolgern took a long swig from the flask in front of him.

"He never did like her. The rumor is that when she was a small child he led the debate on whether or not the other sorcerers should destroy her. He's a paranoid, superstitious man."

"Does Tnasha know about this?"

"Probably not. But I'm sure she can sense it. You always can with people like that." Shadon took a drink. "Did Alena make it back in one piece?"

"Her sharp tongue is still in tact if that's what you mean. She started back at her post this morning."

"Is General Kauf here?"

"Who?"

"The Carinthian?"

"Oh. Um, a Carinthian legion arrived in the early hours of the morning to take up the rear of the Kersian encampment at the North gate. I think that was their retaliation for Zul."

Shadon shifted his weight, visibly unsettled, and took another drink. "No. If they were easily fought off it wasn't retaliation." His eyes narrowed. "It was more likely a distraction."

"From what?"

"I don't know. But once again I have no doubt we're going to find out."

Kolgern put his head down on the table. "Great. Will we be traveling on the left horse black again?"

Shadon lifted the flask to his lips with a smile. "No. I think this time we're better prepared and we have a plan. We'll have expectations the Kersians will gladly meet."

Kolgern sat back up, took a drink, set his flask back on the table and rubbed his forehead. "Is that possible?"

He shrugged his shoulders. "Sure. Why not?"

"I don't know. If we expect we can anticipate every possible move, then we'll be taken by surprise." He paused. "Wait, aren't you supposed to be the paranoid one?"

Shadon laughed. "Maybe I am being too nonchalant about this. It seems straight forward to me."

A stranger approached the table, dropping a folded note in front of Shadon and quickly retreating back into the mid day crowd.

Kolgern sat back, motioning toward the note. "I guess that happens to you all the time?"

"Yes." He opened the note, read it, folded it back up, and shoved it deep into his pocket. "By Natyis, I swear."

"Bad news?"

Shadon put his head in his hands and rubbed his temples. A sure sign he had a headache. He looked up, meeting Kolgern's questioning eyes. "This sorcerers' war has deep roots, Kolgern. We humans are right in the middle of it. If we do not keep Tnasha safe, and we do not find this weapon, the world as we know it will fall into chaos."

"I know. Tnasha said she saw it in the bowl."

"No." Shadon shook his head. "I don't think you do understand. Not completely anyway."

Kolgern responded with a hurt look. "What do you mean?"

"I mean that our lives are about to become very different unless we find a way to stop it. This war goes beyond political struggle and power."

"How so?"

"Genocide and enslavement of the masses." He reached in his pocket, retrieved the note, and tossed it across the table to Kolgern.

Kolgern took it warily. He opened it. Spreading it before him he read, *Beware the Angoran's. The fifth gen will die. The hand of Graneck leads them.*

He re-crumpled the note, tossing it back to Shadon. "The Angorans? What do they have to do with this?"

"They may seem harmless, but being these sorcerers live in a harsh environment I can imagine their hunting and tracking skills might prove useful in an assassination. My guess is...." The spy, Shadon, sighed, seeming annoyed. "The only way they would allow themselves to get involved is if Graneck convinced their elders that she was a threat, or if Graneck offered them a price they could not refuse."

Kolgern said nothing.

"The more people who get involved, the more complicated it becomes. Now we have to worry about the Kersians and the Angorans, coupled with Tnasha's faulty sorcery. Who knows what will happen if the sorcerers in Arkeereon hear of this."

"Arkeereonish Sorcerers?"

"Yes. They are but another faction of sorcerers with their own ways and beliefs, my friend. With so many involved comes the possibility of a war that could quickly turn cataclysmic."

CHAPTER 15

Lucas rode ahead, looking off into the distance.

Behind him, Aithian kept his cloak pulled tightly around him. As he inhaled, the icy air stiffened his nostrils. His breath emerged smoke. The frozen wasteland spread out before them.

Lucas slowed down and shifted his weight to the right, causing his horse to spin on its hind legs in a well-trained maneuver to face Aithian. "What are you doing lagging behind?"

"I'm freezing." Aithian rubbed his hands together vigorously, and blew into them, only warming them for a few seconds.

His friend, whose bright white mana stood out with the elemental properties of air, smiled. "I know *exactly* where we are going to bury it."

"Good. Where?" Aithian's own deep blue mana turned an even deeper blue as he tried to use it as a shield against the cold.

"In the Ankeer Desert," Lucas said in triumph.

Aithian didn't believe it and fought the urge to chuckle. "You expect that we can take the weapon, run all the way to the desert with it, bury it, and return before the Kersians and Danarian's arrive? When they discover it's not here, both of their search parties will head straight for Arkeereon."

"I've already taken care of that. No one has seen it, right?" A sly grin passed his lips and he narrowed his eyes. He reached into the depths of his mana and retrieved something. Upon pulling it out, he furrowed his brow with a nod. "See?"

Aithian examined the stick. At the stick's top a crude claw held a black rock. He smiled, amused. "What, by Arkeereon's pits, is that?"

"The replacement Raven's Claw."

Aithian couldn't help himself. Laughter erupted from his lips, fading into the wind. "It doesn't even look convincing."

"We don't know what it looks like and it was *our* ancestors who made the real one after all. So who is to say the Kersians or the Danarians will know the difference?" Lucas laughed an evil laugh and shoved the crude replica back into his mana. "It's brilliant, you must admit."

"We'll see. How long before we get to Ramathra? We've already endured almost two days of this cold."

"Oh, I don't know. Sundown maybe? We'll camp in the ruins."

"Not a smart idea." Aithian now knew why Natyis sent him. His reason, coupled with Lucas's ambition, made for the possibility of success. "If they arrive, and we are not supposed to alert them to our presence..."

"Eury said Ramathra is big. There are many caverns, temples, and buildings standing. It could take us several days just to find the Raven's Claw anyway. We'll find someplace at the furthest edge of the ruins to set up camp."

Aithian gave in and nodded. "Well let's hurry then because I'm tired and cold."

"You worry too much."

"You keep saying that. And another thing..."

Lucas rolled his eyes.

A wave of concern washed over Aithian. "What if they were there and gone already? What if they already have the weapon?"

Lucas leaned forward, urging his horse into a slow amble. "We'll find out when we get there."

Obviously, it was something Lucas had not considered, which made Aithian all the more anxious. They continued onward, not knowing what to expect, but at least they had a plan.

As they rode, the clouds moved out, and finally, the sun hung uncovered overhead, offering some small measure of heat.

Another question passed through Aithian's mind. He spoke it aloud after it occurred to him. "Why would anyone leave something so dangerous out in the open for anyone to find?"

Lucas did not answer right away. The sound of the horse's hooves rang off the hard ground. The wind passed over them gently. When he finally spoke, it was as if nature fell silent for a brief moment. "Maybe they wanted it to be found."

"That's an inane explanation and you know it."

"Not if you think that the events leading up to something bigger depended on one sorcerer faction obtaining a weapon."

"Now you accuse your father of leaving it here on purpose?"

Lucas did not bother to turn. He kept his head forward and his eyes on the path before him. "My father would do anything if he thought it meant to resurrect the ancestral mana."

Lucas's statement stunned Aithian to silence. It made more sense than it should have. "I suppose you're right."

"Of course I am."

"I just hope your father is right."

Lucas snorted. "We all do. Because if he's wrong…"

"We're all dead," Aithian finished in a somber tone.

"Now I didn't say *that*." Lucas grinned again. "Don't worry; we'll get there before they do. Things will work out."

Aithian sensed Lucas's doubt. No one, not even Lucas, could get a lie past him. As the carrier of the serpent god's mana, as he was known to many of the humans in Arkeereon, Aithian dealt death to lies. His gift for knowing the truth stood out as one of his greatest gifts as a sorcerer. That gift was second only to his uncanny ability to control the ocean, the rain, and his ability to speak with sea creatures and serpents. Knowing that Lucas was also unsure made him feel better somehow. They rode on in silence.

CHAPTER 16

Morvack forced himself to dress and go to the dining hall that morning. He did not want to face his brother, but knew he had little choice. When he arrived, he found Gavgal sitting in front of the platters of meats, vegetables, and eggs. Gavgal wore a genuine smile when Morvack entered. Morvack nodded in acknowledgement, but said nothing. There was nothing to be said.

"How are you feeling?"

"As well as one could expect."

"Will you be well enough to leave in the morning?" A hint of impatience stood out in Gavgal's question.

Morvack nodded, somewhat unsure of himself. "Yes. I expect so." *Not that I have a choice*, he added silently.

"Good." Gavgal took a plate and heaped it with grilled meats, steamed vegetables, and boiled eggs and placed it in front of Morvack. "Eat. You need to keep up your strength."

Morvack sat down, wondering if his brother cared about him at all. He immediately cut into a slice of ham and stuffed it into his mouth. The salted wild boar tasted wonderful. He then realized he had not eaten anything since the previous afternoon.

Gavgal helped himself to a plate. "I am concerned the Danarians may have left already. I have not heard word from Seth, so I am unsure of the seer's destruction."

"He did it," Morvack said. The bland distaste for his brother, Seth, seethed in his voice.

Gavgal's eyes widened with surprise. "Have you had a vision of this?"

Morvack rolled his head with exaggeration, his exhaustion having relinquished his inhibitions. "You know as well as I that he succeeded. Seth is a heartless, sadistic, madman. He would kill you or I if he had the chance."

Gavgal smiled. "I never knew you felt that way about Seth."

Morvack put a tomato in his mouth. Their brother Seth projected his thoughts often. And though Morvack rarely saw him, he had been around his brother enough to know that he was not sane. "He projects his thoughts. More than once he has thought, in front of me, how easy it would be to kill me, and you. He probably feels the same way about Alax."

"So you have seen into his mind?" Gavgal narrowed his eyes.

"Only because he projected it and made no move to hide his thoughts." Morvack continued eating, feeling his mind reaching into Gavgal's. His brother's suspicions were roused.

"Have you ever read my mind?"

"No. Why? Are you concerned I may have heard something you did not intend for me to hear?" He amazed even himself with his response. "I know how impolite it is to reach into someone's mind without permission. You taught me that as a child, remember?"

Gavgal smiled and retreated from the question. "I have your traveling party working on assembling everything you will need."

"Thank you."

He nodded. "It is the least I can do. I would go myself, but your skills are more suited to the task."

Morvack felt a sarcastic response emerging in his brain. *You mean you don't want to put yourself in danger and I'm expendable.* He bit his tongue, unsure where the sudden surge of insolence came from.

The voice returned then. *"He has the ability to materialize from place to place. You have the ability to read minds, and control the winds. Whose skill is more suited to taking a magical weapon from its slumber?"*

I know this. You don't have to tell me, his mind called out to the voice. Morvack looked at Gavgal; half expecting that he had heard the voice and his response. His eyes searched around the room.

Gavgal's gaze followed his. "What is it?"

"I thought I heard something fall and break."

"I heard nothing."

"It was probably just my imagination."

"Well aren't you quick on your feet this morning," the sultry female voice said.

Oh shut up, he thought.

"I hope you know what you are getting into, Morvack," the voice continued.

I hope you will leave me be before I am confined for suspected insanity, his mind told her.

The female voice sounded irritated. *"Fine. Return to your quarters later and we will discuss it further."*

"Fine," he said aloud.

"What is fine?" Gavgal leaned forward, obviously confused.

"Did I say that aloud? I was thinking about the quickest way to get to Ramathra. I should be able to get there by morning after tomorrow. Our ocean voyage will only take a day if I can manipulate the wind properly. Then on horseback, if we drive them hard, we can be there by morning."

"You will not have to drive the horses to death. I have sent ahead fresh horses, and you can switch them, riding through the night."

"Wise planning."

"I like to think it is the reason I am administrator." Gavgal took a sip of wine.

"I will spend the rest of the day resting and packing my things. We will leave early in the morning. Before sunrise."

"Are you sure you are up to this?"

Morvack nodded and forced a grin. "I will be fine. I will not fail you."

Gavgal smiled in appreciation. "I know you won't."

They continued eating and parted ways after the meal. Morvack hurried back to his chambers, closing and locking the door behind him. "Come out," he whispered.

"You could always keep the weapon for yourself," the voice said with a soft sigh.

"What need have I for a weapon?"

"You could destroy Seth and Gavgal, and return the weapon to the Arkeeronish, where it belongs."

"You can't be serious? The imperial hierarchy might use it to destroy us!"

"If the imperial hierarchy wanted to, they would have used it already. If you were the only one left…"

"What about Alax?"

"I do not know enough about him. You think of him rarely."

"He's the quiet one. He keeps to himself presiding over the converted in Exavia." Morvack stopped, shaking his head quickly. What was he thinking? He fidgeted nervously. If the voice was in his head, certainly he would not have to explain Alax to it.

"You fear your own insanity?"

"Am I insane?"

"No," she said matter-of-fact.

He decided quickly that recent events had put him under a lot of stress. The voice had to be his imagination. "You are in my imagination. The Unnamed is testing my resolve and loyalty through questions."

"If you wish to believe that…"

"I will not keep the weapon for myself." His decision sent a pang of guilt through his stomach.

"Who's to say Seth will not steal it from Gavgal?"

He shook his head with a concerned frown. "Nonsense. You are a part of my imagination. I know this for certain, now. Seth would never challenge Gavgal. He fears Gavgal's relationship with the Unnamed."

"Not even you believe that."

"I believe our conversation has ended."

"Very well. Soon, you will learn I am right."

"We'll see."

Silence. He looked around the room, expecting the voice to emerge ethereal from the still air and drift to his ears. Nothing. He sat down on the edge of his bed, took a deep breath, and looked out the window. He did not feel like lying down or sleeping. It was far too beautiful outside to stay in. He stood, took a light cloak from the closet, and left his chambers to take a walk.

CHAPTER 17

Tnasha waited until she was alone with Margore, Kolgern and Shadon. The four sat on horseback near the North gates waiting for the Carinthian, Kauf. Tnasha finally spoke. "Graneck hired assassins to kill me. *Obviously* they did *not* succeed."

Kolgern's eyes went wide and he glanced at Shadon, whose face remained stoic. Margore's mouth dropped open, but nothing came out.

Finally, Shadon nodded. "He's such an inept bastard I knew his plan would fail."

"You knew?" Margore's eyes brimmed with anger. "By Natyis, why didn't you tell someone?"

"I only received word of it yesterday and I was going to bring it up eventually. Besides, it's hearsay unless there is proof. There is no proof. However, I suspect he'll try again." Shadon looked around them as if searching for hidden spies or passers by who might overhear.

Tnasha lowered her voice. "He's right. Without proof, how do you prove it? But I did tell Priestess Caitlan. Now he'll have her wrath to deal with."

"Someone tries to assassinate you and you get his wife after him?" Margore was stunned.

Tnasha laughed. "Have you ever seen Caitlan angry? She'll give him a verbal lashing he will not want repeated. And he won't dare cross her again because he knows she could easily bring the wrath of the elders down on him. Caitlan has more power than people know."

A wide grin slid over Shadon's lips. "I can think of nothing worse for a high priest with no bloodline to speak of."

"You're probably right," Margore said with reluctance, then turned to Tnasha. "You could have at least told your father though."

"So he could panic and bring it up at the sorcerers' council? Enemies from within are much more dangerous than those outside. Suspicions would fly, and a situation like that could pit sorcerers against one another. At that point my family might lock me away from the world for my own safety." She rolled her eyes and smirked. "I don't *need* to be saved."

Kolgern tried to hide the grin, but it came anyway. An evil glint crossed his eyes. "No. You don't need to be saved...from anyone but yourself."

An onslaught of laughter came from the men before Tnasha could retort. Commander Kauf, who had been standing off to one side, interrupted. "We should leave now." His tone was heavy and serious.

Having little choice, the five of them left the comfort and safety of Danaria behind them, through the gates, and North into the Selenia Forest. The journey had finally begun, but first they had to take a detour to Kalath's to ensure, in the very least, that Tnasha received several more days of training while the others planned the route and discussed various strategies.

They rode along the rough path canopied by the forest trees, until finally, the small bridge came into view. For Tnasha, the bridge was usually a welcoming sight that took her back to happier days. Her father used to bring her here. It was always a treat to visit Kalath, and the sight of the bridge always brought back memories of fragrant incenses, warm food, and the comforts of home. But today it seemed repetitive. And something did not feel quite right about it. Not right at all. She looked around them wondering what it was that sent the uneasy cold feeling down her spine. That is when she saw him.

Tnasha dismounted hastily and ran to him. Kalath lay face down on the ground in the clearing just outside the cave. The golden colored sword still protruded from his back. His once white robes seethed deep crimson, almost black. She fought tears back, but it was no use. They came anyway, streaming down her face. Distantly she heard sobs, then realized they came from her.

Margore hurried up to put a comforting arm around her. He pulled her to him. She sobbed softly on his shoulder.

"By Natyis," whispered Kolgern. He also dismounted and bent down to examine Kalath. He shook his head and wiped his own eyes.

"Kersians," said Kauf. His voice stood crisp and filled with contempt.

Shadon nodded in agreement.

Margore patted Tnasha's back, still holding her in his arms. "We should give him a proper sending."

"The pyre could attract their attention if the Kersians are near," Kauf said. He did not seem to care that Kalath had a proper funeral.

His lack of caring turned Tnasha's sorrow to anger. "Well, we cannot leave him lying there."

"I meant no disrespect. I was thinking burial might be better. More subtle." Kauf took a step backward and shrugged.

Tnasha's eyes, still wet with tears, went wide in horror. "No. The traditional sending is the only way. Otherwise his mana will not ascend to rebirth!"

Kauf averted his gaze to the ground. "Oh. I apologize if I have offended your traditions."

Shadon lowered his head and looked at Tnasha. "Tnasha, he didn't know. We will build a pyre."

"Besides..." she hissed. She clenched her jaw, feeling her face contort into an angry scowl. "If they do come, I'll have a little surprise waiting for them." She imagined herself throwing a blate of mana strong enough to destroy the entire salt marsh. She silently vowed then and there that she would make the Kersians regret the day they crossed her.

Tnasha took one last look at Kalath's body, averted her gaze, and went inside. She wanted to put his affairs in the best of order so that when the priestesses came to remove everything, none of it would be missed, and it would be easy to retrieve. The cave seemed strange now. Kalath's mana did not permeate the air as it once did. No fire burned in the hearth, and no candles lit the rooms. She found several new candles and some flint and lit them. Slowly, she began stacking the books, the jars, the eating utensils and bowls…

Her mind wandered back to happier times. She smiled, remembering when Kalath first gave her the amulet she wore. She pulled it from beneath her tunic and gazed at in loving memory. It was his gift to her, reminding her that she was a fifth generation sorceress anomalous, and as Kalath believed, special. While the amulet had caused her recent run in with the Kersians, it was now the only tangible thing for her to remember the old sorcerer by. It meant even more to her now than it had when it was in the hands of the Kersian sorcerers Morvack and Gavgal.

In her mind, she heard the voice of Kalath and a conversation they had in her room when she was a mere sixteen years of age. She remembered his words perfectly, "I bestowed upon you your third name, Delepitore'. Of Sorcery. Quite fitting, would you not agree?"

"I don't know. I'm not really sure I believe in such things," she had said.

"It is always good to doubt. I have read the Crystal Oracle and consulted with Priestess Arasni."

She remembered how he suddenly changed the subject after he said that.

"I understand you have had some trouble with your swordsmanship." It was not a question, but rather a statement as if he had known her predicament with her father and his demanding nature all along. That was Kalath. He always knew.

Tnasha remembered how she gave him a questioning look. She did not always understand Kalath's odd riddles and changes in subject. For he never really came out and said what it was he truly meant. She always assumed he enjoyed the game and wanted her to figure things out for herself. Most of the time, she found that everything he said connected in some way. Yet, all the same she found it somewhat annoying. He was the first person she told about her struggle to please her father. "I think my father hates me because I cannot fight."

The image of his frame outlined in the window was a memory etched in her brain. Kalath did not turn from the window. "Can not or will not?"

"You think I choose not to learn?" she asked, taken aback by the question.

"Yes."

His answer came at her, crisp and matter of fact, slapping her like a cold wave of water. So much so that she was stunned to silence. It took all of her willpower to force sound from her lips. "It isn't so. I, I..."

"You have chosen not to learn just as you have chosen what you will and will not believe. This is what I have come to tell you," he said.

Tnasha said nothing and stared at the stone floor. Kalath was right. She knew that now. Back then he had been talking about her unwillingness to use sorcery and learn how to control the raw power within herself. How she wished she had understood that then. She never appreciated his concern. Another tear came to her eye.

Kalath never did intend to let the subject rest as she had hoped. "So now, the choice is yours. You can either learn what you can, or give up without trying. Which is more admirable? The decision you make could change the world." He gave her one last knowing look and strode from the room, leaving Tnasha with her thoughts. She remembered that look most of all. His eyes were filled with hope and understanding. He had always been like a second father.

More tears streamed down her cheeks. She remembered that she sat for some time staring out the window to the treetops beyond then remembered Kalath had left a book on her dressing table. She opened it. Inside the cover lay the turquoise amulet on a thin silver chain, inlayed with silver markings. The silver inlay was the sigil of Aithian, the sorcerers' serpent god who was the keeper of water sorcery. She rubbed her hand over Aithian's sigil and remembered thinking that Kalath did not make a habit of leaving such things behind. At that moment, she knew he had left it for her. A precious gift. It was then, and still was, the one thing she treasured most. She never went anywhere without it.

She put the amulet to her lips and kissed it, letting her tears fall upon it.

"Tnasha?"

She shoved the amulet back beneath her tunic, wiped her eyes, and turned to Shadon.

"Kolgern and Margore wondered if you wanted to perform last rites before we commence his body to the fire."

Panic overwhelmed her. The reality seemed more than she could take. She swallowed her fear and sorrow. "Can I have a few more minutes? I want to put things in piles so the priests can come retrieve it all. He could have family somewhere..." She knew he did not. She was his only family. "I'll leave a note."

"Do you need help?"

Tnasha nodded, sniffling and fighting back more tears. She looked around, realizing she already cleared the bulk of the main room. It never occurred to her how little Kalath had. But for what he lacked in material goods, he was, no – he had been, wealthy in friends, compassion, and spirituality.

Shadon left for a moment, returning with Kolgern and Margore. Together, the four of them cleared Kalath's cave, making neat stacks of items along one wall. Tnasha sat down in front of the books. One in particular caught her attention. Inside, slips of parchment marked pages. She pulled it from the stack and opened it. Another grimoire. Its pages were aged and crisp. Reading the headings of the marked pages, she paused. "Why would Kalath have marked these? He could never do any of them. Not with his degenerating mana."

The men said nothing. Kauf entered, expectantly. "Are we going to proceed? I realize you need time to grieve, but I believe it is best to finish this and move on. We can make better time, and perhaps arrive in Ramathra before the Kersians."

Tnasha ignored him. She began reading the headings aloud. "Transformation of physical objects. It says here it is possible for some sorcerers to open portals to move from place to place by transforming their physical being, or the physical being of any object, including others, to another location. Provided they know where that location is."

"Then perhaps you can transport all of us to the port at Cabalia and save us the ocean journey," Kauf said with a wry smile.

Kolgern lifted an eyebrow and took a step backward. "I do not think that's a wise idea."

"Why not?" The Carinthian General shrugged. "She's a sorceress."

"Have you ever seen Tnasha work sorcery?"

Tnasha looked up from the book, her eyes still red and swollen from crying. "This is probably not within my abilities. But it could shed light on how Gavgal can move from place to place. Vanishing into thin air. I'm bringing this book with us."

"Anything else interesting in there?" Margore peered over her shoulder with curiosity.

She opened the book to another marked page. "How to render another's mana useless. This is interesting. It could prove useful."

Shadon leaned in to look over her other shoulder. "That could be helpful if we ran into Morvack or Gavgal again."

Tnasha turned her attention to Kauf. In his hand, he held the sword that he pulled from Kalath's back. "That was not the sword used to kill Kalath. That sword was taken. Why was this one left behind?"

Kauf lifted the sword, holding it to the light from the cave's entrance. "It looks like your typical Kersian sword."

Tnasha squinted and stood, still holding the book in her arms. "Let's go outside. I think I can see a trace of mana on it. I want to know which one of them killed him."

The five stepped outside into the bright mid morning light. Several feet away, upon a large, flat stone, Kalath's body lay covered with a blanket. Kindling and dead branches stood heaped beneath him. She kept her gaze on the sword, afraid to look upon Kalath. The thin layer of mana on the grip of the sword shone a slight orange color. She did not recognize it. "This mana is different. It is not Morvack or Gavgal's. It's orange."

Shadon sucked in a deep breath. All eyes settled on him. "It has to be Seth or Alax."

"How many more are there?"

"There are only four Kersian sorcerers left that we know of. Gavgal, Morvack, Seth, and Alax. Morvack and Gavgal are pests. Alax is very passive, but Seth..." Shadon's eyes traveled the circumference around the cave. "Seth is aggressive. He would have been the one if Gavgal sent anyone to assassinate

Kalath. I don't think Alax or Morvack would have the stomach for it unless it was ritualized. Gavgal never does his own dirty work."

Tnasha sniffed again. The warm salty air filtered through her nostrils rank and sour. "You wouldn't happen to know the color of his mana?"

"I'm sorry, no."

"This is orange. The airy part of fire, and elemental mana at that."

Margore shrugged. "Or maybe his mana is benign like yours. What did the book say about neutralizing mana?"

Tnasha took her gaze from the sword, a calling card left by the Kersian sorcerer Seth. "Copper bracelets, copper bolts shot into the mana, and by forcing negative energy into the mana to block it. Those are the most common ways of neutralization."

Kauf stomped one foot impatiently. "Should we continue with the last rites?"

"Are you aware how annoying you are?" Tnasha gave him an angry glare.

His voice softened. "I am considering how much time we are wasting standing here discussing things when we could already be on our way. Leaving sooner could put us ahead of schedule."

"Had Kalath been alive we would have stayed several days because he was suppose to give me further training in magick," she said, disgusted. "You would have had time to plan, strategize and so on. So why are you getting impatient?"

The General let out a deep sigh. He stepped aside without word and with a look of resignation.

Tnasha stepped past him and up to the large flat boulder they had used to serve as the pyre altar. She laid a hand over Kalath and closed her eyes. She wished she could make things right again. That she could bring him back to life. She felt the tears begin to well up in her eyes again. "By Natyis and all the gods, may your soul and mana return from whence it came so that it may be re-born. You were loved in life, and will forever live in our memories and hearts. Be at peace for I will avenge your wrongful death."

She stood over him a few more moments in silent prayer then stepped back when Shadon and Margore approached with torches. They lit the pyre aflame, and with the flames Kalath's mortal body burned and went through a rebirth in the smoke that rose to the sky. The scent of burning flesh, death, wafted to her nose. She wiped her eyes again. The men stood in silence.

Tnasha took the book to a nearby stone and sat down. She opened the book and scanned the scores of marked pages. Among the pages Kalath marked were incantations to block blates and throw them back at the castor. Another page dealt with narrowing a blate for stronger impact. She smiled, looking up at the stream of smoke lifting to the sky. Finding comfort in knowing that Kalath had marked the pages for her, she stood and returned to the horses. Whether or not she'd be able to perform the spell was another question entirely. The book could prove to be completely useless, which was why sorcerers did not bother hiding spell books from one another. Spells working depended on the sorcerers' natural mana element, the strength of that mana, and the sorcerer's discipline in being able to focus that mana properly. A sorcerer could have strong mana, but it could easily be the wrong element. Or the sorcerer may lack the ability to focus the mana properly. Even knowing this, she put the book alongside the other one Kalath had given her, inside her saddlebag. There was no harm in trying, and with her anomalous mana, most things did work for her, though not entirely in the way they were supposed to. What Tnasha lacked was experience and focus. With such strong mana, it got her into more trouble than not.

She finally turned to her companions. "Let's get out of here. Kauf is right. There is no sense staying here when the Kersians are most likely already on their way."

The men nodded. Once they remounted, they made their way East, toward the Western Ocean where a small ship waited to take them to Cabalia.

CHAPTER 18

Two Angoran sorcerers ambled though the streets of Morasta, moving toward the ports. They figured they were at least one day ahead of the sorceress. Oron spotted their ship. "There's our transportation. You will invoke the wind so we will arrive in Cabalia long before they do. We will wait until we are just outside Ramathra before we attack."

Arick's voice emerged monotonous. "Why can we not simply take care of them here?"

"We must make it appear as though she was destroyed by the Kersians," Oron said, in a similar flat voice. "We must do it that way or we will not be paid, and our tribe will face another harsh winter with limited provisions. We cannot afford to lose more children this year."

Nodding in agreement, Arick stepped ahead of him.

They led their horses across the pier to the moored ship. It was smaller, with just enough room for a crew of ten men. With passengers, they would be crowded. "Are we *sure* the sorceress is dangerous?" Arick finally asked.

"Graneck thinks so. I am apt to believe him. Why would he lie? He is a member of the priesthood and has been ordained by the gods." Oron looked over at his friend, wondering what he was thinking.

"I hope he is telling the truth. Even the gods' chosen spiritual leaders can sometimes be corrupt with power."

"Possibly. But *she* could destroy us all with *her power*. Perhaps not intentionally, but I've been told she has no control. She is untrained. With as much unfocused, uncontrollable energy she has, she is a danger to herself and all of us." He shuddered as a cool ocean breeze swept over him, sending chills down his spine.

Arick gave him a sideways glance. Clearly, Arick had doubts all along. "If we are wrong, the three-fold retribution of all that is will be swift and unmerciful. The gods will retaliate."

Oron nodded, realizing for the first time that if they were doing the bidding of a wayward priest rather than an honest member of the clergy, the gods *would* have their say. No amount of money or supplies could save their tribe from *that*. He made a decision then. "We will see her for ourselves, maybe even talk to her before we destroy her. That is the only way we can be sure."

Nodding again, a slight smile crossed Arick's lips. "I would feel much better about that."

They hurried to board their ship. With Arick's wind magick, they would be in Cabalia by the following morning.

●

Caitlan cornered Graneck in his study. She stomped toward him, stopped, and put her hands on her hips. Her eyes clouded. "You swine!"

He looked up from the letter he was writing. "By Natyis, woman! What?"

She spared no words. "You sent assassins to kill Tnasha? You put Malarissa's life in danger so you could get Tnasha out of the city to kill her? What is wrong with you? I swear I wonder how your mind works!"

He sat back in his chair. "What, by Natyis, are you talking about?"

"Do not feign ignorance with me." Her eyes glowed fierce gold in angered intensity.

"I would never do such a thing. I, I..."

"You are at a loss for words," she finished. "Do not lie to me. I am not an ignorant woman, Graneck."

Graneck stood and held out his arms with shrugged shoulders. "Why would I do that?"

"You were the one who said she must die. Remember? You sang those words to Kalath and I the night he arrived from Sherok. Well, your fool plan failed. So I guess my question is- do you have more assassins after her now?"

Graneck looked down at the floor. He had never been good at keeping things from Caitlan. She did know better. There was no point in lying now. His fate, his life, was in her hands now and he had no way of knowing what she would do. "Yes."

"Ugh!" She pounded her small fist on the desktop and leaned into him, her eyes still blazing with fury. "Who?"

"The Angoran's," he said in a subdued voice. Once he realized that he had just confessed, he forced his mouth shut. He had never intended to confess outright.

Her hands darted into the air unexpectedly and he jumped back. "Call them off. Now!"

He found his spine. "She is going to destroy us all, Caitlan. She is a danger to herself and all of us. Her power will never be matched, and she has no control! I am not the only one who feels this way. There are others who agree with me. She could destroy our race with one misdirected blate or blundered incantation!"

Caitlan's fiery gaze bore into him, vicious and unyielding. "You say that as though she could never learn."

"Can she?" His eyes plead for her concurrence, but she offered none.

"We will not know unless she is given the chance. We never could force her to learn sorcery, but she is trying to learn *now*. You have not wanted to give her a chance since she was a child. You fear her because *you* do not understand her."

"How can we know she is not dangerous?"

"I know because I know she has a kind heart. While she may be somewhat sarcastic, hasty, and undignified at times, deep down I believe she really is a loving and caring person who is knowingly putting her life in danger to save all of us. She did not *have* to agree to any of this. And in the end, Graneck," Caitlan paused to make sure he was listening. "In the end, she may be all that stands between our survival and our destruction by the hands of the Kersians. Could you live on knowing that you doomed all our kind to extinction because you killed the one sorceress who could stop those Kersian madmen once and for all?"

Her final words slapped him cold across the face. He stared down at his desk, wondering if Caitlan would go straight to the council. "I will send a messenger to stop them."

She glared at him, her eyes unforgiving. "See that you do." A glint of satisfaction crossed her eyes. "I will keep this between us for the moment because I want to believe the best of you, Graneck. I want to believe I married a man whose judgment is merely marred with fear and stupidity. So here is what you are going to do - you are going to call your minions off. I expect to see the note before it is sent, and we will send it with *my* private messenger. Tnasha will have enough obstacles in retrieving the weapon. What were you thinking? I will be watching you and if you try something like this again, I will inform the sorcerers' council and you will be put on trial for attempted murder – if you survive that long once the others learn..." She shook her head, turned on her heal, and stormed from the room, slamming the door shut behind her.

Graneck sat back down, partly shocked at Caitlan's reaction, and put his head in his hands. He had no choice but to do what she told him. It was, possibly, the only way he could save his own life. With some reluctance, he dipped his quill into the ink and set the tip against a fresh sheet of parchment, wondering if Lord O'Jashan could or would help. If Caitlan was wrong, they were doomed. But if Caitlan was right, the lives of thousands of sorcerers depended on one anomalous fifth generation sorceress. He sighed and began writing. If they were fortunate, the note would reach the Angoran sorcerers in time. He swallowed the lump in his throat, knowing it was already too late and hoping for the first time, that the Angorans didn't succeed.

CHAPTER 19

Lucas and Aithian arrived in Ramathra early that morning. The sky stretched out all around them, and what remained of the city stood open to the harsh elements of the Northern wasteland. Aithian looked over the scattered ruins. "What a disaster. How are we going to find it in this?"

Lucas contorted his face in thought. "Maybe we should start at one end and work our way through."

"You're serious? That will take days!"

His friend shrugged his shoulders. "I don't know. What looks like a temple?"

In front of them, the ruins spread for a mile or more. Hundreds of stone buildings lay fallen and dilapidated with partial walls rising from the ground. Aithian let out a heavy sigh. "I cannot tell where one building ends and another begins. Nothing looks like a temple. Do you see a temple?"

A cold breeze swept over them. "No. I see mounds of rock everywhere. It is freezing." His teeth chattered. "Maybe we need to find a campsite, make something hot to drink, and discuss a plan of action over a warm fire."

Aithian nodded, knowing they had an almost impossible task before them. Lord Natyis could have at least given them some idea of where the weapon was. Even a general location would have been better than nothing. Natyis' reasons remained unclear. Had he wanted it to be difficult for them to find it? Clearly, Natyis did not want Lucas to hide the staff. After all, they were only supposed to see *who* took it and report back. Those were Natyis' orders and Natyis only gave orders like that when he knew something they did not. Of course there was nothing to prevent them from taking it either. In the end, however, Aithian knew they would find it and that Lucas would succeed in his plan to hide the staff. He did not know how he knew. He just did. "Let's search for a campsite out of the way, to the East. Something with most of the walls still standing preferably. Big enough for the horses."

"Agreed."

They moved on through the rubble still shivering and spreading their mana in front of them in attempt to block the frigid winds. The horses picked their way through the fallen stone and overturned pillars. Whatever happened to Ramathra, if it was indeed a single disastrous event, had destroyed everything. As if hearing Aithian's thoughts, Lucas asked the question. "I wonder what happened here. You don't think it had something to do with the weapon, do you?"

Aithian shrugged, pulling his cloak tighter around him. It didn't help. The cold slipped through his mana, through the heavy dark wool fabric, through his clothing and skin, and straight into his bones. "Who knows? Maybe our ancestors simply abandoned it. This place has poor tactical advantage."

"Yes, I'm noticing that. Or maybe it was too cold. I know *I* would *not* live here willingly. The weather leaves a lot to be desired."

He nodded. That certainly seemed like reason enough. He wondered then if spring ever came to Ramathra. The far side of the ruins seemed leagues away. They pressed on. "Where do people usually build temples?"

"In the middle of a city," Lucas said quickly.

"I was thinking the Northern most point in the center. Those seem the likely places where we should start our search." He paused. "Once we have a chance to warm up we'll look there first. Whose idea was it to ride through the night again?"

"I figured if we kept moving we'd stay warm."

Aithian smiled at Lucas's reasoning. It sounded logical. "You knew we would have to stop and rest the horses."

"Yes. But I didn't realize how cold it would be. Unlike my father, I do not see all." That last bit of sarcasm put a satisfied grin on Lucas' face.

"I hope we have enough grain to last as long as it takes to find the staff." Aithian's blue eyes traveled to the pack mare carrying their supplies. She moved, weighted down with grain and packs, at an even pace.

"You're worrying again."

"You would be, too. Especially if you thought things through more."

"Are you saying I don't think things through?" Lucas sent a questioning look toward him. "Who had the foresight to bring the weapon replica?"

Aithian laughed. Lucas's face bore a look of unreserved pride. "You're right. You brought the replica."

Lucas joined in the laughter, which drifted over the desolate graveyard of fallen stone spread out in front of them. Directly ahead, they saw a building with four crumbling walls. It boasted a doorway large enough to bring the horses inside. "Perhaps we should stop here." Lucas dismounted, leading his horse toward the entrance.

Aithian agreed. His stomach growled with hunger. "This looks good, and maybe we can prepare something to eat."

They entered the ruined building to find a large, clear space with several inside walls still standing. Lucas' grin widened. "This is perfect. We can put the horses on the far side, and we can keep warm in that corner area over there."

Aithian's eyes followed to where Lucas pointed. The small area had three walls and opened to the South. He rubbed his gloved hands together in anticipation then turned his attention to pulling the packs from the mare's back. "You take the horses and I'll start the fire."

Together, they set about building their camp. Before long, a campfire sparked to life with warmth within the crumbling walls of the ruins of Ramathra.

•

After they had eaten and spent several hours sitting next to the inviting fire, Lucas and Aithian emerged from the building on foot. They looked around.

"I have one question." Lucas looked around and frowned. "How can we tell where the center is?"

"Maybe we should search for the sorcerer gods' sigils. If we can find them, chances are they will lead us to the temple."

Lucas nodded.

They walked slowly, picking their way through the crumbling walls of the ancestral city, their eyes downcast, studying the fallen stone for any sign of sigils or ancient writing. With each step, their task seemed more hopeless. After searching for hours Aithian realized it was noontide, signaled by the sun's place mid sky. That is when he saw it. The symbol glinted gold on one standing wall directly ahead of him. He hurried to it, careful of the uneven stones littering the ground in his path.

"Here," he called over his shoulder. A lone sigil, the sigil of Liale, god of earth and steel, shimmered in the noon sunlight high above him. "Liale."

Lucas came up behind him and looked up. His optimism showed itself clear on his face. "This could be it."

Both men made their way inside, traversing the dangerous labyrinth of rock and mortar. On the far North wall, on a slowly crumbling overhang high above them, more sigils of the sorcerer gods gleamed out at them. Broken steps led to a stone platform where upon three stone pedestals stood, untouched by the decay of time. When they reached the stairs, they shared a brief knowing glance. This was it.

Ascending slowly, Aithian reached the platform first. His eyes slid over each pedestal and his face contorted into a look of confusion. Etched into each pedestal's top, ancient writing stared back at him. Within each pedestal, something emerged from a hollow cutout within the center. He stepped closer to further examine them. Lucas stepped up behind him, looking over his shoulder.

"There are three?"

"Looks like it." Aithian's blue eyes filled with resignation. "How do we know which one it is?"

Lucas, as always, had a solution. "We could take them all and leave the fake."

"And we would have to destroy the pedestals for the other two, hoping we destroyed the right one, or they would know there were others." Aithian shook his head.

"So two are fake?"

"I don't know. How is your ancient Arkeeronish?"

"Umm, you know I don't speak, let alone read, ancient Arkeeronish." Lucas gave him a tight smile.

"It figures. I'll see if I can make it out." He went to each pedestal, pausing for a few moments to study each one. Then he stood and stepped back. "According to the writings, and if my ancient Akeeronish is correct, one of these is the Raven's Claw. Another is the Eagle's Talon, and the other is the Crow's Foot. The problem is, according to the text, they've been..." he paused, holding his hands in front of him and wiggling his fingers. "...jumbled up."

Lucas wrinkled his nose in amusement, stifling a laugh. He stepped up to each pedestal, examining each for himself. He stepped back and turned to Aithian. "The claws on each of them look different. I know for sure the one on the left is the Eagle's Claw or Talon rather."

Aithian eyed him suspiciously then turned back to the pedestals. He'd never taken an interest in bird or animal tracking. "Are you sure?" He knew Lucas was sure, but he had to hear the confirmation from Lucas's lips.

"Yes. Eagle's feet are scaled and raven's feet are ribbed. But both of these two are ribbed and I cannot tell which is which. They're a lot a like and evidently the person who carved these did not see a difference between ravens and crows."

Aithian shook his head. He sat down on the step. "You do realize that your replacement weapon isn't going to work, right?"

"Maybe not. Or maybe it still will. It is possible the Kersians aren't that intelligent. We have to at least try. This makes it easier for us."

Aithian shook his head. "It's not the Kersians I'm concerned with. Besides, wasn't it you who was telling me only a few days ago that I should never underestimate my enemy?"

As mid day faded to late afternoon, the Arkeeronish sorcerers studied the remaining staves long and hard. A decision had to be made, and it had to be made soon.

S. J. Reisner

CHAPTER 20

Morvack and his men left early that morning. Now the ship moved along at an even pace, slicing through the water with the help of the conjured wind. He leaned over the railing on the deck, staring into the gray waves. Ever since sunrise the voice refused to leave his head. She asked questions and taunted him. He let her comments pass without answer.

"I have learned new things," she cooed.

Finally he had enough. He answered her in his mind. *"You know nothing."*

"I know that Gavgal killed your mother and the other sorceresses because they were unable to produce his offspring."

That is nonsense. A plague killed them.

"Did it?"

Why is it you torment me?

"I do not mean to torment. I mean to help you," she said gently.

You can help me by going away.

"I cannot. You are the only hope…"

For what?

"To save yourself."

"From what?" he asked aloud. Morvack closed his eyes. He felt cursed.

"From yourself."

116

Her riddles were beginning to annoy him. "You keep insisting I must be saved from myself," he whispered beneath his breath.

"You are not like your brothers. You have a warmth burning deep inside you and you only seek what pure hearted men seek."

Which is? he asked in his mind with sarcasm.

"A family, love and peace." Her voice drifted off, fading into the soft sounds of water and wind.

She did not lie. Family, love and peace were things Morvack had wanted since his youth. Once he retrieved the weapon, those dreams would manifest.

Her voice emerged from the oceans depth and rang sharp and clear in his head. "That is what you thought last time, Morvack. And you were wrong then as you are now."

He squeezed his eyes shut and ran his hands through his long brown hair, trying to shut her out. *I am not wrong. This is the only way!* his mind screamed.

"One day you will know I am right. But by then, I will have died and you will have no one to share it with." The voice faded again, into the wind.

With his eyes still shut, he summoned a stronger wind that pushed hard against the unfurled sails. More than anything he wanted it to be over. He wanted to get the weapon, take it back to Zul, and be done with it. Then he would go back to the Danarian mainland. His home. He missed his cottage hidden deep within the forest. That was gone now, he remembered. The Danarians had undoubtedly destroyed it once they discovered the small village was where the Kersians hid from them.

"I will find a new home on the mainland where I will not be bothered," he said under his breath.

Morvack allowed his imagination to move forward. Constructing a home for himself and a new life. But as always, the dream included a lovely wife and at least two perfect children. He felt ashamed for thinking such things. He pulled himself from the fantasy feeling the wind slide up his sleeves. With a final sigh, filled with sorrow, he retreated below into the cabin in hopes he would find some of the warmth he so desperately sought.

Several mugs of strong wine later, the chill retreated. He sat back and looked over his men. Hushed whispers and unspoken gazes filled the room. Their uncertainty spoke without words. He raised his mug to them. "For all that will soon be ours."

The resounding lifting of mugs and cheers, void of enthusiasm, left the room even more silent than before. Morvack sighed. If only the voice would leave. He could still feel her, hiding in the back of his mind, watching and listening. His previous confident demeanor had fallen into an oblivious pit filled with perpetual darkness. He stared off distantly.

"Your Holiness?" One of the young men from his party sat down across from him. He waited patiently for Morvack to bring his full attention to him before speaking. Once he had it, the young soldier wasted no time. "The men have noticed your distance lately. Is everything all right?"

Morvack tipped his head, contemplative and reserved. He tried to find his confidence, but he could not gather it. "Even I struggle with duty and the orders given me. While I may not always understand the Unnamed's divine plan for us all, I do understand that my loyalty lies with him. Therefore I understand my duty."

The vague response seemed to satisfy the young Kersian sitting before him. A spark of hope flickered in the young man's eyes. "Thank you, Your Holiness."

Morvack nodded and lifted his mug to his lips. He had not realized his own melancholy was so evident that even the humans could see it. Forcing a grin with a stiff upper lip, he addressed them again. "I am merely tired of traveling, and wish for those days past when I sat at home reading the great words of the Unnamed."

Many of the men surrounding him nodded in agreement.

"But the life of a soldier of the Unnamed is a hard one. The Unnamed tests my resolve as he tests yours. That is his nature. Soon we will receive everything we have fought for for so long. Our day is coming, soon. When we have finished, the Kersian Empire will rise, and all will convert and embrace their purification." He half believed himself as he said it.

The morale among the men immediately lifted. He could hear their projected thoughts. With their fears curbed, the conversation picked up, and around him, his men laughed and talked believing that they were chosen and blessed. Morvack stood and yawned. Using his mana to summon the wind had only tired him. He retreated to the sleeping cabins where he drifted quickly into a dark dream world. In a meadow overlooking the ocean, the unknown sorceress waited for him. Her hair, silken black, flowed behind her. She wore a long, maroon dress that brought out the soulful depths of her deep brown eyes. Morvack went to her.

auf led the way through un-traveled paths hidden deep

CHAPTER 21

Kauf led the way through un-traveled paths hidden deep within the Selenia Forest. Finally, as late afternoon announced its presence high above them, they emerged from the forest to the lowlands leading to the sandy white beaches. They were South of Morasta now. From where they were they could see miles out over the calm ocean.

Tnasha looked around, studying their faces. She had a terrible feeling accompanied by a swift and fleeting vision that took her by surprise and she shook it from her head. A sense of urgency rushed through her. With some uncertainty she said, "We are not going to make it in time. If we had only left yesterday…"

"You were injured yesterday," Margore stated in a flat voice. "Why the sudden interest in getting there so quickly now when yesterday you were upset that Kauf wanted to get moving so quickly? Revenge for Kalath?"

"Getting there any faster will not ensure revenge and we cannot change the past," Shadon added.

Tnasha sighed heavily and inhaled the humid air. A sense of sorrow and grief plagued her. Without Kalath, all hope seemed lost. She imagined Kalath's reply to that. 'Nonsense, girl,' he would have said. She forced a smile and turned to Shadon. "You're right, of course. But something is wrong. I just know we've waited too long."

"Let's stop here to rest the horses for awhile." Kauf dismounted, and immediately loosened the girth of his saddle. The gray mare he rode nickered softly as if to thank him, and began grazing.

"Not with the bit in her mouth," Kolgern said in protest. "It will get all mucky."

Kauf raised and eyebrow, said nothing, and allowed the mare to continue eating.

Tnasha dismounted and pulled the new book from her saddlebag. She dropped the reins, allowing her own horse time for grazing. After loosening the saddle girth, she found a spot of lush grass beneath a young tree where she could read. She re-opened the book to the page wherein it explained Gavgal's uncanny ability to dematerialize himself. The idea crossed her mind and she tossed it aside. But it would not leave her and reared its head again. "Kauf, how well do you know Arkeereon?"

Kauf looked up from his pipe. "Very well. I used to work military intelligence in that part of the world in my younger years. I've been past Ramathra numerous times on my way to Elishta."

"Do you know Cabalia well enough to project an image to me? Well enough to see it in your head?"

Kolgern peered out at her from behind one of the horses with a hoof pick in his hand. "Oh no. *That* is out of the question."

Shadon and Margore exchanged glances, but said nothing, and continued with the chore of checking all the horses' hooves.

A slight grin appeared on Kauf's face and his eyes narrowed. "Why not? She's a sorceress. *That*, I assume is a spell book? And she's right that the Kersians are likely days ahead by now. I'd rather arrive at Ramathra before they do, and avoid a confrontation with them altogether. Wouldn't you?"

Kolgern smacked his lips together and chose his words carefully. "I think I know her better than you, General. What I do know, that you do not, is that her sorcery is...," he paused with a tight smile. "Could use... needs refinement."

Tnasha shot him a warning glance.

"What? Are you going to deny you sent us through a hurricane and *accidentally* raised a serpent? What about the flood?"

Kauf's eyes went wide with curiosity.

She shook her head. "It wasn't *that* bad. A few mistakes that worked in our favor. Besides, I think I have more control now. The *last* serpent was intentional."

Shadon snickered.

Kolgern pointed at him. "See? Shadon and I know better."

Shadon lifted his hands in front of him in protest. "Don't get me involved in this discussion, my friend. I know nothing of sorcery."

Kauf had since lit his pipe and held it between his teeth. "What is it you plan to do?"

"I want to try moving us from here to Arkeereon with magick. The incantation is right here. It says you need a clear picture of where you want to be, and I can extract that from you by reaching into your mind."

"Can you do it? I mean," Kauf paused, as if choosing his words carefully. "I mean, is that within your ability? I know that different sorcerers have different abilities according to their mana..."

Kolgern's face contorted into fear. "No! We'll end up in the middle of the ocean or worse, back on Zul. Or dead! I am *not* agreeing to this."

Tnasha rolled her eyes. "My mana is benign, which means I can do things sorcerers with a definitive element cannot. Most of the time anyway." She gazed into the distance thoughtfully. "Water and earth magicks come easier to me and this *is* an earth spell..."

Kauf nodded, seemingly supportive of the idea. Kolgern groaned.

"I'll send Kolgern and Margore first." She smiled with reassurance. "If I was not confident I could do it, do you think I would sacrifice my own flesh and blood?"

Margore peered over the back of his mare, smiled and shrugged his shoulders. "Why not? Let's give it a try."

"No." Kolgern said flatly, crossing his arms over his chest in defiance.

"Yes." Tnasha smiled. She did feel sure she could do it. After all, she had more mana than the Kersian Sorcerer Graneck, and her last encounter with him had proven he could do it. "Let's get the horses ready to go, gather your things, and when you are ready, just stand over here."

With reluctance, Kolgern did as she told him. Margore stepped up beside him without so much as a blink.

"Hold on." She browsed the page with her brown eyes. "This should be simple enough."

"Ha."

She lifted an eyebrow at Kolgern. "Relax. Margore's not afraid, are you?"

Margore shook his head. "Nah. Come on, hurry up."

As Shadon and Kauf looked on Tnasha summoned Kauf to her side. "Think of the place we need to be, picture it in your mind, and let it fill your thoughts."

The General closed his eyes in concentration as she instructed.

Kolgern squeezed his eyes shut while Margore picked at a hangnail on his thumb.

She reached down and took Kauf's hand into hers, saying the words. "Lamec hern anu kana. By Natyis, so be it."

In a shimmer of golden light Kolgern and Margore faded and disappeared.

Shadon's jaw dropped. "Where did they go?"

The General's eyes flew open, searching their surroundings for the missing men. "Impressive."

She smiled in triumph and jumped up and down in excitement, ignoring the fatigue that began to settle into her muscles. "It worked! Now we'll join them. Come on."

The three huddled close together with horses in tow. Once again, she took Kauf's hand into her own. He thought of where they needed to be, and she recited the incantation. A cool blast of wind startled them.

"By Natyis!" said Shadon. Clearly in shock, he checked his horse, then immediately pulled a heavier cloak from his saddlebags. He put it on, still startled.

Tnasha's own eyes went wide with amazement and traveled around them. A small part of her did not want to believe she could do such a thing. As nonchalant as she could manage she said, "We're here."

Kauf opened his eyes with a practiced calm that often seemed innate among generals. "So we are."

"There's only one problem." Shadon searched around them, pausing to look at the rising spires of temples indicating a city in the distance. "Where are Kolgern and Margore?"

Tnasha whirled around, her eyes darting in all directions. Her gaze finally settled on Kauf. "Were you thinking of the same place the first time?"

General Kauf shrugged. "I thought so." He fell silent and bit his lower lip. "What if my mind wandered for a second?"

She narrowed her eyes. "A second? To where?"

He pointed South. "A few miles down the coast from here."

"You didn't."

He shrugged and stepped away from her. "I tried to focus, I did. But I am certainly not a sorcerer."

A deep, nervous chuckle escaped Shadon's lips. "General, I think *you* made a mess of the only sorcery she has never botched up."

Tnasha shook her head in anger. "Now what? We can't very well go searching along the coast for them. They have no idea where they're going. They're stranded!"

"They are within a short distance of Cabalia. They will soon discover where they are because they'll see the city." Kauf nodded toward the city in the distance and gave her a sheepish smile.

"By Arkeereon's pits, I swear." She followed Shadon's lead and retrieved a heavier cloak, and gloves from her saddlebags wondering why nothing ever worked out in her favor. Now, they were clearly outnumbered and without the protector and the warrior what were their chances of retrieving the weapon? She sucked in one cheek and bit it until the pain was unbearable. It was all she could do to keep from losing her temper.

"We should continue without them." Shadon said. "If your feeling is right, the Kersians are either ahead of us, or a short distance behind us undoubtedly."

"How are your swordsmanship skills?" Kauf asked him.

"Good enough, I suppose."

"Well, brilliant General. We are now outnumbered, I'm sure," she said, not able to hide her disgust. It wasn't really Kauf's fault. It was a mistake even she could have made. With a deep breath and a yawn, she patted her horse on the neck, wondering if the bay gelding felt the cold.

"I am sorry. I made a mistake. Will you hold it over my head this entire journey?" The General glared at her.

"Ugh!" Leading her horse by the reins, she stomped off a short distance. In truth she felt terrible for blaming Kauf. His memories had gotten them here after all. She remembered her father scolding her for her temper and knew she should apologize.

Shadon sighed. "She'll get over it. She's just upset it didn't work as she intended," he whispered, unaware that Tnasha could hear every word.

"There is a reason Carinth only allows certain women in their military," Kauf said with a frown. "They're too tempermental."

"Don't let her hear you say that. Especially if you'd like to keep your teeth." He shook his head. "Which direction?"

Kauf paused, and turned to Tnasha. "Well, wait. Can't you just transport all of us to where they were?"

Another yawn escaped Tnasha's lips. She used her last ounce of strength to remount her horse. "No," she said inside another deep yawn. "Not unless I want to imbalance myself and die. They'll figure out where they are and can follow us."

"All right. We go North." Kauf turned away from the city, checked the girth on his saddle, and mounted his horse. "Let's be off then."

Tnasha and Shadon followed. All the while Tnasha's thoughts, though murky in her present state, were with Kolgern and Margore. In the very least, she hoped they would understand the mistake and forgive her. Especially Kolgern.

CHAPTER 22

Lucas stood and decisively went to one of the pedestals. After examining the staff, he drew it from the center of the stone. With a shrug, he pulled the decoy from his mana and put it in place of the staff he removed. "This is the one."

"How do you figure?" Aithian looked on, curious and analytical.

The left one says it is the Raven's Claw, but the staff it holds is obviously the Eagle's Talon, evident by the scaled claw. The center one says it is the Crow's Foot. It cannot be the Crow's Foot, because it would make no sense to put the Crow's Foot in a properly marked pedestal. The right one says it is the Eagle's Talon, but we know the Eagle's Talon is on the left. So, we are left to deduct, with good reason, that the center staff is the Raven's Claw. Which would make sense because it is the one that is important; therefore it sits in the center."

Aithian nodded. At this point, he didn't care. He shivered within the temple wishing they could just go home. Central Arkeereon was surely much warmer. "That makes sense."

"Are you satisfied with my choice?"

"Does it matter?"

"Well, yes. Give me a reason to doubt myself and we will sit here longer."

"It sounds logical to me. If I think of any reason it wouldn't make sense, I'll let you know, and we can come back and choose the other."

Lucas tipped his head to one side. "Maybe we should make two more decoys and take them all."

"Where would we find the materials?"

"Anywhere. Fashioning a crude staff wouldn't be a difficult task." He shrugged. "That one took me a short time to make."

"And it looks like it." Aithian stood, stretching his arms over his head with a yawn. "Let's take the one and leave. We will be here for a few more days anyway. I would rather be warm inside the camp. We can debate whether or not we'll come back and take the others."

"All right." Lucas led the way out of the temple. Aithian followed, hoping the staff he now carried was indeed the right one.

They retreated to their campsite, settling in near the warm fire. Together, both men studied the staff. Aithian ran his hand across it. Its long, smooth wooden shaft led to the claw, which grasped a perfectly round, smooth black stone. The others were mirror images. Only the claws remained different.

●

That night, as they lay asleep within the ruins of the building, Aithian woke in a sweat. He could feel it; the presence of another sorcerer overwhelmed him. The hairs on his arms stood straight up. He shook Lucas awake. "Someone is coming."

Lucas's eyes flew open and he sat straight up, reaching for his sword. "Where?" he whispered.

"They're not here just yet. But someone is on their way."

Lucas rolled his eyes. "Damnit, Aithian. I thought you heard something."

"Can't you feel it? It's unsettling. I won't be able to fall asleep." He tossed a few more pieces of broken wood onto the fire.

"I feel nothing." Lucas rubbed his shoulder, set his sword beside him, and closed his eyes. "I want very much to be in my own bed with a raging fire in the hearth."

"You aren't allowing the feeling in."

Lucas opened his eyes suddenly. He did feel it. Aithian could tell by the startled look on his face.

"See?"

"Okay, I felt that. If this sorcerer is on his way, then he would have to be strong for us to feel him. He must be close."

Aithian looked around. They listened to the haunting echo of the wind as it whipped around them. "It looks as though neither of us will sleep tonight."

"If we don't sleep we will not have enough strength to endure this cold."

"If we continue sleeping the sorcerer could arrive unannounced and possibly find us and the staff." He looked around, taking a defensive posture.

Lucas nodded. "We will sleep in shifts."

Aithian nodded in agreement and shivered. "I'll take the first one."

CHAPTER 23

Oron and Arick arrived at the port of Cabalia early that morning. The busy streets of Cabalia, spilling over with the carts of merchants and the bustle of buyers, pulled them to attention. The ship had been void of the numerous voices and the sounds of carts and horses. Oron's eyes searched the crowd. He stopped short. "They are here already."

Arick stopped behind him. "How do you know?"

"That man over there." He nodded his head to their right. "If looks do not deceive me, that brown haired man looks very much like the sorceress' kinsman. Those of the O'Schoitt bloodline bear distinctive features, and I have been in Danaria enough to know one of them when I see them."

"He has no mana." Arick squinted, trying to see where Oron made the connection.

"It is internal. His mana is very slight outwardly. There is a green color emanating from him, see?"

Arick looked closer and finally saw the faint hint of mana on the surface of the man's skin. The Angorans had very few sorcerers with internal mana amongst them, but knew that those with internal mana had limited abilities. Oftentimes their only ability was to create more sorcerers with stronger external mana. "I see him," he finally said. "He's breeding stock and not worth much else. The sorceress should be near. Why do I not sense her?" He pushed his mana out in an attempt to find the sorceress then pulled it back with a jolt and turned to his left. "She's not here, but the Kersians are."

Oron turned to see the Kersian sorcerer and his men leaving their ship. "It looks as though we have arrived on time. But where could the sorceress be and how did she arrive here before everyone else?"

Arick shrugged and whispered, "Perhaps she can work stronger wind magick, or maybe she left these two behind as a diversion."

Oron shook his head and narrowed his eyes. "I don't think so. I think she has more power than I originally assumed. Wait, what's this? Another Kersian Sorcerer?"

"Where?" He followed Oron's gaze, seeing a taller, Kersian male, a sorcerer with strong, deep orange mana, greeting the Kersian group.

Oron's lips contorted into a sneer. "Seth."

Arick's stomach did a flip. His heart pounded heavy in his chest. "I've heard about him. Nothing good."

"We need to hide our mana before they notice us. Now."

Together, their mana faded into invisibility. Arick shook off the light feeling that consumed him. "This will only wear us down."

"We have no choice if we want to survive. The Kersians cannot know we are here if we want to avoid a confrontation."

"What's the plan now, Oron?" If anything, he was even more concerned. If the sorceress was not a danger like Graneck had said, and the Kersian Sorcerer Seth was involved, things were about to become even more complicated.

Oron put his hands on his hips. "We will follow the Kersians. Get the horses."

Arick turned to leave, but paused. "That would be certain suicide."

"Perhaps they will do our job for us." Oron turned to his friend with a scowl. "But we still have to follow to make sure."

"If we follow, they will see us. Eventually."

"No. We will find a good disguise. We'll pretend we are with a merchant convoy taking supplies to Northern Elishta. It's a Northern outpost past Ramathra."

Arick lowered his head with a sigh of resignation. "I hope it works."

"We will need supplies. A cart for the horses, and some local clothing." He tapped Arick on the chest. "Come on. We'll both get the horses. We don't want to be too far behind them."

Once they gathered their horses, supplies and bought a cart, they finished hitching the horses and waited. After they were sure the Kersians were a few hours ahead of them they moved North out of the city, following at a safe distance. All the while they hid their mana. The time passed quietly until the sound of horses came up from behind them.

CHAPTER 24

Morvack stepped off the plank leading from the ship onto the Cabalian dock. He moved forward at a steady pace knowing his men followed by the sound of their footfalls echoing off the wood planks behind him. Something did not feel right. Nothing had felt right since the sorceress destroyed the temple at Zul. A sick feeling made its way to the pit of his stomach.

The voice jumped out at him from the noisy docks and streets around him. "Beware," she said in a wisp of wind.

That is when their eyes met. His brother Seth started toward him, taking long, even strides. He wore full battle dress and made no move to hide the obvious Kersian blade sheathed at his side.

"You're late," Seth said with a disapproving glare.

Morvack felt his own expression turn sour. "I am not late, brother. I am precisely on time. What are *you* doing here?"

"Making sure *you* do not fail this time." Seth's steely gaze traveled from person to person as merchants passed them.

"Then why am I here at all?"

Seth said nothing, looking like a king examining his subjects. Finally, he turned to his brother with a sly, insincere grin. "I sense another sorcerer."

Morvack's eyes followed his brother's. He saw nothing. "You are paranoid."

"The sorceress is already here," he said with a growl.

"How do you know?"

"I can smell her," he snarled.

Morvack found it hard to believe Gavgal mistrusted him this much, but it shouldn't have surprised him. His brothers had always treated him this way. He was simply too trusting to accept it. Clearing his throat he chose his words carefully. "Go home, Seth. I will deal with the sorceress and the weapon. I am quite capable of doing this on my own."

Seth shook his head. "I disagree, brother. I cannot risk you or Gavgal failing again. I either go alone, or we all go together."

"The Unnamed did not ask this of you. He asked it of me." Morvack felt the hot flush of anger fill his cheeks.

"No worries, brother. I have no intention of taking any honor from you. I am only here to insure you do not fail – again."

Morvack winced at Seth's continual use of the word 'fail'. He decided to change the subject rather than try to argue failure with his elder brother. "What of the seer."

Seth shook his head again. "You will never learn, will you? When I am given a task, I complete it. I *never* fail. The seer is no longer a problem. He is dead, and no one, not even your untrained sorceress could have changed that."

"You do not have to keep mentioning my failure. Don't you know I know I've failed?" Morvack wanted to lunge forward and break Seth's smug jaw. Especially when Seth smiled.

"I'm glad you understand. Now, what shall it be? Will you come with me, or will I go alone?"

"Fine. You can come along." Morvack hid his anger, all the while wondering how Seth managed to arrive in Cabalia ahead of him. He decided not to ask. His brother was infamous for his volatile temper. Anything could set him off. And Morvack didn't want to be the one to do it. They mounted their horses together and headed North. All the while Morvack found himself probing into Seth's mind.

Inside, he found angry visions and delusions of grandeur. Seth fancied himself a formidable warlord, a force to be reckoned with. A trait, Morvack surmised, that would eventually lead to his downfall. His anger at his brother's arrogance forced against his insides. Finally he decided to ask the question. "How did you arrive here before me?"

Seth did not turn to him. Instead, he sighed in annoyance and answered the question with the obvious intention of belittling his younger brother. "I left long before you did, brother. I did as I was instructed to do, and made my way here as quickly as I could. I lost three horses doing so."

"What of your armies?"

"They were purified in glorious battle in the Unnamed's honor."

Morvack's stomach twisted thinking of the lives lost— the lives of men that Seth found expendable. "Oh." He still did not understand Seth's desire to make sure he obtained the weapon. Morvack's failures had never been so high on his brother's list of worries before.

Seth rode ahead with his chin held high.

Morvack scowled after him. He relaxed, allowing his mana to flow freely. He could feel them. A few hours behind them, other sorcerers followed. But none were the sorceress and her friends. He made no move to warn his men, least of all Seth. Chances were that Seth felt them, too. But in all of his arrogance, he would not be bothered with it. Other sorcerers, to him, were beneath his self-exalted station. Morvack snorted, scoffing the idea. Seth's natural abilities were strong and destructive. There was no doubt about that. At the same time, to think he was better than other sorcerers because of those abilities seemed almost stupid.

He urged his horse forward, finding himself at Seth's side again. "What will you do if we arrive and find the sorceress there?"

Seth turned to him with a malicious grin. "I will destroy her, of course."

"Gavgal never said to destroy her. She's good breeding stock."

A sharp laugh escaped his brother's thin lips. "Gavgal would not know good breeding if it were ordained by the Unnamed, himself. Do you know why our brother has this grand fantasy of converting the heathens to our ways and why he wants the sorceresses? Do you think he cares about you or I continuing our family bloodlines?"

"I do not know what to think sometimes."

"Well, brother, were you aware that it was Gavgal who killed our own mother? And destroyed all our sorceresses?"

Fear filled him. The disembodied voice had said the same. "To what end?"

"To father his offspring, of course. You can be so naive." Seth waved a hand absentmindedly in Morvack's direction. "Gavgal's problem, however, is that he is incapable of reproducing. His seed cannot siege the fortress, if you understand what I mean. Or should I use more plain terms?"

"I am not the idiot fool you take me as."

"Ha." Seth shook his head, still wearing a smug grin. "If you had any spine, you would not worship Gavgal nor hold him in such high regard."

Morvack said nothing.

"Shocked by this revelation brother?" Seth smiled, then lowered his voice. "Were it not for your brother and his foolish religious lies, you would have a family, I would have a family, Alax would have a family. He thinks because he is the eldest, that right should be extended to him first. And if not him, none of us. If he cannot find a sorceress to produce his offspring, we will be denied the same."

Morvack hung his head. Never before had he felt such sadness, such anger.

"You suspected it." Seth's eyes bore into him. "I propose we take the weapon back to Zul and use it to destroy him. It is the only way any of us will ever be free."

"What about the Unnamed? And *His* will?"

"Do you honestly think Gavgal has the power of all goodness within his grasp? That it is only for the Kersians to take? All religion is simply a way to control the masses, Morvack. If you want to live a prosperous life, you should let go of religion. It serves no purpose for men like you and I. It is a weakness. One *we* cannot afford if we wish to see our family bloodline survive. Gavgal knows this and uses it. You and Alax have fallen into his trap. He means for you to do his work for him so that he can achieve his own ends."

Morvack could see into his mind and he knew that for now Seth spoke his true thoughts. "Then why do you follow his orders as well?"

"By following his orders, he does not suspect I know his true motivation, brother. He also does not suspect that I intend to use his own tactics against him. Nor will you tell him." Seth glared and Morvack, expecting an answer.

"I will say nothing."

"Does what I have told you anger you?"

Morvack clamped down his jaw until the pain became sharp and shot through his teeth. "Yes."

"Good. It should. You and Alax still have a choice. You can choose to stand by me, and receive what you have been promised all along, or you can stand by Gavgal and chase false hope until your dying breath." Seth rode ahead again, his silent thoughts cursing Gavgal's very existence.

Morvack pulled his mind from his brother's. He did not trust Seth. At the same time, Seth offered more than Gavgal did. But if Seth were lying, things would be no different. At that moment, Morvack had a change of heart, and Seth's campaign to defeat Gavgal started to sound better and better as the day wore on.

CHAPTER 25

"If we're in Cabalia, where, by Natyis, are Tnasha, Shadon, and Kauf?" Margore looked around expectantly.

Kolgern threw his arms in the air. "Great. We're lost in the middle of nowhere. I *knew* this would happen!"

"Relax. Look over there." Margore pointed at several thin lines of smoke rising high into the sky. "It's a city. All we have to do is reach it and we'll know where we are."

The ride seemed to take longer than it should have. They rode in silence until Kolgern finally spoke. "At least we're still in one piece."

Margore chuckled. "That's the right attitude to have. Tnasha may not be a *great* sorceress, but she did manage to transport us from one continent to another."

Kolgern cocked his head in contemplation. "Do you think she'll ever learn how to use it?"

He shrugged. "If you mean control her mana and the power behind it, I think so. She may be an old woman before that happens, but eventually she will master herself. If there is one thing I know about my cousin it's that she's persistent and doesn't give in to failure easily."

Kolgern snorted. "I know that for a fact."

They reached the city late that afternoon, happy to discover they were in Cabalia. They found an inn and slept for the night. The next morning they ate, gathered their horses, and stood near the docks searching the sea of people for familiar faces. "Maybe they're here, too?" Kolgern suggested.

"No. I suspect not. I would have seen a trace of Tnasha's mana. I *can* see mana, you know. Maybe we can find someone to guide us there."

They saw them from a distance. Kersian soldiers stepping off the docks. "Oh no. Don't stare. Kersians," Kolgern said, bowing his head and pulling the hood of his cloak over his matted blonde hair.

Margore followed his example and pulled the brown hood over his own head. "Look to your left."

Kolgern did as instructed. "What?"

"Two more sorcerers. They're not Kersian though. They have spotted the Kersians and just hid their mana. What in Natyis' name?"

"More sorcerers? What are they doing?"

"I dunno, but they seem very interested in the Kersians."

"Are they Danarian?"

Margore shook his head. "No. I don't recognize them."

"That doesn't mean they aren't Danarian…"

"No and they're not wearing Danarian clothing. They look like ruffians."

Kolgern raised an eyebrow and turned to him. "Ruffians?"

"Angoran Sorcerers. They live in the Onyx Mountains in their nomadic tribes. They don't care for the Kersians either, but they also keep to themselves and don't consort with sorcerers outside their own tribal bloodlines."

"Maybe they want the weapon, too?" Kolgern thought about that for a moment, wondering what the outcome would be now that there were three sorcerer factions involved. "If that's the case, we need to find Tnasha and the others as soon as possible. They're clearly outnumbered."

"We are outnumbered either way. I guess the best we can do is follow them." He paused, then added, "At a distance."

After the Kersians left, Shadon and Margore kept their distance; stalking the remaining Angoran sorcerers like assassins lying in wait. After the Angorans purchased a cart, they harnessed their horses to it and started off, after the Kersians, heading North.

Margore mounted his mare. "Let's go. It looks like they are disguising themselves as merchants. We can approach them and ask if we can ride along with them. Maybe we can find out what they're up to."

Kolgern mounted, following him. "What if they see through our plan?"

"There are two of them and two of us."

"They *are* sorcerers. They can throw mana blates, we cannot." Kolgern's forehead crinkled with uncertainty.

"Hey?" Margore turned to him, hurt. "I *am* a sorcerer you know. I *do* know a thing or two about sorcery. Besides, maybe we can use diplomacy. The Angorans are not entirely barbaric people."

They rode a short distance behind the Angorans for several hours before daring to approach the men in the cart. Margore urged his horse into a canter, coming up alongside them. "Aya!"

They did not stop and kept their eyes averted straight ahead. Margore's tone turned brave. "May I ask where you are going?"

"What business is it of yours?" The tall man driving the cart kept his eyes cast forward on the well-cut dirt road.

"My friend and I need to get to Ramathra, but we do not know the way. We wondered if we could travel with you."

The men in the cart exchanged glances. The second looked Margore up and down, then turned to Kolgern and did the same. "We are going to Elishta, North of Ramathra. However, I do not understand why you would want to go to Ramathra. Nothing there but ruins."

The man driving threw his partner a sideways glance.

"Delivering supplies?" Margore gave them a friendly smile.

The man drew the horses to a stop and turned to the men riding alongside them. "I know who you are."

Margore smiled again, this time with appreciation for their honesty. "We know who you are, too. The Kersians are likely to see through hidden mana. They will still feel it."

139

The men exchanged glances again, as if they shared the same thoughts.

The passenger tipped his head, holding out his hand. "I am Arick, this is Oron."

"We have come to offer support to your cousin. She is untrained and outnumbered by the Kersian sorcerers," Oron said. He cracked his whip, urging the horses forward again.

Margore and Kolgern continued to ride alongside. "I was not aware the Angoran concerned themselves with the Sorcerers' Council politics," Margore said, his voice laden with curiosity.

Arick shrugged. "This time the outcome could affect us. We saw a need to become involved and offer our support."

Kolgern winced. His own suspicious nature told him the Angoran sorcerers were not telling the entire truth. He set aside the uneasy feeling that washed over him.

"How is it you are not traveling with the sorceress?" Oron asked.

Margore easily slid the lie in unnoticed. "We stayed behind to take up the rear."

"You arrived quite quickly," Oron said.

"My cousin has an affinity for working strong weather magick."

Oron bit his lower lip in what seemed a brief moment of contemplation before he replied. "She is powerful. You know, there are some who believe she is dangerous."

"Not on purpose," Kolgern blurted. Tnasha's closest friend, and biggest critic, suddenly felt the urge to defend her. "She just hasn't gotten a grasp on how to hold back yet. She's great at letting it loose. But control comes with time and practice. She just started practicing magick recently. We cannot expect her to be an adept sorceress overnight."

Margore turned to Kolgern with his jaw set and his eyes wide, shocked at Kolgern's outpouring of information. He had not intended on them being honest.

Oron did not seem to notice Margore's reaction and nodded. "I suppose not."

"So you do not believe she is dangerous then?" Arick asked, gazing out over the flat wastelands before them.

"No," both Margore and Kolgern said in unison.

Margore scratched at his unshaven chin. It was too late to be secretive now. They had to risk trusting the Angorans. "My cousin is a perfectionist; she'll get it right eventually."

Kolgern nodded in agreement. "Tnasha is a good person. She would never use her magick to hurt anyone unless it was in self-defense. Even then, she might hesitate. Or rather, she *does* hesitate..." he corrected.

Oron and Arick exchanged glances again and turned their eyes forward, back to the roadway. If all went well, they would arrive in Ramathra the following morning, hopefully with the Angorans as true allies.

CHAPTER 26

A cold wind slipped up Tnasha's tunic. "It's freezing! It must be colder than Exavia here!" She wrapped her cloak tightly around her shoulders and chest. They had spent the night before camped behind some large boulders near a river. The boulders offered little protection from the wind and the river made it that much colder. The chill feeling from the night before had continued with her through to the next morning, and until now.

"Does this place ever warm up?" Shadon asked.

Kauf rode ahead, in silence. Finally, after a few minutes, he twisted around in his saddle. "It is always very windy here. Even in summer it's still cool."

"How much further is it?" Tnasha asked. She could not help but complain. The arid, cold climate was more than she could bear and her muscles ached from the long ride.

Kauf's chapped lips turn upward into a half-hearted grin. "Not until late tonight if we want to ride through without stopping. We can find someplace to camp among the ruins and begin our search for the weapon at daybreak. Between the old wells and the river there should be enough water for the horses and we have enough grain."

Tnasha sensed them, the Kersian sorcerers, and shuddered. Her stomach did a flip. "They're not far behind us."

Both men looked at her. "You can feel them?" Kauf asked.

Tnasha nodded. "I feel Morvack, but there is another sorcerer with him. I don't know who it is."

Shadon crinkled his forehead with concern. "It better not be Seth or we're done for."

"There are ways to handle men like Seth," the General grunted. "One way would be to cut off his head and burn his corpse."

She scrunched her mouth in a look of disgust. "Not if he kills you first. He's a sorcerer, remember?"

"You are ruining my fantasy, Tnasha fen Schoitt," General Kauf said with a smile.

Shadon leaned over and untwisted the brow band on his horse's bridle. "You said we would have to search for it? How big is Ramathra?"

"The ruins spread out for miles. The buildings are difficult to distinguish one from another."

Tnasha looked at Kauf, wondering what was going on in his head. For the most part he was a silent man, unless he had something to say or he was spoken to. It made her nervous. She wondered then if he had sent Kolgern and Margore someplace else on purpose. Being as forward and direct as she was, she decided to ask. "Did you send Kolgern and Margore further down the coast on purpose?"

He paused a moment before answering. "No. I give you my word that my mind merely lost focus for a moment. But I have been considering the benefit of the mistake." He gave her a hopeful look.

"How so?"

"If they were sent just South of Cabalia, and they were smart enough to find out where they were, they should be behind us as well. With any luck, they will be behind the Kersians and can track their movements. And, they could take the Kersians by surprise and intervene if need be."

Shadon nodded in agreement, but the look on his face showed uncertainty. "Unless the Kersians catch them. Morvack and Kolgern have some bad blood between them."

Tnasha took a deep breath. As always, Shadon brought up a good point. "Kolgern would be smart enough to keep himself hidden. He has common sense."

"He's a prankster and a risk taker." Shadon smiled.

"Yes, but he knows when to be serious. I doubt he would find running into Morvack a jovial situation."

Kauf slowed his horse so they could catch up to him. "I have faith in your cousin. He seems very practical."

Tnasha nodded. She trusted Margore. While his romantic pursuits were less than successful, he had a way with diplomacy and tact. She recalled, from childhood memories, more than one occasion where Margore had used his wise tongue to get himself and his brother out of trouble. She laughed. "He broke his mother's favorite glass bowl when he was ten. She was angry until he told her he had no control over the direction the wooden block went when Martiga knocked it from his hand. Then he explained how sorry he was, and that he had learned rough play with his brother indoors was not a practical thing to do, as it could result in such mishaps. She was so amused with his honest assessment of the situation that she did not stay angry with them."

Kauf chuckled.

A wide grin spread over Shadon's lips. "It really is miserable out here."

A sudden surge of energy and happiness engulfed Tnasha. If they were going to be miserable, the least she could do was try to make the situation less weighted with melancholy. "Let's race. First one to that big rock up there does not have to help set up camp tonight." She leaned forward, urging her horse into a full gallop.

Shadon followed with, "Oh no you don't!"

With the realization he was far behind, Kauf reluctantly went after them.

In a pounding of hooves and rush of wind, Shadon passed her, making it to the boulder before she and Kauf did. Shadon let out a chiding laugh and patted his gelding on the neck. "Ha. It looks like I get a night off."

Tnasha reined her mare to a stop, throwing her weight backward in the saddle. The horses frothed at the mouth, and their necks were slick with lather.

By his eyes, she could tell Kauf clearly disapproved. As if reading her mind he said, "Perhaps we shouldn't have done that. The horses need water and the next river is an hour's ride off yet."

Tnasha pulled one of the heavy water skins from her saddle, dismounted, and poured it into the one bucket they carried. She offered it to her horse. "We can go without water for another hour."

"I won the race," Shadon repeated.

"Gloat all you will." Tnasha giggled. She patted her horse on the neck, pulled the grimoire from her saddlebag then went over to the rock, sitting down next to it. The rock took the wind off her for a while at least. Opening the page, on a whim, she turned to page seventy-five.

"What are you doing?" Shadon yawned and stretched.

"Just looking."

Kauf approached her, looking over her shoulder. "Anything in particular?"

"No. You seem awfully interested in sorcery though."

"It is not as common place in Carinth. I find it a curious subject." He continued looking over her shoulder. "How to conjure bats?"

Tnasha smiled, noting that Kauf seemed to be warming up to them. "You never know when you'll need bats."

He laughed.

Shadon joined them. "Maybe there is something in there that will keep us warm."

Tnasha's eyes lit up. "That's an idea. I should have thought of that. I wonder if there is an index." She flipped through the back of the book. There was none. It figured. She wondered then why some books were indexed while others weren't. It was probably due to how organized the sorcerer who wrote it was, she finally decided.

"Go through page by page," Kauf suggested. He shrugged at Shadon, who returned the shrug.

She started at the beginning and turned the pages, quickly scanning each page as she passed it. "Oh, here is one to calm the wind."

Shadon rubbed his shoulders and fidgeted. "That's a start."

She left a finger on that page and continued. "That was on page thirty-six. Remember that." Continuing through the book, she found another. "To bring out the sun."

"Mmm. Yes, that sounds lovely," Kauf said.

Shadon nodded.

She placed another finger on that page. Finally, she reached the final pages. "I wonder."

Both men looked at her expectantly.

"I wonder if sorcerers endowed with the fire element can keep themselves warm."

"I don't know. But hurry and try the two you found. Maybe you can calm the wind in the very least," Shadon said.

Mumbling in agreement, Kauf stepped in closer to her.

She read over the incantation several times, then closed her eyes and recited it aloud, focusing on the wind, imagining the air calm. In the immediate area surrounding them, the air became still. But outside the space in which they stood, the wind continued. She rolled her eyes. "That won't do us any good."

"Yes, but it's fine for now." Kauf looked up at the gray sky. "Now, what about the sun?"

Once again, she opened the book, this time to the second page. "Anry anka Flery, Solaris," she said in a loud and boisterous voice, with a silly grin.

The men lifted their eyes with curiosity and expectation. Nothing happened.

Tnasha sighed. "What did I do wrong now?"

"You said the words right, didn't you?" Shadon looked over her shoulder. "Maybe you mispronounced something?"

"No. The words are just a focus tool. They mean nothing. Maybe I wasn't focused enough." She closed her eyes, whispering the incantation beneath her breath. She looked up at the sky again. Nothing.

Kauf stuck out his lower lip. "Maybe the incantation was recorded wrong."

"No, it's not the words." She looked up at him, stretching her neck back as far as it would go in order to meet his eyes. "Thank you for being so kind. But I must come to accept that fire magick is not my greatest strength."

"One out of two isn't bad," Shadon said with reassurance. "At least we have a little protection from the wind."

Closing the book, she stood. "Should we be on our way again?"

Both men mumbled in agreement. Together, they remounted their horses and moved on. Strangely, the wind whipping all around stood blocked by the field of sorcery still surrounding each of them. They all agreed it was much warmer.

CHAPTER 27

Morvack felt her now. Undoubtedly the sorceress and her companions stopped more often to rest their horses. He drew his men to a halt. Seth turned around. "What are you doing?"

"We should stop and rest the horses. I would hate to have to make the rest of the journey on foot." Morvack tried to keep the emotion out of his voice. He did not know why he wanted to stop. He just did.

"They will be fine for several more hours."

Morvack held his ground. "Fine, you go ahead. But if your horse parishes because you have pushed it too hard, you will be on foot. There are no replacement horses, Seth. In case you didn't notice, we're in the middle of a desolate wasteland."

Listening to the voice of reason, Seth turned around and dismounted, handing the reins to one of the soldiers. "Very well, have it your way, brother."

Morvack followed him away from the men. "Why is it you insist on undermining my authority, and *my* mission?"

"*Our* mission," Seth corrected. He turned to his brother, towering over him by a foots-length. "If we continually stop, the sorceress will reach the weapon before we do."

"That would not be good." Morvack stared off into the distance. "She is more powerful than Gavgal and I together."

"This time she will not be able to raise serpents. The ocean is too far." Seth's upper lip stiffened. "I heard she was powerful."

"She is also quite..." Morvack chose his words carefully. "Defiant. Stubborn."

A deep, hollow chuckle emerged from Seth's throat. "Most women are, brother. But they are also just that. Women."

"Are you saying women are weak?" He did not hide his amusement. After all, Seth had not been up against the sorceress and was working on an assumption. Morvack knew better. He had been there.

"Perhaps not in the sense that they cannot fight. But they are weak by their very nature. Their emotions deceive them every time. When we confront the sorceress, you shall take up the rear, and I will approach from the front. You forget, Morvack. My mana blates render other's mana useless for a time. I can stall it, imbalance it, and even take it away if I choose."

Morvack nodded, wondering if Seth was merely reiterating something Morvack already knew or if he was making subtle threats. "Ah, yes. I suppose I did forget," he said, his voice dripping with sarcasm. "I think I'm going to go stretch my legs."

Seth's gaze followed him for a few moments then left him in favor of watching the men tend to the horses. Once Morvack knew Seth's attention was away from him, he breathed a sigh of relief.

"He mocks you." Her disembodied voice came out of nowhere, hitting him in the face like the coldest of winds.

"What should I do about him?" he asked through clenched teeth.

"Tolerate him, for now. Another opportunity will present itself to you, for he will deceive you. You will fall by his hand."

He tried to mask his surprise so that anyone watching him would not notice a change in his demeanor. "He is going to kill me?"

"He will try. But he will fail. The sorceress will protect you. She will shield all of you."

"He would leave my men and I for dead?"

"Why shouldn't he? He does not need you to destroy Gavgal. He needs the weapon. *You are expendable.*"

Morvack growled. "I hope both Seth and Gavgal kill one another."

"That is possible," she whispered. "However, the weapon in the hands of Seth makes it improbable."

With another deep sigh, Morvack returned to his men and Seth. After a brief rest, they remounted and continued toward Ramathra.

CHAPTER 28

Stopping for the night, Oron, Arick, Margore, and Kolgern set up camp in a dry creek bed. It dipped deep into the landscape with high, steep sides at some spots, offering some protection from the wind.

After a sparse meal of broth and dried bread, Oron and Arick slipped off around the creek's bend for privacy.

When they were finally alone, Arick whispered in a discreet voice, "I think we would be making a grave mistake following through with Graneck's orders, regardless the monetary prize. The sorceress' family is wealthy and might donate the supplies we need for helping her."

Oron nodded with reluctance. "Perhaps you're right. I do not want to make a rash decision."

"But we *have* made our decision. We won't do it. Right?" Arick prodded. "I do not want to pay for a rash misdeed through eternity. I could never live with my conscience."

"We have the word of her friend and cousin that she is not dangerous. I still think we need to see the sorceress for ourselves. Talk to her. We can make a decision at that time. After all, cousins and friends can be blinded by the bloodlines and emotion that bind them."

"Will we have that kind of time?" Arick's eyes filled with anger. He reached into his pack and pulled out a small, leather-covered book, and opened it to a passage marked with a slip of torn red cloth. He read, "For all wrong doing there is consequence. For the universe must maintain balance. Harmony is one with the universe and so are we all."

Oron's eyes fell downcast, to the ground.

Arick closed the book and continued. "If her mana is meant to be, and we destroy her, then the universe could become imbalanced, throwing everything into discord. The retribution of the universe, and the gods…"

Oron nodded. "I still wish to speak to her and make the judgment for myself. You do not have to involve yourself if my decision goes against yours. I will bear the weight of my own actions and take any punishment due me."

Arick fell silent and walked away, leaving Oron alone with his thoughts.

•

Kolgern watched the men intently from afar. "What do you think they were talking about?"

"Is it any of our business?"

"They seem at odds with one another."

"Is it any of our business?" Margore repeated.

"No, I suppose it isn't. I just hate secrets." He sat down with a heavy sigh and commenced pouring several small rocks from his boots. "How did those get in there?"

"I don't know that we can trust them, but you gave us no choice." Margore frowned.

"How?"

"What do you mean, how? You started blurting out information…"

"I didn't mean to. It was an accident." Kolgern looked at him through narrowed eyes. "Isn't it better that we're close and watching them?"

Margore noticed one of the Angorans returning and nodded toward his approach so Kolgern would shut up. "Maybe."

Arick returned and sat next to them near the fire. "We will sleep in shifts. We have to wake early to catch up with the Kersians."

"Agreed," Margore said with a nod of acknowledgment.

Kolgern narrowed his eyes and leaned forward. The Angoran seemed disturbed about something and that unsettled him. "Is something wrong?"

Arick rested his head on his hand. "Oron and I have a disagreement in how to handle the Kersians if things become... difficult."

"You mean magical warfare?" Kolgern frowned, wondering if these sorcerers were more adept than Tnasha.

"Precisely. We may not be able to defend you both if we are defending ourselves."

Margore snorted. "We can take care of ourselves. I am not concerned with that."

"I did not mean to insult you. It must be difficult being a sorcerer with internal mana."

"*I have* certain abilities." A mysterious underlying tone filled his voice. "Things I can do to protect myself."

The Angoran lifted an eyebrow. "Really?"

"Sure."

"I didn't know internal mana allowed such abilities."

Margore drew in a deep breath. "I *can* see and sense mana as you do. I have heightened coordination, and my eyesight is perfect. I also get strong *impressions*."

"Can you throw a blate?"

Margore shrugged as if it wasn't important. "I don't know. I've never tried it because I was always told I probably couldn't. I guess I never felt the need to find out. Maybe I can."

The Angoran smiled with a chuckle. "Maybe you should try it ahead of time to make sure you can." He turned over his shoulder. "Oron, come here. Margore is going to try and throw a blate."

Oron wandered over and stood behind them. He pointed ahead of them. "That rock over there."

Kolgern waved a hand at the Angoran, feeling the need to participate in some way since he had no sorcery to show off. "You first."

Arick stood up and looked down at Margore. "Let me show you how to do it."

Margore's jaw visibly tightened. Being a sorcerer with internal mana almost always guaranteed a man was seen as less than a man in the eyes of other sorcerers and Kolgern felt his own jaw set in response. He felt sorry for Margore for the disrespect he must have tolerated from his own kind. Kolgern had experienced that kind of disrespect before and his natural instinct was to stand up for the cousin of his best friend. "How do you know he needs you to show him?"

Margore lifted a hand to quiet Kolgern and said to Arick, "All right. Blast it."

Arick cupped his hands together. The blate built slowly between his palms pulsating a glow of light. With outstretched arms and palms forward, the blate escaped like silver lightening, crashing against the rock in a flash of sparks.

Kolgern smiled, feeling reassured that the Angoran had such control. "Impressive. Who's next? Oron?"

Oron stepped forward. He built his blate more quickly, hurling it before anyone had a chance to see it form. It flew through the air like a ball of fire, taking the top of the rock off in pieces when it hit. He smiled, content. "Not bad if I do say so myself."

The Angorans looked at Margore expectantly then. Margore stood. Taking a deep breath, he filled his lungs with the cold night air. He closed his eyes. Kolgern assumed Margore was imagining a burning ball of mana in his hand, an angry yellow fire seething with all his pent up frustration. That's what Kolgern would have done. Just then, Margore opened his fingers, shoving his palms forward, throwing the mana outward. Two thin lines of greenish-yellow light emerged like far away lightening, merely scorching the rock, leaving black soot marks. Unsteady, Margore lost his balance, regained it, and putting his hands to his head he sat down. He visibly shivered.

Arick picked up a blanket and put it over Margore's shoulders. "Not bad. I expected nothing at all."

Oron patted Margore firm on the shoulder. "With a little practice you'll be throwing full force blates in no time, my young friend."

Margore put on an obviously forced smile. "Maybe."

With a snort, Kolgern sat beside him. "If you ask me, that was pretty damn good for someone who never threw a blate before."

The Angorans both nodded in agreement, exchanging a brief glance before settling down. Margore said nothing. He looked exhausted.

That night they took watch in shifts and slept likewise. Well before sunrise they arose, cleared their camp and moved on. Upon the first rays of golden morning light, the ruins of Ramathra stood outstretched before them.

S. J. Reisner

CHAPTER 29

Having not slept past the mid of night Tnasha kept herself busy tending the fire. With daylight not quite upon them, she decided to make a hot pot of tea. A sense of urgency overwhelmed her. She shook Shadon by the shoulder and whispered in his ear, "Wake up. We should go soon."

Shadon rolled over wearily. He opened his eyes, rubbing them. The wind spell had since worn off. He shivered. "What happened to our wind protection?"

Kauf bolted upright, reaching for his sword. "What's wrong?"

"Nothing," she said. "I made some tea. We should go soon. Before the sun is up."

Shadon sat up and yawned. With his eyes half open he reached out and took the metal cup she offered him.

"We have to leave soon. The Kersians are getting closer." She handed the second cup to Kauf.

"We should have ridden further last night. We could have camped in the ruins." Kauf looked around, trying to hold back a yawn.

"The horses needed rest. Not to mention the wind magick tired me. Weren't one of you two supposed to be keeping watch?"

Shadon sipped his tea and stared at the ground. "I was up until after you fell asleep. Kauf was still awake."

156

After finishing the tea, they all rose and began packing up their things. Clearing the camp took little time, and they soon found themselves riding North again toward Ramathra.

Just before they ascended the slight incline leading to the expanse of the ruins, Tnasha felt the presence of other sorcerers. Not the Kersians this time. It hit her in a wave of indefinable feeling, exploiting her senses. She could feel them, smell them, and even taste them. Taken aback, she reined her horse to a complete stop. "Wait. Someone is already here."

Kauf reached for his sword. "Kersians?"

"No. Someone else. I feel two distinct individuals."

"Sorcerers?" Shadon asked.

"Yes." She shivered, but not from the cold. Rather their very presence.

Kauf eyed her strangely.

"Sorcerers can feel one another. It's an innate ability," Shadon explained.

Kauf's eyes clouded. "Who else would want the weapon?"

Shadon lifted an eyebrow and met Kauf's questioning gaze. "The Arkeeronish? Imperial hierarchs possibly. It *is* their family artifact we are after."

"The weapon belongs to the Arkeeronish?" Tnasha could not hide her surprise. It was a detail Priestess Caitlan had conveniently left out. Or perhaps she simply forgot.

Shadon nodded. "We will have to find out who it is sooner or later. Let's go."

"Hurry, the Kersians are gaining ground. They should arrive shortly." She looked back over her shoulder, expecting to see them.

"What will we do then?" Shadon looked genuinely worried.

Tnasha shrugged, but kept her calm demeanor. "We will work that out when something happens. I don't think this is a situation that can be planned for, is it?"

Neither man answered. From the look on Kauf's face, she could tell he was uncomfortable with her approach. But they had no choice. Not that she could see. Her mana was still too depleted to transport them with magick. Priestess Caitlan's

words rang in her mind. *The warrior's blood still runs red.*
Never before, not even on her excursion to Zul, did she realize it
as she did now. Immortality was not hers. The possibility of
death seemed very real indeed.

They rode on, finally reaching the ruins that stretched far
in all directions in front of them. Kauf's description had not been
an exaggeration. She could not tell the buildings apart nor
distinguish the ancient streets. Ramathra in and of itself was ruin.
Like a candle extinguished by water, she extinguished her mana.
Suddenly, the early morning darkness seemed even darker.

CHAPTER 30

Voices and the hoof-falls of horses pulled Lucas to alertness. "Aithian!"

Aithian jumped, and stood fully awake in mere moments. "They're here."

"More are on the way." Anxiety sat on the edge of his voice. He pressed his lips closed for fear breathing would attract attention.

"Hide your mana."

He promptly obeyed Aithian's order, fighting his golden elemental mana into blackness. Taking a deep breath, he peered around the corner of the ruin doorway into the darkness beyond. "I cannot see anything."

Aithian came up behind him and pointed. "There."

Lucas looked hard and finally saw them. Three people on horseback made their way through the ruins, though none of them displayed mana. "One of them?"

"I have an idea. Did you hide the staff?"

"It's hidden back in the ruin, beneath my blanket."

"We don't want them too close to it, but I'm beginning to think we have no choice."

"We are supposed to remain hidden. Who is disobeying my father now?"

"I have an idea. Come on." Aithian stepped out of the doorway and crept his way to the next crumbling building wall.

Lucas shook his head. It was not like Aithian to act so rash. The idea of getting too close made him nervous and he hurried to follow.

Finally, Aithian stood full height and stepped from around the side a building wall and in front of the three travelers. "Who are you?"

Lucas stepped up beside him. He could feel the invisible mana from the other sorcerer hit him like a brick in the chest. Aithian felt it too, he could tell because his friend took a step backward, then forced himself to step forward again.

●

Tnasha looked down at the men, both tall and dark haired which was telling of their Arkeeronish background. The man in front could hide his mana, but not the brilliant blue of his eyes. They glowed like many sorcerers' eyes glowed in the darkness. Just as she was sure her own eyes might hint at the violet color of her own mana. She fought harder to hide it even though she knew it was useless. "I am Tnasha fen Schoitt of Danaria. This is my friend, Shadon, and General Kauf of Carinth. Who are you?"

It was then Aithian realized it was not a sorcerer they sought, but a sorceress. "We are Arkeeronish. I am Aithian, and this is Lucas. We heard people were coming to retrieve our sacred artifacts and our elders wanted to know who. Is that what you're here for?"

She narrowed her eyes. "Perhaps." She paused and thought about her answer for a moment, painfully aware that all eyes were on her. "Or maybe we are here to make sure the artifact does not fall into the *wrong* hands."

Aithian turned to Lucas with a glint of uncertainty in his eyes. It was obviously not the answer he expected. He turned back to face them. "We can protect our own."

Kauf and Shadon moved their horses aside and Tnasha rode forward. "You have done a fine job so far, but the Danarian elders and priesthood have asked me to retrieve the item and make sure it is safely locked away where the Kersians cannot get to it. You should tell your elders that they shouldn't just leave magical weapons in the open where *anyone* can get at them."

Aithian nodded in concurrence and held out an arm to help her dismount. "Let me show you where it is."

She gave Shadon an amused smile and dismounted. Kauf and Shadon dismounted as well.

"It is too easy," Shadon whispered in her ear as they followed the sorcerers, horses in tow.

"Why would they lead us to it?" Kauf furrowed his brow, stumbling on some stones on the path. He regained his footing with a curse.

Lucas followed Aithian warily. "What are you doing?" he asked beneath his breath.

"If we take them to it, they will take one and leave."

Tnasha stopped momentarily and pulled one of the torches from her saddlebag. It was still too dark to see the path clearly. She lit it with an incantation and held it in front of her, making it easier to see the sorcerers who paused and looked back every so often. She found both of them to be attractive, well built men. Aithian in particular. He had a strong jaw and high cheekbones, and he was tall and muscular. Healthy. All of these traits were indicative of selective breeding. She pulled herself from her admiration and forced her concentration back on their reason for being there.

As they reached the temple, a figure surrounded in orange light, emerged from the shadows. "Well. This is not what I would have expected."

Shadon gulped and his face went white. "It's Seth."

Seth stepped into the light. "Indeed, it is *I*. I am pleased my reputation precedes me."

Tnasha felt Morvack behind her. She whirled around only to find both Shadon and Kauf surrounded by Kersian soldiers.

"Lynae was it? Or perhaps it is Tnasha. Daughter of Warlord O'Schoitt. A fifth generation sorceress. I will not fall for your hidden mana a second time."

Seth scoffed. "Ha. She fooled you with that? Why am I not surprised?" He turned his attention to the Arkeeronish with a wild look in his eyes. "And these two? I've never seen them before."

Aithian stood square and unmoving. "Are you here for the artifact as well?"

"Are you here for the artifact?" Seth mimicked. He licked his lips. "You would give it to the Danarian whore first, wouldn't you? Quit hiding like spineless whelps, all of you."

Tnasha's mana emerged a bright flash of violet light in a spark that lit their entire surroundings. She forced it outward, engulfing all of them in its brilliance. "If that's what you want."

Just as quickly, the Arkeeronish let their own mana, brilliant blue and gold flash forth in bright blasts of light.

Morvack took a step backward. "Two elemental sorcerers and an anomalous fifth gen." He pulled his blade from its sheath and rushed Tnasha, putting a blade against her throat.

Tnasha made no move to stop him. No fear crept into her eyes. Her entire body and mind felt numb. Her response surprised even her. "What are you going to do Morvack? Kill me?"

Seth looked at her. "I see what you meant when you said she was defiant." He turned back to Aithian and Lucas. "Give us the staff or we'll kill her."

Aithian shrugged. "Kill her. Why should we care?"

Shadon stepped forward, finding his chest facing the blade of one of the Kersian soldiers. "Don't give it to them."

"It seems no one cares if you kill me. So that plan is not going to work," she said flippant and matter-of-fact, noting that Morvack's grasp on her did not seem genuine. She glanced, from the corner of her eye into his. The conviction that had once filled those eyes was no longer there. She whispered over her shoulder, "What happened to you?"

Morvack said nothing.

"Shut up," Seth hissed. "Show me the weapon. Now."

"Don't," Shadon said.

Aithian took a deep breath. "I did not hear *please*. Did you, Lucas?"

Lucas tipped his head in thought. "No, Aithian. I didn't hear *please* either." Lucas pulled his sword and turned with his right side facing the Kersian sorcerer Seth.

"I have no time for this nonsense." Without warning, Seth sent an orange mana blate blazing from his palms, knocking all of them to the ground, including Morvack.

Tnasha felt the force of the blate and then the pain in her head. Too late to block the blate's force, she fell backward and the blackness surrounded her.

●

Seth stood back and admired his work. Around him, bodies littered the ground like dead leaves blown by the wind. His eyes fell on Morvack and he shook his head. It was a deserving fate for one so weak. He didn't bother to stop and check if they were dead because he didn't care if they were or not. There were more important issues at stake and his brother, the sorceress, and the Arkeeronish meant little in the grand scheme of things. He was more powerful than all of them. Without emotion, he turned from the fallen and entered the ruins of the Arkeeronish temple. He looked around. "So this is where the mighty Imperial Hierarchy of Arkeereon fell," he said aloud to no one. A sly grin slid over his lips.

As morning's first light ascended from the East, he approached the pedestals, examining each staff. The center pedestal obviously held a fraud. He smirked when he saw it. "The Raven's Claw," he whispered. His eyes traveled over the remaining two. "This is an eagle. But the other is not."

He pulled the final staff from the pedestal on the right. Satisfied, he left the ruin behind him. Once again outside, he looked over the mess of fallen bodies one last time, turned toward the temple, focused his mana through the weapon, and in a deafening blast, brought the remainder of its walls crumbling down. Satisfied, he mounted his horse, and turned back toward Cabalia at a full gallop. He could not wait to see the look on Gavgal's face when *he* returned with the staff.

CHAPTER 31

Just before they stepped into the ruins, a lone sorcerer on a black horse galloped past them, not pausing. The Angoran sorcerers turned in their saddles to watch him pass.

"Should we stop him?" Margore asked, stunned.

Kolgern shook his head. "No. But if that was one of the Kersian sorcerers, then where are Tnasha and the others?"

"Was it Morvack?"

"No." Kolgern remembered Morvack even now. The man who had ridden past was not the same Kersian high priest who had almost killed him back on Zul.

Margore finally spoke up. "He had orange mana. *That* was Seth."

The Angorans urged their horses forward through the ruins. Ahead of them, several horses were down, and Kolgern could make out the outlines of bodies. "By the gods," he whispered, the fear clear in his voice. "By Natyis."

Upon their approach, they saw Tnasha, Shadon, and Kauf lying still upon the ground. The bodies of fallen Kersian soldiers, including Morvack also lay there. Kolgern jumped down from his horse and ran to Tnasha's side, lifting her limp body from the ground. "Tnasha," he said frantically.

Margore came up behind him with fear clear in his voice. "Is she breathing?"

Kolgern's eyes welled up with tears. "I can't tell."

Oron knelt on the other side of her, ignoring the Kersian Sorcerer, Morvack, beneath her. He felt her wrist. "Her heart still beats." He looked beneath the sorceress' head. "She hit her head on this rock."

A gasp for air and a grunt pulled their attention away from her. To their left, Aithian struggled to rise. His chest heaved as he fought to inhale. Finally, his breathing evened out. His eyes darted around wildly until he found Lucas. He shoved him. "Lucas."

Margore bent down, helping the Arkeeronish sorcerer to sit upright against a heap of stone.

"Lucas!" Aithian said again, this time with more force.

Lucas moved ever so slightly, turned on his side and heaved upon the dry ground. Margore went to him, helping him to sit as well.

"You took the wrong damned staff." Aithian looked at the temple in disgust. The ruined wall that once stood there was now a gaping hole and the stone fine dust.

Kolgern patted Tnasha's cheek. "Wake up, Tnasha."

Oron shook his head. "She's unconscious."

Morvack groaned from beneath her. "I can't breathe!" he gasped.

"Good." Kolgern shot him a glare of disgust, and lifted Tnasha from atop the Kersian sorcerer. He looked around for a place to set her.

Aithian held out his arms. "Bring her here."

A wary look slid across Kolgern's face.

"My mana has healing properties. Combined with her natural healing abilities, I can probably bring her around."

Kolgern handed her small, petite frame over to him with some reluctance and went to help Margore with Kauf and Shadon.

Once Arick finished tying Morvack's hands behind his back, he turned to Oron. "The blate only knocked them all unconscious." He pointed to the fallen horses and humans behind them, who were also coming to. "Even the horses were unconscious."

Lucas scowled. "That blate should have killed the humans and the horses."

"It was her mana that saved all of us." Morvack's voice emerged resigned and void of emotion.

"How do you know?" Kolgern asked.

"She, the voice, told me."

Oron pulled Kolgern back from the Kersian sorcerer. "You hear voices?"

"*A* voice. She told me my brother would do this."

Oron's eyes widened then narrowed. He mouthed something inaudible to Arick. It looked like, *stay away from that one.*

Aithian spit, the look on his face suggesting there was a foul taste in his mouth. "No one said the Kersians were sane. Eh?"

Tnasha, who was just coming to, lay in his arms moaning in pain. "My head."

Aithian placed his hand on her forehead where a thin line of crimson mana pulsated within the violet. The color shifted to blue and the pain subsided.

"Where is the weapon?" she asked in a faint voice.

"The Kersian sorcerer has it because *Lucas* took the wrong one!"

Lucas' eyes widened. "Sorry! I thought for sure it was the right one."

"You didn't know?" she asked in barely a whisper.

"I thought it was the one in the center because they were all mixed up."

With her eyes barely open, she looked at him in question, clutching Aithian's shoulders. "They?"

Lucas's voice rose in pitch and protest. "There were three of them. My father did not bother telling us which was which. We made a guess reasoning that if the one on the left was the Eagle's Talon, but marked the Raven's Claw, that the one in the center and the right must have been switched, too. Who knew the staff in the pedestal marked the Crow's Foot was actually the Raven's Claw when the Crow's Foot was marked the Eagle's Talon?" He shook his head, confused. "We should have taken all of them."

"What do we have? The Crow's Foot?" Aithian felt just as confused.

Tnasha shook her head. "I cannot think with my head hurting like this."

Oron kneeled down on one knee in front of them. "He would have noticed one was missing."

Lucas shook his head. "I put a fraud where the Crow's Foot was."

Kolgern jumped up with his usual *I-have-an-idea* look. "What do the other staves do?"

"We don't know. I was able to translate the ancient Arkeeronish that labeled the pedestals, but I couldn't read the runic writing."

"Maybe they're weapons, too." Kolgern nodded with raised eyebrows. He pointed a finger at them. "We could go after them and use the others to get the weapon from him."

"No." Tnasha said. "We cannot go on a hunch. Take me into the temple." She looked at what was left of the temple. " I hope none of the pedestals were destroyed. I can read runic, but only because my grandmother insisted. It's just like any language."

Oron stood and took her weak body from Aithian. "All of you should take time to rest. Arick and I will take her into the temple."

He walked into the temple with Tnasha in his arms and Arick close behind him. "What happened?"

"They took us by surprise. We were already stunned to find the Arkeeronish here waiting for us. Then Seth went crazy. He threw the blate. Usually they build and you can see a sorcerer is going to throw one." She took a deep breath and winced in pain. "I didn't see it coming. I'm not an adept."

"Not all of us can have the foresight to see all the obstacles facing us." Oron moved toward what remained of the platform, locating the pedestals after some searching. "We will have to move some debris."

Oron set her down on the steps. She looked up at them, squinting as if it eased the pain. It did not. "Who are you?"

"I am Oron, and this is Arick. We are Angoran."

She fought to keep her eyes open. "Oh."

They cleared the pedestals, finding them thankfully intact. Oron picked her up again. "Your reputation has grown in the past few months."

"Yeah. I've been living one great big adventure." Sarcasm dripped from her voice.

"Are you trying to say you are an unwilling participant?" He smiled at her.

"If we find time, perhaps I'll tell you the story."

He nodded, carrying her to the first pedestal, which still housed the Eagle's Talon. She noticed the talon holding the black stone crowning the staff. Tnasha reached for it. "Take the staff out."

Arick followed her command, gripping the staff firmly in his large fist, examining it.

Her eyes studied the writing in the pedestal. "It says here the three staves were created by an alliance of sorcerers from many different lands, and placed here for protection. That is all this one says."

They moved to the next. "A weapon, a staff to negate ill magick, and one that can be used for a variety of things."

She motioned him to the third. When she finished her brown eyes met Oron's. "We have two of the three, and two of them can help us recover the third. But I will need the help of sorcerers more adept than I. I think the Arkeeronish should be involved. They're the ones who left it here, unprotected, after all. We cannot allow Seth to return to Zul with that staff. If they use it, we are facing a sorcerers' war that could destroy the world as we know it."

●

A chill ran up Oron's spine. The sorceress was right. Wondering what High Priest Graneck had been thinking, he glanced at Arick who nodded. "We should listen to her."

Oron forced a grin. Arick was right, the sorceress was no more dangerous than any sorcerer despite her impressive abilities. "We will help, but first, we need to make all of you healthy. You are no good to us half unconscious, bruised, and hurting." He glanced back at Arick to make sure he still had the staff. They could not risk losing another, especially if the remaining staves could help them. Together they left the temple and returned to the motley crew waiting for them assembled outside the temple.

CHAPTER 32

They returned to the ruins of the building where Aithian and Lucas' camp stood. There, within the walls offering some protection from the wind, they gathered around the fire. The Kersians sat against the far wall with their hands bound behind their backs. Kolgern and Margore brought supplies from the Angoran's wagon while Arick made a metal pot of spiced tea.

Tnasha leaned her head on Aithian's shoulder. His mana eased the slicing pain pounding through her head. Her eyes studied the staves lying next to her. Both were crowned with black stones, perfectly round and polished. She reached out and picked up the Eagle's Talon. "This staff." The men quieted. "This one gives the ability to see the future and to project mana across great distances. The Crow's Foot protects the person who holds it from another sorcerer's attack."

"What did the pedestals say about the Raven's Claw?" Lucas gave her a solemn look.

"It gives the bearer the ability to project blates through it, amplifying a blate's power twenty fold." She pulled the rough wool blanket covering her legs up around her shoulders. Aithian put a comforting arm around her.

"So how will these two help us?" Kolgern did not understand.

She felt her muscles relax and she yawned. "We can use the Crow's Foot to protect us from any blates Seth throws at us. We can use the Eagle's Talon for long-range attacks to slow him down, or maybe to see where he is so we can follow him. That depends on if any of us has the abilities. That's the only drawback..."

Aithian looked down at her with deep blue eyes. "What?"

"The only sorcerers who can wield the staves are those who already have the natural ability to do what the staff can do. They are merely tools to amplify an existing ability. The problem with the Raven's Claw is that any sorcerer, chiefly of the fire element, who can throw a blate of mana, can use it. Which means almost any sorcerer with ability for fire magick could use it. The other two are more complex than that. Not all have the ability to see. Blocking an attack of sorcery, while possibly common, is a learned skill. If a sorcerer does not have that skill, it cannot be amplified."

The sorcerers exchanged glances. Morvack scowled. "You are all wondering who can do what. I will tell you now that my abilities, to my knowledge only extend to wind magick and thought reading."

Lucas narrowed his eyes. "Then you know how much we all hate you and your people."

Morvack lowered his eyes to the ground.

She watched the Kersian sorcerer. Something about him was different. She could not quite gather what it was. His eyes. She sank even further into Aithian. "Morvack, what has changed?"

Morvack looked up.

"His no-name god has forsaken him." Kolgern snorted and tossed another piece of wood on the fire.

Morvack met his comment with a scowl. "My god has shown me the error of my brothers' ways. He would never sanction..."

Tnasha interrupted him. "What does your brother, Seth, plan to do with the weapon?"

His eyes met hers with deep sadness. "Seth intends on destroying Gavgal and use the weapon for his own motives."

"Which are?" She sat up. Her teeth ached from grinding them.

"Seth wants power. He wants to be feared. He wants to have people fall before him, trembling, begging for his approval and mercy."

She persisted. "What are Gavgal's plans for the weapon?"

Morvack sat silent for a brief moment before saying anything, then blurted, "He planned to test the weapon against the imperial Hierarchy of Arkeereon. If the test was successful, he plans to use it to convert the humans into servants and soldiers of the Unnamed, and to use those human armies in the siege of Danaria."

Kolgern started to say something, but Tnasha held up a hand to quiet him. "To what end?"

"In hopes the Danarians would send their sorceresses and their children away from Danaria so they could be captured, and to destroy the sorcerers." Morvack averted his eyes from her gaze.

"Forced, captive breeding?" Tnasha had known the truth all along. Somehow, hearing it from an inside source made it that much more real.

Oron grunted. "To create eventual inbred bloodlines that would ultimately destroy our kind?"

She shrugged and felt a sharp pain slice through her left shoulder. "I don't think he thought that far ahead. Gavgal never does, and yet he persists. It's interesting how four Kersian sorcerers have managed to escape the Danarian sorcerers when we outnumber them. It has to be stupid luck."

Lucas shrugged. "Would it not have been easier for the Kersians to merely attempt peace with the other sorcerer bloodlines through marriage treaties? That would make more sense in the struggle for self preservation."

Morvack nodded. "Were his convictions and delusions of moral superiority not so strong, he may have. But his mind is clouded with self-righteousness."

"The Kersians are all insane." Kolgern looked away, disgusted.

"For our religious beliefs?" Morvack glared at him with his jaw set firm. He ground his teeth.

Kolgern looked at him with contempt. "If your religious beliefs were not so destructive..."

Tnasha stopped him. "Our own nomadic ancestors made sacrifices to our gods up until one thousand years ago."

"But that was a long time ago, Tnasha. Human and sorcerer sacrifice is considered barbaric in our present time."

She tipped her head and sighed. "So they're not as evolved in thought..."

"Whose side are you on?" He shook his blond head in defeat.

"I'm not trying to absolve their actions, Kolgern. I am simply stating that all our peoples have the ability for violence and destruction of our own. When we war with one another we kill all the time."

"And that's self defense."

"Yeah, but it's still killing."

"There is a big difference between killing to survive and killing just because."

She gave Kolgern a dumb look. "I understand that. I guess what I've been trying to say is that the Kersians have not learned the difference yet. But they will. They will have to... eventually. Pardon me for my lack of lucidity."

Kolgern clamped his jaw shut and folded his arms over his chest. Tension found a home in the silence.

Oron moved closer to the fire, putting his square hands near the flames to warm them. He rubbed them together. He grunted, suggesting he had questions of his own for the Kersian Sorcerer. "What powers do your brothers possess?" he finally asked.

Morvack scoffed. "I have already said too much, though I suppose I have no choice now that I'm your prisoner." He didn't sound convincing.

The voice whispered in his ear, "They must know. You must give in to save yourself."

He lifted his eyes to meet Oron's. "Gavgal can transport himself through thin air from one place to another. He also has the powers to see, but he cannot willfully conjure an image on his own. Seth, however, is more dangerous. He can negate other sorcerer's mana, rendering it useless against him. His blates are destructive. He has no conscience. It is the reason he commands Gavgal's armies."

"What about your other brother?" Kolgern asked.

"Alax? Alax is a sheep," he said, obviously disgusted. "He will follow whoever seems strongest for his own preservation. His abilities are persuasion and healing. It is the reason he was placed in a position of the priesthood."

"He can convince people to convert willingly," Aithian said absentmindedly.

Tnasha felt a cramp in her back and winced. She leaned back on Aithian and closed her eyes. "I thought the Exavian monarchy gave up their religion too easily. Why did Gavgal not utilize Alax's abilities to convert other sorcerers?"

"Gavgal believes Alax's abilities are still too weak to use against strong willed sorcerers." Morvack kept his eyes cast on his lap.

"What should we do with them?" Arick asked, nodding toward the Kersian sorcerer and the seven men with him.

"Nothing," Tnasha said with her eyes still closed. The answer to Arick's question seemed obvious to her. "They are going to help us get the weapon back, sacrificing their own lives if need be."

Morvack choked back his exasperation. "We *cannot* and *will not* help you. If my bothers believe we have betrayed them, we will all be murdered."

"One of your own men could be conspiring to kill you right now for giving us so much information," Oron pointed out.

The Kersian sorcerer looked his men over. "These are men loyal to me, who have stood by me for many years. I personally handpicked them to help me acquire the weapon. Their loyalty lies with me *and* my link with the Unnamed."

"Are you trying to convince us, or yourself?" Oron gave him a dull look. "You realize your brother Seth left you for dead? That he intended to kill you just as he intends to kill Gavgal? He never had any intention of saving you and making you a part of his plan. The same goes for your loyal men."

"Because Seth knew you were in the midst of a change of heart," Tnasha added thoughtfully. It was the only reason she could think of to explain the unfamiliar look in the Kersian sorcerer Morvack's eyes. She believed people could change. No, she knew they could change, and at that moment she softened to Morvack, silently forgiving him and giving him a small bit of trust. "He probably sensed you were unsure as to why you were doing it. Then he saw you pause when you could have killed me at the temple. He knew then you were too strong-minded to be easily led. A man like Seth doesn't have time to fight enemies from within and enemies from the outside."

A flicker of realization entered Morvack's eyes, as if suddenly he knew the sorceress was right. It was clear to everyone that Seth wanted him out of the way.

Oron furrowed his brow. "You see now. You have no choice. If we let you go, you would be hunted by those you have wronged in following your brothers. If you help us, you may redeem yourself and if you die, you would certainly die with more honor."

"Perhaps you're right," Morvack said with some reluctance. He took a deep breath. "We will help you, but I want to make a deal."

The sorcerers exchanged glances, and Tnasha's eyes popped open. "A deal?" she asked, surprised at Morvack's nerve. She admonished herself then for giving that small bit of trust, recalling how Morvack held her over a pit of fire. Only a month ago he wouldn't have given it a second thought before throwing her into that pit. Had Kolgern and Alena not arrived in time, she would be dead. *But people can change*, she reminded herself sternly.

"If any of my men, or I, survive, we can seek asylum in Danaria and live the remainder of our days as protected citizens, free from religious persecution."

"That depends." Tnasha tried to hide her shock at his request, but could not. She felt her eyes remain wide and unmoving. "You do recall you almost succeeded in killing me, right? Do you plan to continue to practice your religion by killing women and children?"

In a small voice, Morvack answered, "No, I do not intend on the continued practice. As for almost killing you, I..." His voice trailed off. Obviously he knew he could not redeem himself to her for *that*.

"How do you expect us to believe that you won't slip back into your old ways?" Kolgern stood and began pacing. "Do you feel any remorse for your crimes against our people? Do you have any idea how many families you have hurt? How many mothers have emotional wounds knowing their children died horribly? What about the children and husbands of the women you have murdered? And you," Kolgern started toward the Kersian sorcerer and stopped himself. "You stabbed me in the shoulder... I don't think we could guarantee your safety unless you lived quietly, in a remote place. I never want to see your face again!"

Tnasha held up a hand to calm Kolgern. "Just calm down. But Kolgern is right. We could not offer you a life free from persecution. There are many Danarians who would just as soon have your head on a pole rather than a weak apology for the atrocities the Kersians have inflicted upon the Danarian people." Tnasha shook her head. She still did not believe what Morvack asked of them. Redemption was one thing...

"I have been blind to my actions most of my life." The Kersian sorcerer paused, his face a mask of genuine remorse. "Until now. All I can give you is my word that I will never sacrifice another Danarian. I cannot make you believe me or trust me. I have earned neither."

Tnasha felt her eyes stretch even wider. She knew Morvack had changed, but this she did not expect. A part of her, a small part, feared he was lying. "Why is it you are willing to risk everything, including your own life, to help us in hopes you can live the rest of your days in peace within *heathen* territory?"

He nodded toward Oron. "As your friend pointed out, I have no choice but to help you. My brothers will hunt me until they find me and destroy me. I want nothing more than what anyone wants. I desire a family, a permanent home and happiness. Something both of my brothers promised me, but could never produce."

She almost felt sorry for him then silently berated herself. Could it be the Kersian before her had done everything he did in hopes he would some day have a family? Then a strange thought struck her. Morvack did not know love. His family, undoubtedly, was void of it. Love was the one thing he yearned for. Her sympathy for him grew despite her attempt to ignore it. "I will see what the Danarian Council is willing to offer you, *if you survive*. That's a big *if*."

Silence enveloped them for a short while and Aithian wrapped his arms tightly around her. She closed her eyes and drifted off to sleep wondering if a man as callous as Morvack could truly change – almost overnight.

CHAPTER 33

Aithian sat quietly, listening. The weight of the Kersian's honesty surprised him. He finally spoke, noticing his voice woke Tnasha. She opened her eyes. He rested his cheek on her head, and ran a hand through her soft, thick auburn hair. "We should discuss what each of us can do so we know who can wield which staff," he finally said.

Tnasha smiled up at him. "Well you obviously have some healing abilities. I haven't slept that good since I was at home in my own bed beneath several layers of quilts."

Kolgern snickered.

"What?" She closed her eyes again.

Aithian smiled slightly. Her beauty astounded him. His heart yearned for her and he did not want to let her go. He tightened his grasp around her waist. "I can do water magick, and I can speak with serpents."

Kolgern sat sharpening his sword. "Really?" He motioned toward Tnasha. "She can, too."

She opened her eyes. "I can see by scrying, too. But I've never tried to conjure something on my own. I was able to see what Kalath saw when he scryed." Her voice took on a sad note.

Kauf had remained silent until now. "She can transport people from one location to another as well."

"Is this true?" Oron looked on in obvious surprise.

Tnasha stretched and opened her eyes, sitting up. "I read how to do it in a book. It wasn't that hard. But it did make me tired."

Arick sat back with a mug of tea. "You *just* learned you could do this?" She didn't respond so he continued. "Well, I suppose you are still learning everything you can do. I wonder what other abilities you have."

Oron nodded. "Perhaps we should test you."

"Test me?"

Lucas leaned forward and scratched his knee. "If we do that, we'll only exhaust her and that seems counterproductive."

"We weren't leaving until tomorrow morning, were we?" Margore looked up. The day was still early. He smiled, as if suddenly remembering something, and a sense of pride washed over his face. "Oh Nasha, I didn't tell you. I can throw a blate!"

Tnasha smiled with a light laugh. "Now *that* is amazing. The Sorcerers' Council persists in their belief that sorcerers with internal mana have limited abilities for magick, and they discourage sorcerers like Margore from trying. When you get home, you'll have to prove them wrong. I'd like to be there for that."

"Don't worry. You will be." He looked down at his boot and rubbed at the dirt.

She paused and looked at each of them. Shaking her head, she crossed her legs in front of her. "No. I am sending you, Kolgern, Shadon, Kauf, and the Kersian soldiers, as prisoners of course, back to Danaria."

Margore gasped in protest. "You can't do that."

"It's too dangerous for all of you. We must work sorcery against sorcery. It's doubtful there will be a call for hand-to-hand combat. You have no protection against sorcery. This is magickal warfare."

Margore put another piece of kindling on the fire, pouting like a child.

"I will transport all of you back so you do not have to make the journey."

Without word, he stood, and stomped off toward the horses to help Shadon. Kolgern gave her a thankful, knowing look and followed him. Kauf stood soon after, leaving the sorcerers to discuss their business.

She turned to Oron and Arick. "It's the only way."

Oron nodded. "I agree. They will only be underfoot and more for us to worry about. Arick and I can provide protection with blates, but I fear those are the only abilities we can offer."

Aithian narrowed his eyes. He could detect a mistruth a league off. Detecting lies was an ability he chose not to share openly. "You do not expect us to believe that is all you can do. Even Lucas can control the winds, aside from releasing a violent, destructive blate."

"Wind working is a common skill. I suppose Arick can do the same," Oron agreed.

"What about you?"

Oron lifted an eyebrow. "I can temporarily stop the flow of another's mana by touch. But I cannot project it long range. Just as you have the ability to detect half truths."

Aithian smiled, admiring the Angoran's intuition and honesty. "True."

"So, it seems, three of us can work wind magick, two of us weather magick, all of us are well versed in throwing blates…"

Tnasha winced, but this time it was not due to the pains from her injuries. "I'm not very good at it."

Oron continued, not acknowledging her comment. "The question is, can any of us repel a magical attack?"

"I have never had to protect myself from a magical attack," Morvack said.

"Neither have we," Lucas said, nodding toward Aithian.

"We haven't either," Oron said in agreement.

All eyes fell on Tnasha.

Oron motioned toward her. "She somehow managed to save all of you from a close range blate meant to kill." His eyes met hers. "How did you do it?"

Tnasha shook her head and shrugged. "I don't know that I did anything really. It just…happened. On its own."

Arick fidgeted nervously, lost in his own thoughts. "If we leave in the morning, Seth will be far from here. We will not be able to get to him before he arrives at Zul with the weapon."

"Gavgal cannot be saved," said Morvack. He stared into the flames. His human soldiers did likewise and kept quiet. Morvack looked them over then turned back to the other sorcerers. "It is likely Seth will need several days to secure Zul after that. Once he does, and he destroys anyone who opposes him, then he will begin planning his dictatorship."

"Do you think he plans to take over the world?" she asked. "I mean, that's what most egocentric warlords want, right?"

"I imagine that might be his eventual task." Morvack paused. "But I don't believe he will rush to conquer the world," he concluded.

Aithian scooted out from beneath Tnasha and stood. She looked up at him. He looked down on her apologetically. "I need to stand for awhile. Perhaps I'll take a walk."

Lucas looked up. "Me, too. You don't mind, do you?"

"Not at all."

●

Once they were outside, away from listening ears, Aithian turned to Lucas. "So what do you think?"

"What are we doing?"

"What do you mean? We're getting that weapon back."

Lucas pursed his lips, crinkling his forehead. "We were told to find out who received the weapon. That's it."

"Who was the one willing to hide the weapon in the first place?"

He narrowed his eyes. "You're attracted to Tnasha. You are trying to win her over by playing the hero."

"And you're suddenly afraid now that it will take magical warfare to get the weapon back?"

"It is not our job to get the weapon back, Aithian." He sighed. "I realize she's beautiful. But we can't help them."

"We have to. It was our ancestors who left the weapon here for this to happen." Aithian looked down at his feet.

"Your heart is clouding your judgment."

"Coming from you, *that* sounds strange. Especially since you allow your own convictions to dictate all you do without thinking your actions through."

"Have you thought *this* through?" Lucas's tone hinted his irritation.

"Yes. If Gavgal can manage to overpower Seth, he will attack Arkeereon with the weapon. *Our families*, Lucas. If Seth has his way, how long before he decides to do the same? What do we do then? Go home and wait for the Kersians to show up outside the gates? Wait until they kill the few of us left? We're a dying a race. This goes beyond my attraction to Tnasha. This is about self preservation."

"We should, at the very least, tell my father what we're doing."

Aithian felt his eyes widen in surprise. He could not believe Lucas' sudden concern for his father's approval, especially when it was Lucas who was the one set to go against Natyis' wishes in the first place. "Why. So he can stop us? I can't believe you're saying this after you preached to me about disobeying your father to hide the staff!"

Lucas tipped his head in thought. "That was different."

"How?"

Sighing, Lucas nodded. "You're right. But what if…How do we know he did not intend for this to happen?"

"He could not see. Her mana blocks him from seeing events regarding her. She *is* anomalous."

Lucas rolled his eyes. "Indeed. Even in your case."

"Are you jealous?" Aithian hated that Lucas knew what he felt for the sorceress.

Lucas smiled. "No." He put his hand on Aithian's shoulder. "I'm sure she has sorceress friends. Do you think she would mind introducing me to them once this is over?"

Aithian smiled. "I don't know, but I'm guessing it's a good bet. Maybe we'll find out."

●

Oron licked his cracked, dry lips, feeling the peeling skin with his tongue. His gaze moved from Tnasha to Morvack and back again. "We should see how far your abilities go," he said again.

Tnasha nodded. "After I send my friends home."

"You could take us directly to Zul when we are ready to leave," Morvack added.

"I could. But all I remember of Zul are the docks, the city, and temple. My memories are a bit scattered like Kauf's were."

"You could use mine. We will find a less conspicuous place to arrive."

Tnasha looked at him. "I do not know that I would trust your memories, though you do have a point. Your memories would be more specific and less apt to wander."

Oron rubbed his hands over his forehead. "Are we going to see what you can do, or not?"

"You have no patience, do you?" Tnasha gave him an angry glance. "Maybe we should all practice protecting ourselves against attacks. It seems to me that would be more useful. Whoever it comes more naturally to will carry the Crow's foot and protect us all. I will use the Eagle's Talon to *see* if I am able, but you can use it to project your ability to stop mana flow if necessary. It increases the range of the user's mana, too, remember?"

"I'm sorry. I'm not trying to be difficult. I have a strong sense that we have little time."

"I know. So do I." She stood. "I am going to gather up Aithian and Lucas." She left the shelter. It felt good to stretch her legs. She met Lucas just outside the door. "Where is Aithian?"

He nodded behind him. "He found some old bowls in the ruins. He's looking at them."

"Is everything all right with both of you?" An odd sense of familiarity connected them. Tnasha could feel it. It seemed a bit odd to her that all of them had become so comfortable with one another in a few short hours. It was as if... she fought back the urge to laugh at herself. It was almost as if they were kindred and the bond between them was natural.

He looked at her with a raised eyebrow.

She shook herself back to the present moment, realizing that she had been standing there for at least a minute staring off into nothing. "I realize it wasn't your intention to get involved in this."

He grunted. "We were involved the moment we discovered the possibility our own weapon could be used against us."

"Do you need to discuss this with your family elders?"

Lucas forced a half grin. "I wanted to, but Aithian does not think it is wise. They may not want us involved."

"I can speak to them if you wish. If you think it would make a difference."

"Convince Aithian of that. If they did want Arkeereon involvement, they may choose to send some of my brothers, who are more experienced with warfare, instead."

"That would be fine," she said.

He shook his head and looked up at the sky. "Aithian wouldn't have it."

Tnasha knew he was hiding something. "Why?"

With narrowed eyes, he let out a laugh and a broad grin made its way across his face. "He has grown fond of you." With that, he stepped past her.

Aithian appeared carrying two clay bowls. He smiled when he saw her, lifting the bowls up. "I found these. I should take them back for my mother. She collects old bowls."

"Why?"

He shrugged. "She likes them, I suppose."

Tnasha coughed, clearing her throat of the thick black mana that had settled there. "I was thinking that perhaps we should inform your family elders of our plan to take the weapon back."

His face fell. "They would not allow our involvement."

"By our, do you mean you and Lucas, or do you mean Arkeereon's sorcerers as a whole?"

A hint of crimson surfaced in his cheeks. "Lucas and I. We feel involved and want to see this through. I would be disappointed if it were taken out of my hands and put into someone else's."

Tnasha felt a wave of emotion flow over her. She smiled playfully. "It is not as though you'll never see me again. I seem to be traveling a lot these days."

He grinned and looked away. "Promise?"

She felt her cheeks glow crimson and tried to shove the feeling aside. The last thing she needed was to fall for an Arkeeronish sorcerer when there were more important things at hand.

CHAPTER 34

Natyis paced his chamber. Once again, the scrying bowl had not changed. The black mirrors and crystals remained dark. He could not see anything and that bothered him. Lucas and Aithian should have started back by now, and yet he could not feel their approach. He could not feel it because they had not started back.

Eury stood at the far end of the room, watching him. "You cannot worry, Lord Natyis. You knew that eventually the sorcerer would come here and cause you to lose your sight completely."

"It's unnerving. I am blind." He turned to his friend. "Why is it so hot in here?"

"Your own heart beats furiously with worry. It warms your blood." Eury made his way to a chair and sat down. "Sit with me. One of the women will bring tea soon."

"I would rather have coffee." Natyis turned from him and stared into the hearth, hoping to see something in the bright blaze of the orange gold flames.

"Lucas and Aithian can take care of themselves. They are not children anymore," Eury reminded him.

"It seems only yesterday they were."

"You protect them too much."

He whirled around suddenly and went to the scrying bowl. "If the sorcerer will prevent me from seeing my son, then I will look in on his people. Perhaps that will give me insight."

Eury shook his head. The serving girl entered with the tea tray. She set it on the table and left.

Ignoring the slight interruption, Natyis tried to conjure the image. He strained, pushing at the blackness, almost forcing something. The glass fogged then turned black again. He closed his eyes. In every direction, and in all lines of vision, a thick cloud stood in his way. He growled, pounding his fists on the table, knocking over a glass goblet that fell and shattered on the stone floor.

"You must sit down and try to relax, Lord Natyis." Eury attempted to make his voice soothing. "I do not feel death. I would feel it if either of them perished."

Natyis sighed and dropped into the chair with a heavy thud. He leaned back, taking deep, even measured breaths. Closing his eyes, he spoke. "I am blind."

"What you see, the things around you are the only things myself and others see. You are no more blind than any of us." He poured two cups of tea from the kettle. "But I understand how strange it must be for you. Having had a wider vision all your life you only feel blind. Once the sorcerer's presence on Arkeereon fades, you will be left with your sight again."

"What power does he possess that he can prevent my gifts from meeting their potential?"

"I do not know. I wish I did." Eury stared at the stone wall across the room. His eyes drifted to the deep gold and brown tapestry hanging there. "I wonder if the sorcerer means us harm, but I cannot bring myself to entertain that particular thought for too long. Or perhaps the sorcerer is on our side. Either way I expect we shall find out soon enough."

Natyis turned his white eyes on Eury. His mana turned a lighter gray. "Indeed."

CHAPTER 35

Tnasha concentrated on the Temple Dagon in Central Danaria. A white light encompassed her human companions, her cousin, and the human Kersian prisoners. She extended it with her mind, placing them on the temple's stairway leading to its entrance. Their presence diminished in a dazzle of light, fading into nothing. Now, the sorcerers stood alone in the ruined temple with their horses. She closed the book and looked at the awed faces around her. "What?"

"That's quite amazing," said Oron. He glanced over at Arick who wore an expression of wonderment.

Morvack shook his head. "My brother Gavgal has that ability. He may escape Seth that way. It is the same way he has escaped the Danarians all these years."

"Yes, well, not if Seth renders his mana useless," she said.

"True." Morvack attempted to stretch his wrists in the rope that bound him. "May I have my hands unbound?"

Tnasha pulled a knife from her belt. Lucas put his arm in front of her. "Are you sure that's a wise thing to do?"

"Why not? He can work wind magick and he can read the thoughts of others. He is no harm to us."

He leaned in to her. "He can also throw blates."

She looked into Morvack's eyes. Fear stared back at her. He was just as alone as any of them. Now, more than ever, he needed allies. "The only way, Lord Lucas, to find out if you can trust someone is to extend them that trust."

He stepped out of her way with a wary glance at Aithian who made no move to stop her.

She stepped up to Morvack and sawed at the rope, unbinding him. He pulled his wrists in front of him, rubbing the irritated and swollen red markings where the rope chaffed him.

Arick went into his pack and pulled out a small jar with salve in it. He handed it to Morvack. "So what now?"

Tnasha clapped her hands together. "We go to the city of Arkeereon and meet with the elders of the Imperial Hierarchy.

A sinking feeling, emanating from the Arkeeronish sorcerers, washed over them in a wave of melancholy.

Oron bit his inner cheek. "The hierarchy may not allow these two to accompany us."

"I know. I will speak with them myself." She looked around hopefully, letting her gaze rest on Aithian. "Let's gather our things and bring the horses. Perhaps for the night we'll have a warm place to sleep?"

Aithian nodded, handing the staves to Lucas.

Once everything stood gathered, Tnasha opened the book again. Taking Aithian's hand into hers, she read the incantation, and closed her eyes allowing her mana to encompass all of them. She took a deep breath and let her eyes fall open. Her knees collapsed beneath her. As she fell to the floor, Aithian and Lucas caught her, helping her to her feet. She looked around and yawned. The magick usurped her strength, but it had worked. Now they stood in a great entryway of the Arkeeronish holding, horses and all. The ceilings overhead stood tall, giving the foyer a hollow feel. A chill drifted through the air, and she shivered.

Lucas went ahead with the two remaining staves. "I will let my father know we're back."

Aithian helped her to a bench. Oron, Arick, and Morvack followed, leaving the horses standing in the midst of the hall patiently.

"I'm sorry," she whispered. Her face went pale. "Too much has happened today. I just need to rest."

"I will see about having the women tend to the guest rooms." Aithian turned and disappeared through one of the doors on the right.

Oron and Arick settled in beside her on the long wooden bench. Morvack moved closer to them.

"You feel uncomfortable?" She looked up at him expectantly.

"Of course I do. I have never been invited into a house of this size notwithstanding my brother's palace." He glanced nervously toward a stairway leading to a door. The one Lucas had gone through only minutes earlier. "Especially the home of... others of a different faith."

"Thank you for choosing that phrase over heathen," Oron said with a straight face.

Tnasha let out a giggle and Arick began laughing. Oron's lips turned upward in a wide grin. Tnasha stopped laughing and looked up at Morvack. "You realize we are not as different as you may think."

"With regards to?"

"Our religions are not entirely different. You have one god who encompasses everything. We simply break our whole into smaller, more palatable bits. Or many gods. Each of our gods is a mere aspect of the whole, or *the one*."

"Religion, in its ceremony and pageantry, is nonsense. The rituals are mere formalities." Oron said matter-of-fact. "The Universe is the only god. The good thing about the universe, however, is it doesn't expect rituals or prayers. It simply is and it doesn't talk back."

Arick nodded in agreement, then hesitated as if he wanted to disagree. But he let it go.

"Yes, I would have to agree. It is the reason I never went into the temple to train for the priesthood like our council of elders wanted me to."

Morvack smiled. "Nonsense. You simply enjoy defying authority."

She sighed. "More likely is the fact that I hate being told what I can and cannot do. When someone says I cannot do something, I feel an urge to prove them wrong."

Oron chuckled. "That dissipates with age. You're still young."

The door to their right opened and Aithian emerged, followed by several other sorcerers. When they saw her, they stopped short, looking to Aithian for some explanation.

"This is Tnasha. She is a Danarian soldier. Those two are Oron and Arick, representatives of the Angoran. And this," Aithian put a hand on Morvack's shoulder. "This is Morvack, a defector from Kersian Zul."

Tnasha nodded in acknowledgement, feeling uncomfortable in the midst of so many sorcerers with strong mana.

"This is Liale, Berith, and Flery. We do not have many servants in our home. We do for ourselves here. But since you are guests, and we rarely have guests, they have agreed to take your things to your rooms, and make the horses comfortable in the stables."

"Thank you." Tnasha's eyes widened and she studied Liale. It was Liale she called upon when she needed strength. Lately, she had not needed him. To see his mana incarnate in a physical being like herself amazed her.

Aithian stepped in front of Liale with a slight hint of jealousy in his eyes, and averted her attention. "Let us find a warmer room to wait in."

He helped her to her feet. With some of her strength renewed, she leaned on him and he visibly relaxed. They ascended the staircase at the end of the entry hall and went through the door.

The door led them to a less formal room with chairs lining the walls. On the left wall, a fire raged in a hearth. No chill filled the room. Instead, it felt inviting and warm. Tnasha slid into one of the plush chairs. She felt like closing her eyes and sleeping. "This is so much better."

Aithian smiled down at her. She looked up at him, wondering if he wanted to pull her into his arms and hold her while she slept. He turned from her and walked across the room, and Tnasha shoved the thought from her mind. There she went again, putting her attraction for the Arkeeronish sorcerer ahead of what was truly important.

•

Morvack came up behind Aithian. "You yearn for her," he said is a quiet voice so the others would not hear.

Aithian looked into the Kersian sorcerer's eyes and leaned back against the wall. "It would be forbidden. Lord Natyis would never allow it."

"Perhaps it is for the best." His eyes followed Aithian's and fell upon the sorceress. "She could be injured, or may even die in our attempt to return the weapon to your people. We all might. And if not, her family may not consent to such a union either."

"She will not die if I have anything to do with it." With a frustrated sigh, Aithian turned from him and strode from the room.

Morvack shook his head. If the Kersians did not start a sorcerers' war, Aithian would.

CHAPTER 36

Lucas knocked on the chamber door. As expected, Eury opened it. "Lucas," he greeted.

He nodded in acknowledgement and stepped past the pale sorcerer elder to his father's chair-side. "Father."

"Ah. You have returned." There was relief in his voice.

"Yes."

"All is well I trust?" he asked, his voice filled with hope.

"No. The Kersians have the weapon."

Natyis pulled back the cowl hood covering his head. He gazed up at his son with white eyes. "What about the sorcerer?"

"The Kersian sorcerer attacked us when he took it."

"Not the Kersian, the other."

Lucas's face contorted, confused. "The only other sorcerers were the Angoran's, Oron and Arick. They arrived with the sorceress' companions."

"Sorceress?" Confusion crossed Natyis' face.

"Yes. She's here. She would like to speak with you."

Natyis visibly shivered as if a chill had descended his spine. "Which of their mana is strongest?"

"The sorceress'."

"Are you sure?"

"It's blatantly obvious, Father." Lucas exhaled an exasperated breath. "Her mana stands more that a foots length from her body and shines a brilliant violet color. She is hard to miss. She's the only reason we all survived the mana blate the Kersian Sorcerer Seth threw at us."

Natyis' confusion turned to disapproval and he glared at his son. "Why is she here?"

"She wants your approval to take Aithian and me to Zul with her to retrieve the weapon from Seth."

"Have you agreed to this?" he asked in a gruff voice.

"Not exactly…"

"Eury, leave us." He waived his hand. Once Eury had gone, he spoke again. "I will not risk your lives. You know this. You were not supposed to engage anyone who arrived at Ramathra. You deliberately defied my instructions. Where is Aithian?"

"Making our guests comfortable."

"You do not understand…"

"No, Father, you do not understand!" Lucas kneeled down beside him. "This sorceress has abilities that go far beyond anything I have ever seen. She is not malevolent. Besides, Aithian enjoys her company."

Lord Natyis shook his head. "You I would expect this from. But not Aithian."

"And Aithian is not capable of any wrong doing?" He threw his hands up and stood. "You can be so untrusting. Do you wish to meet with her or not? Should I throw them out and tell them they are not welcome, per our elders' orders?"

A knock resounded from the other side of the door.

Natyis wrung his hands furiously. "Enter."

Aithian poked his head around the door. "Am I interrupting?"

"Get in here and close the door behind you, please."

Aithian did as instructed and came over, standing next to Lucas.

Lord Natyis cocked his head to one side and furrowed his brow. "I am concerned."

"Why?" Aithian looked at Lucas with confusion.

"You both have brought feral sorcerers into this house without your elders' permission. They could be assassins."

Lucas brought his right hand over his eyes and shook his head with a deep sigh.

"Feral is not exactly how I would describe them. The sorceress is a soldier for the Danarian military. As a sorceress, she's a neophyte. The Angorans seem genuinely concerned about the welfare of everyone with regards to the situation. And the Kersian sorcerer…"

Natyis jumped from where he sat and took two paces toward them. "The Kersian sorcerer? You mean to tell me you brought a *Kersian* sorcerer here?"

"If he gets out of line, Tnasha can send a blate or two in his direction." Aithian shrugged, obviously still confused.

"Tnasha?" Natyis narrowed his eyes and gave Lucas a knowing glance. "I see."

"What?" Aithian looked at Natyis, then Lucas. "Let me guess, you told him some nonsense about me being in love with her?"

"Well, *you are.*"

"Just talk to her. If you want them to leave I have no doubt they will oblige." Aithian crossed his arms over his chest.

With a deep breath, Natyis settled back into his chair. "Fine. Bring her in here and tell Eury to join us. We want to talk to her - *alone.* Leave the others in the sitting room and watch them closely."

Lucas and Aithian hurried from the room. Moments later they entered the sitting room only to find the four sorcerers lounging comfortably in the deep, upholstered chairs. They looked up.

Tnasha forced a smile. "Will they see me?"

"Lord Natyis and Lord Eury will see you." Aithian paused. "Alone."

"All right." She stood, glancing back over her shoulder with a look of regret. She followed Aithian and Lucas back to Natyis' chamber door.

"Is there anything I should know before I go in there?" she asked.

To Aithian's surprise, Lucas nodded. "My father is a stubborn, difficult man. He sees all outside sorcerers as a threat. Be cautious. He could throw you out of this holding tonight."

Tnasha's eyes grew big. "Are you serious?"

"Unfortunately." He turned from her and knocked on the door.

A voice from the other side bade her to enter. She turned the knob, feeling the latch click and release. She stepped into the dimly lit room, closing the heavy door behind her. "This is pleasant."

Natyis grunted and turned to her. He choked, and began coughing.

Eury stood and rushed to his side.

"Is he all right? Does he have an illness or something?"

Eury turned to her with a serious expression. "No."

Natyis spoke then. "You surprised me, that's all."

"Oh, umm, I'm Tnasha fen Schoitt of Danaria. I apologize if I startled you." She smiled as genuine as she could manage, glancing around the room and from Eury to Natyis not knowing what to expect.

Natyis stood. "I am Lord Natyis, and this is Lord Eury. We comprise two of the nine elders of the Imperial Hierarchy of Arkeereon."

"It is good to meet you." She bowed her head in acknowledgement of their high positions.

He motioned her to a chair. "Likewise, though we are left to wonder what it is you want with us."

She went to the chair and sat, leaning forward. "I am here to ask if Lucas and Aithian could help us reclaim the weapon that was stolen from Ramathra. They would be valuable in making this a success."

The elder sorcerers exchanged glances. Natyis' gaze traveled back to her. His white eyes did not show any emotion. "I hear you saved them from the Kersian Sorcerer Seth's attack."

"Yes, but... it wasn't entirely intentional." She forced a smile. "Not that I wouldn't have intentionally saved them... but..."

Eury leaned forward as well. "What do you mean?"

Her voice emerged small, with a hint of embarrassment. "I was not trying to save anyone. I am not sure how I did it. You must understand, I am, for the most part, an inept sorceress. Hence the reason I could use the help of an adept sorcerer or two. I'm not sure I could do it by myself. We do have the other two staves."

Again, Natyis and Eury' eyes left her, they exchanged glances, then returned to her. "What other staves?" Natyis asked.

"The Eagle's Talon and the Crow's Foot," she said, unsure as to why they looked at her with confusion. "There were three staves."

"When the Kersian sorcerer threw his blate…"

Tnasha cut him off. "He used the third staff, the Raven's Claw." She stopped short, remembering her manners. "I apologize for interrupting."

For the first time that night, Natyis smiled, amused. "Have you read the works of the Sorcerer Rylara, Tnasha?"

"No." She paused, not knowing what to say, but knowing they were waiting for her to continue. "I never went into the temple as the priestesses wanted. But I have two grimoires given to me by the Sorcerer Kalath."

"And this Sorcerer Kalath is your teacher?"

She bowed her head, feeling that same somber feeling she had every time Kalath was mentioned. She fought back a tear. "He *was* my teacher, yes. The Kersian Sorcerer Seth murdered him days ago in the Selenia Forest."

"Days?" Eury seemed confused.

Even though the question was not asked, Tnasha knew what he meant. "I used one of the incantations in the book to transport myself and my friends here to avoid a journey by sea."

Natyis sat back with a stunned look on his face. "What else can you do?"

She shrugged. "I am only now learning that I can do these things. I do not know the extent of my abilities."

"Then you also do not know that your mere presence in Arkeereon has rendered my ability for sight useless?" His tone hinted a sudden surge of anger.

"I'm sorry," she said, not knowing what else to say. "It's not intentional, I swear it."

Yet again, the sorcerers exchanged glances. A wide smile appeared on Eury' lips. "I suspect you really do not know, do you?"

"No."

Natyis took another deep breath. "You can bring your request to the entire council of elders in the morning."

Tnasha breathed a deep sigh of relief. "Thank you." She stood, then paused, not sure if the conversation was finished. "Umm. Do you want me to go now?"

The elder sorcerers nodded in acknowledgement, and Tnasha retreated from the room finding Lucas and Aithian waiting for her.

"What did he say?" Lucas looked concerned.

She closed her eyes and took several measured breaths. "I thought for sure he was going to throw us out. But instead I was granted permission to seek audience with your elders in the morning."

"It is getting late. Rumor has it Aithian's sister made her famous stew." Lucas put his hand on her shoulder as they returned to the sitting room.

Aithian pushed him away with a tight grin. "Then we will show you to your rooms."

Tnasha smiled, amused by Aithian's jealously. "Thank you."

"No gratitude is necessary. The elders have not agreed, *yet*." Lucas opened the door for her.

CHAPTER 37

Morvack paced the small room their Arkeeronish hosts provided. He felt uneasy inside the holding. Here, he left himself wide open to attack.

"Relax, would you?" came the female voice from behind him.

"Not again!" He whirled around, coming face to face with a petite, dark haired woman with pale skin and soft brown eyes.

"As I have been trying to tell you all along, you must listen to your heart. You are a kind person at heart." She smiled up at him with warmth.

"Who are you?" His voice betrayed his hidden disbelief.

"I am Annah Ashtar, daughter of Lord Aramon who is a son of Natyis. All this time you struggled with your sanity, did you not?"

"Is this some sort of trickery?"

She held out a thin, soft hand as pale as the rest of her. Her mana seethed an even brighter white from her skin. "I can communicate with others over long distances and see into the future. These are my only gifts."

"Why is it you sought me?" His eyes could not help but slide over her small frame, noting how the thin nightdress she wore showed off her voluptuous curves.

She saw this and pulled her robe around her. "I performed a rite to find my soul pair bond. It was the incantation that brought our minds together." She wiggled her outstretched hand at him. "Come with me."

"Where?"

"I must show you something."

"If I am caught with you, they will surly kill me."

"She trusts you." She smiled with near perfect lips.

Morvack narrowed his eyes. He knew who she meant. "Tnasha."

"Yes. She trusts you. She is the one the prophecy for this generation speaks of."

He took her hand, allowing her to lead him from the small room and through dimly lit corridors. Finally, they stopped at a door leading into a small chamber with an altar on the far side of the room. On either side of the altar were niches holding statues of gods long since forgotten. "What is this place?

"This is my sanctuary. Where I come to meditate and perform rites to my gods."

He pulled his hand from hers. "What types of rites?"

She looked back at him over her shoulder, then kneeled, saying a prayer beneath her breath. She stood and approached the altar. "I worship gods of nature."

His mind raced back to Tnasha's words only hours earlier. She had said their religions were much alike. The god was the same, only broken down into smaller parts.

"She was correct. You know, in your heart, that it is true."

"What is truth but our perception of it?" He smiled wryly at her back.

She turned to him. "Exactly."

He let out a heavy sigh. "Why is it you always speak to me in riddles?"

"I do no such thing."

"You do."

"Come, sit near the altar." She picked up a book from atop the altar, bringing it to him. "You must read the prophecy for yourself. Only then will you know it's true."

"How can I know it is true by reading it? I do not believe everything I read."

"That is wise." She handed him the book. "However, you may find this interesting considering you have lived the first prophecy of the three already."

"Why are there three?" He took the book, but he did not look at its pages.

"Each generation brings three prophecies. This happens nine times, and then a formidable change occurs. The process repeats. It is cyclic. This particular prophecy is the ninth. Which means it will bring change."

A cold chill ran up his neck. His eyes fell to the book's pages. He read.

"The one who holds great power shall find that in mistakes, the will of the One speaks. For in mistakes there is growth. The one will cause the beginning of the war, and will bring it to the end. So the cycle of change completes. For the Daughter of our Lord, formed in someone else, but of the same hue as Her mana, Delepitore, of sorcery. In those who oppose her, there are three, and the pawn. One shall be treachery, one greed and the other deception. The last, who will be cleansed of a fatal wound by the sorcery of all, shall be spared. For he brings tolerance and love, where many thought there was none. Three nations shall be united in the aftermath of war under one nation, but first three things must come to pass.

The first shall be a test of the One's strength and fortitude to obtain a piece of what was taken.

The second shall be a test of bravery to take back the power of destruction stolen from the sacred temple.

The third shall be a test of trust and love, in the face of adversity."

He closed the book. There was nothing more. "It is not specific. It could mean anything."

"This particular version may not be as detailed as others, but the substance is there. You are the one who has been spared by the gift of her power. You coming in contact with Tnasha is no accident. It was meant to spur the events now taking place."

The chill became sharper, and deeper, chilling him right down to the bone. "Then what should I do? Forsake my faith?"

S. J. Reisner

"You have already questioned it. Now you must take what is left over and piece it together into something meaningful to you and you alone. No one can impose a faith on others."

"You speak in riddles again." Annoyance stood on the edge of his voice.

"You understand me quite well." She lifted a dark eyebrow at him. "There comes a time, Morvack, when each of us must develop a personal relationship with the Whole. Regardless of what we believe, or how we choose to worship, the Whole is ever present and strong within us. We are just as much a part of Him as He is us. We all come from the same source. And yet the beauty of our nature is we are all a unique part of that source."

Morvack nodded, handing her the book. She took it and placed it back upon the altar before retreating the way they had come.

"I will always be with you," she said, leaving him at the door of his room. Then she disappeared into the dim corridor like a ghost that had not been there at all.

CHAPTER 38

Tnasha woke early the next morning. A lump sat at the base of her throat. She did not know why she felt this way. Speaking to the elders of the Imperial Hierarchy of Arkeereon seemed easy enough. Her heart sank. Would they provide help? The only way she would know is if she asked. Leaving her room, she found Oran and Arick standing in the hallway. "Where is Morvack?"

"He was out late last night."

"Out?"

Arick snickered, and not in a pleasant way. "With a woman."

"Really?" Unable to hide her own surprise, she went to Morvack's door and knocked.

Morvack opened the door bleary eyed and half dressed. "I'll be out in a moment."

"Late evening?" she asked. It seemed like a logical question. Oran and Arick produced half-cocked smiles.

Morvack's eyes passed over each of them. Without word, he shut the door.

With all of them finally assembled, they found their way to the dining hall where half a dozen sorcerers sat eating. Tnasha found the familiar faces of Lucas and Aithian quickly. With the Angoran's and Kersian in tow, Tnasha sat next to their

Arkeereonish friends at the long table, ignoring the stares of the others.

"How long before I can meet with the council?" she asked in a mere whisper.

Aithian kept his attention on his plate, only half awake. "A few hours. Are you in a hurry?"

"I really don't want the Kersians to have the weapon any longer than necessary."

Morvack shook his head and wiped the sleep from his eyes. "We have plenty of time. Seth is methodic. He will wait until he feels his plans are perfect before using the weapon against anyone else. You know as well as I that it is too late to save Gavgal, if we ever wanted to save him."

Tnasha scratched her neck, then took a plate from the center of the table, filling it with fresh fruits and bread. All the while she contemplated Morvack's profound change of heart. Somehow, she knew she would never understand. "I suppose you're right," she finally said.

They finished the meal in silence.

Several hours later, Tnasha found herself waiting outside the elder's chamber door. Lucas sat with her.

"You seem nervous," he finally said.

"I am contemplating why I am doing this."

"Why are you doing this?"

"Because I have no choice." She put her hands in her lap.

"We all have choices. You do not have to do anything you choose not to. Why not someone else?"

"If we all waited for someone else to do something, we risk that nothing will be done at all."

"So you feel it's your duty?" He sounded amused.

She let out a heavy sigh. "It *is* my duty. It was a task given me by my people. I do it for them, myself, and for my future children," she paused and looked at him then added, "and yours."

Lucas put his elbows on his knees and rested his head on one cupped hand. "What if you and I die?"

"We won't die, will we?" She gazed at him in question. Caitlan's voice came back to her. *The warrior's blood still runs red, does it not?* She shrugged. There was that mortality again. "Fine, we *could* die. But we'll try our best to survive."

Lucas let out a laugh. "I would certainly hope so."

Her leg bounced nervously. "What could they be doing in there?"

He lifted his head and rubbed his hands together. "Going over the last meeting's business I suspect."

"This is so much more important."

"To you, perhaps. My father saw this coming years ago."

She felt her eyes widen in horror. "Then why didn't he stop it then? He could have at least brought the weapon here."

"And risk all of Arkeereon to a war with the Kersians?" He laughed. "Not my father. He's much too cautious. He also believes that everything that happens, happens for good reason. That the future is a fate we cannot change and must all deal with."

She raised an eyebrow at him. She had been taught that each person created his or her own reality and she believed that.

"Meaning he believes the Kersians would have gotten the weapon no matter what. He felt he had to make the choice of whether or not to risk our lives in the process."

"The staff still could have been hidden better."

"Then they would have come here searching for it, using torture and murder as their devices to find the weapon."

She had not really considered that possibility. "So if your elders do let you or someone from your hierarchy come with us, how are we going to successfully retrieve the weapon?"

"We will transport to Zul using Morvack's memory, find Seth, which is where the weapon will most likely be, and take it from him forcibly." He gave her a half-hearted grin.

"It won't be *that* easy."

"Of course it won't. But then nothing is ever as easy as it sounds. It's the best plan we can hope for. The specifics will be worked out as we go."

"I knew you were going to say that," she said bitterly.

"You sound disappointed."

"It reminds me of the last time I was on Zul. Flying by the seat of our britches. Traveling on the left horse black."

He smiled. He obviously knew the story. "That's how we live most our lives anyway, isn't it? By instinct?"

"I pray for my normal, boring routine life. Right now I wish I was home, sleeping in my own bed, and going to the central base every day, getting my orders, patrolling the streets, and coming home at night to something comfortable and familiar."

He put his hand on her knee. "That's what we all want, but that's not life."

They both looked up as the double doors of the council chamber opened. Eury stepped out. "The Council will see you now."

They stood. Lucas patted her on the shoulder. "May the gods look upon you kindly in the elder's decision."

"Thanks," she mumbled, following Eury into the chamber.

The high ceilings and marble floors made the room feel formal and uninviting. On a raised platform adjacent the doors, the hierarchy sat. Sorcerers with strong mana of various shades, sat patiently, watching her. They all had the same long, black hair, several with grey streaks. Undoubtedly many of them were over one hundred years old. She felt small beneath their scrutinizing stares.

Natyis cleared his throat. "This is Tnasha fen Schoitt, a Danarian soldier. She seeks our approval to involve members of our families in a war."

Her eyes went wide. "Not a war," she corrected, horrified. "I am asking your help in retrieving the weapon from the Kersian Sorcerer Seth. In his hands, the Raven's Claw is dangerous. We have a reliable source that suggests the first place Seth will attack is his own brother on Zul. But after that, Arkeereon, Danaria, and the Onyx Mountains, which are home to the Angoran, are all open to attack. We have no way of predicting what he'll do with it."

One of the sorcerers, who vaguely resembled Aithian she noticed, spoke. "Why do you need our help? Surely Danaria is home to others of our kind. Why can they not help? Disposing of Kersian armies should be a simple task."

Tnasha stood stunned for a moment. She did not have an answer for him. "I, I don't know. We have certain ethics," she stammered. "We will not use our sorcery against humans, and it seems, our council of elders and members of the temple have been unsuccessful in stopping the Kersian sorcerers because of their specific talents."

"Cowards."

"They thought I could handle it alone I...." She lowered her eyes to the floor, looking into the waving pattern of gray fading into black in the floor's marble tiles.

"You cannot?"

She took a deep breath, feeling the confidence in herself rise. "I'm an untrained sorceress and an inexperienced soldier. My abilities seem to be strong, but I do not know what I can call at will and what I can't. I'm still learning. With so much at stake, it would be inane for me to attempt this without support. If I tarnish one incantation, this could escalate to a sorcerers' war that will involve *everyone*. Not just Danaria. The Angorans were smart enough to realize this. They sent two of their own to help. One blast from the weapon threw all of us into unconsciousness! I'm no good to anyone unconscious. Especially if I am alone."

Natyis lifted a hand to silence her. "What makes you think it would be any different if you were with others? No one could withstand a concentrated mana blast from the weapon. You would all be doomed."

Tnasha had to think and think fast or risk losing support. At that moment, she wished she had not sent Margore home. He would have had a diplomatic answer for everything they asked. "Not if he was under the impression I was the only one to survive his first attack. I could find something to mask his ability to sense the others. They could come up behind him as he used the weapon against me and we'd have him!" she finished with triumph, knowing that her answer was rather stupid.

"Ah. It sounds promising. But would it work?" Eury narrowed his eyes with a smile, looking around at the reaction of the other assembled elders.

"Who would you want to take?" Natyis asked.

She knew he already knew. "Aithian and Lucas."

"Why have you chosen them?"

Tnasha shrugged, completely unprepared. It was just another question she could not fully answer. "Because they were there for the first attack. They would both recognize Seth, and the weapon if they saw either." She paused and watched Natyis' eyes for some sign of his true feelings. Nothing. "Plus, I, we already know them and feel comfortable with them."

"What about the Kersian defector?"

"He's on our side." Her palms felt sweaty and she wondered if she really believed it.

"Are you sure of this?" Eury asked. He looked at Natyis for some validation.

Natyis cringed. He motioned to a lone armed man standing by the door. "Bring Aithian and the Kersian in here. Aithian and Luithian will be able to tell if his intentions mean to harm us or help us."

Tnasha stood solid in uncomfortable silence. Her eyes searched the room for something familiar and comfortable. When Aithian and Morvack entered, she sighed with relief. Their familiar faces and their support were the closest she could get.

"Aithian, you have talked with the Kersian Morvack?"

"Yes," he said flatly.

"And what are your impressions of his desire to help?" Natyis cocked his head, pursing his lips.

Without missing a beat, Aithian answered. "They are genuine. Even if he is self-serving and motivated by fear."

Natyis turned his attention to Morvack, who looked uneasy within the hierarchy audience chamber. "What are your motivations, Morvack?"

"I have seen the error of my ways and wish to live my life in peace. Free from my brothers and their violent ways and false promises." Morvack stared straight ahead. Not at any council member, rather at the back wall.

"Do you trust us, Morvack?" Luithian asked.

Morvack shot him a piercing look of contempt, then glanced at Tnasha, averting his eyes to their previous position fixated on the back wall. "I trust her. And Annah. No one else."

"Annah?" Natyis furrowed his dark brow in puzzlement. "My granddaughter Annah?"

"Yes."

A low growl emerged from his throat. "How is it you know my granddaughter?"

Tnasha could not mask her own look of surprise. *Oh, Gods!*

Morvack's expression softened. "She introduced herself to me on Zul. Through mind-speak. It was she who helped me find my way."

"They have become friends," Tnasha said suddenly, hoping Morvack would shut up.

The frown faded from Natyis' face. Amusement replaced the anger. "Have they?" he asked. "I never expected Annah would find a person like you…to her *spiritual* liking."

"That is, perhaps, one of the things we have most in common. She made me see that our beliefs are not so far removed from one another."

"I can imagine that was a task." Lord Natyis laughed then his expression turned suddenly sober. "Where is Lucas."

Lucas must have been listening outside the door, for he opened the door and poked his head in almost immediately. "Did you call for me?"

Several chuckles surfaced from the stoic elders.

Lucas's father shook his head. "Come in here and bring the Angorans. Close the door. Is there anyone else out there listening?"

"No." He averted his eyes to the ground as a slight blush colored his cheeks. He entered the room with Oron and Arick trailing closely behind him.

"Tnasha believes she can distract Seth long enough for the rest of you to come to her aid in time to kill him." Natyis looked at the motley crew in question.

"We won't know until we get there if that is a viable plan. I have no doubt we can get the blasted staff back, but what shall we do with the weapon?" Oron asked.

"We will have it brought back here where we will destroy it with sorcery," suggested Luithian.

Tnasha's eyes went wide and she threw her hands up. "Why didn't you do this years ago?"

Natyis shook his head. "If we could have, we would have. We cannot destroy it."

"Why not?" she asked.

"Destroying it could cause the destruction of the world and the universe. It was created by the elements from the nature around us. Hence it would destroy that very nature."

She sent him an exasperated look. Then an idea crept into her mind. They couldn't destroy it, but maybe they could deconstruct it. "Then maybe we need to commit it back from whence it came. We will disassemble it and toss the claw and stone into a deep part of the ocean weighing it down with an anchor, and then we will bury the wooden staff in a grave somewhere. Whosoever does each task will not be allowed to tell the other where the item went. And that knowledge will die with the person who completed the task."

Eyebrows lifted around the room and a rush of voices filled the air.

Natyis nodded. "You think quickly."

Not really, she thought, *otherwise I wouldn't feel so unsure of myself.* Instead of speaking her thoughts, she gave him a polite smile. "Thank you."

"But first, it must be agreed that you will train with Ronove." He motioned his hand toward the man on his left. "On the art of protecting yourself. If the first blate thrown from the weapon was merely a trial on Seth's part, he may have found a way to make the blates stronger with time and practice. If you cannot protect yourself, the next blate could very well kill you."

Tnasha nodded in understanding and looked at Ronove. "You would not happen to have an incantation or something I could use to cover the presence of those who will travel with me, would you?"

Ronove shrugged. "I will search the grimoires."

"I will look in mine as well." She gave him a grateful smile.

Natyis stood. He looked around the room, pausing to meet each elder's eyes for a brief moment. Finally, he turned back to her. "It is settled then. This meeting of the council of elders is adjourned. You may all leave now, and do what you will."

Around her, the elders filed from the room. She stood, baffled for a moment, until she realized they must have made the consensus with mind-speak. Ronove approached her. "When would you prefer to start your training?"

"How much time do we have?" She looked to her companions for an answer.

Aithian shrugged. "Morvack no longer believes we need to hurry. Hurry, don't hurry – I don't know what to believe at this point. So my guess would be we have enough time for you to become adept in protecting yourself in the very least."

"I agree," said Oron.

With a nervous smile, she turned back to Ronove. "How about in the morning?"

He nodded graciously and took his leave.

"There is one thing I would like to request, however." Arick stopped them.

"What?" Lucas asked.

"That Tnasha also learn how to throw some of that protection our way if necessary," he said with a wide grin.

"You got it!" She smiled at them. "So shall we do the rest of the day?"

"Would you like to see Arkeereon? The city I mean," Lucas said.

They all agreed and set off for a day of rest.

CHAPTER 39

As dusk approached, a small merchant ship from Cabalia docked at the port on the Kersian Island of Zul. Gavgal did not expect Morvack to return so soon. He waited impatiently near the entryway, expecting to see Morvack bound up the stairs, staff in hand, with a broad smile from ear to ear. Instead, it was Seth who entered, and he was not smiling.

The corners of Gavgal's mouth turned downward. "What are you doing here, Seth?" As he said it he saw the staff in Seth's hand. "Where is Morvack?"

"My brother has gone and gotten himself murdered. By a sorceress no less." Seth passed him and said in his ear, "A sorceress I believe *you* know."

Gavgal's previous impatience melted with a bit of sadness and plenty of anger. A small part of him, he wanted to think, had enjoyed Morvack's company. The sorceress, she was the one who angered him. He turned and followed Seth down the corridor to a courtyard garden. A soft breeze blew around them. "Then we shall perform last rites at once. Where are his remains?"

"Gone. She vaporized him with a blate seething of fire. Nothing but ashes remained and they were swept away by fierce gusts of wind." Seth smirked.

"You saw this with your own eyes?" Gavgal was shocked.

"Indeed. I was holding the staff at the time. So, I took it, held it in front of me, and let go a blate. She and her companions died quickly. Now, we will probably have reason to worry about Arkeereon and the Angorans as well."

"Why?" Gavgal leaned toward him with a menacing frown.

"Unfortunately, each faction sent several of their sorcerers to stop us. What they did not realize is I could not be stopped. I avenged our brother with this." He held the staff out.

Gavgal moved to take it from him. Seth pulled it away.

Seth's eyes started glowing a deep orange. "I killed the seer as you asked."

"Were there any problems?" Gavgal took a deep, angry breath.

"None. It was flawless."

"Good, you have done well, my brother. Now give me the staff. The Unnamed will reward you with more than you ever imagined." He smiled at his brother reassuringly and held out his hand with a look of expectation.

Seth laughed cold and uncaring. He held the staff out at arms length, grasping it firmly. "No. The Unnamed will reward me nothing. This staff, however, will give me everything I desire."

With a mere thought, Seth's mana surged forward a fiery orange. Absorbed by the staff it burst forth from the stone and struck Gavgal dead. It *was* that simple. Gavgal's corpse lie still on the ground as smoke drifted upward from the charred gaping wound in his chest over his heart.

Seth smiled at his own handiwork. "Amazing."

General Luig and several other soldiers came running. "What happened?" the General asked. His eyes fell to Gavgal's fallen body.

Seth shrugged with a smug look. "He was holding the staff and something emerged from the stone, killing him." He sighed, bored. "Have his body prepared for last rites and have one of the priests bury him. I have more important things to attend to."

His cold demeanor left the soldiers in shock.

Seth didn't care. He wandered casually inside the palace and surveyed what was now his. Retreating to his new study he sent for two things. A messenger and a serving maid. First, he decided, he would contact Alax and have him return to Zul. Second, he would eat. Perhaps later he would bathe, and tomorrow, he would decide how to make the world his.

CHAPTER 40

The cozy library reminded Tnasha of her grandfather's study. As a child, she would curl up with a book in the corner near the window while he worked. There she could fantasize for hours about ponies and mythical beasts with no one to bother her. The warmth from the fire and the smell of cinnamon made her feel welcome. It only increased her longing for home. She sat down in one of the thick, deep blue cushioned, high backed chairs. If left alone, she knew she would fall asleep comfortably.

The door clicked open behind her and Ronove entered. He smiled briefly. "You're early."

"Anxious to start, I suppose." Tnasha wiggled one foot with nervous fervor.

"I can see that. Did you find anything within your own grimoires that will help you block Seth's senses of the others?" He looked down at the books in her lap with wondering, gray eyes.

"No. I did not find *anything*." She let out a heavy sigh. Her lack of a plan reminded her what a poor soldier she really was. Why hadn't her training prepared her for this? She turned her attention back to Ronove, who looked on expectantly.

He rubbed his hands together with vigor. "I was just outside. It is still quite cold."

She tipped her head to one side, shoving her self-pitying thoughts to the back of her mind. "Does it ever warm up here?"

He forced a chuckle. "The winters here are bitter cold, and the summer months sweltering. The humidity, however, remains fairly consistent."

She half smiled. "In Danaria it is cold only a few months out of the year, and hot several months out of the year. But the other months the sun is always shining. It is much warmer. The humidity varies from location to location. Where I live, it is somewhat arid unless we've had plenty of rainfall."

"Ah. It sounds like a place I would like to visit during the colder months." He sat down at a table and pulled a book to him. His gray hair glinted in the daylight seeping in from the window.

She could tell his hair was once deep black like the other Arkeeronish sorcerers. His face was once devoid of wrinkles. In his youth, she was sure he had been quite an attractive man. Of course she found him attractive now, but in a different way. Strangely, he reminded her of Kalath. A sense of sorrow overwhelmed her and she pushed it away. No one could ever replace Kalath, not that she was looking for a replacement. Was she?

He opened the book, flipping through the pages searching for something. When he found it, he turned the book to her and pushed it across the table. "Here. This entire section should explain protection well. While you read that, I will go through several of the more rare grimoires and see if I can't find something to block his senses."

Tnasha nodded and pulled the book to her, placing her own upon the table. She started to read. She merely glanced up when Ronove returned with another stack of books.

"Well, what do you think?"

She pulled her attention from the book. "It does not tell me anything I did not already know. You pull your mana from the center of your being no matter what you do. You project it. Only this time, I'm supposed to visualize a wall. Around myself, or anyone I wish to protect." She turned the page, expecting an incantation. "But there is no incantation."

He laughed and sat down with a thud. "You really are inexperienced."

"Yes. Did you think I was lying?"

"No." He gave her a wide smile. "A person's view of his or her own inexperience is quite telling of the person. It seems to me you simply lack self confidence along with experience."

She shook her head. "Self confidence is not my problem. Sorcery is. I either project too much and cause chaos, or I hold back and nothing happens."

"Ah." He leaned toward her on his elbows. "I thought by now you would have realized that an incantation holds no power on its own. It is merely a tool used to keep the inexperienced sorcerer focused on the outcome."

"Well, I know this, but I often *need* the focus an incantation provides. And I wonder, why are they always in strange languages that are barely pronounceable?"

"They come in several varieties. Some incantations are written in lost languages so that only the sorcerers know what they mean. If, for example, you wanted to invoke wind you might say 'Rena uba Lucia Kan' which means 'Bring me the wind'. If the sorcerer knows this, by saying it in a different language it forces him to focus on the words being said. He is less distracted by that which is common. Other incantations consist of mere nonsense words. The sorcerer memorizes the nonsense as a way to evoke wind. In memorizing, he creates a picture of what he expects to happen. Once again, it keeps him focused and less likely to surrender to distraction."

She narrowed her eyes. "If that's true, that means I could create my own incantations."

"Yes, it does."

"So if that's the case, and the staff is only a tool, how does it concentrate mana into a powerful stream?"

He inhaled deeply. "Magical items are more complex. Through a sorcerers will, certain properties of the creator's mana become entrapped in an object. The object is saturated with it. That is the reason most magical items can only be used by their maker or someone with similar mana."

"So, Seth has the proper mana to wield the Raven's Claw?"

"Evidently so. I'm surprised none of you were killed."

She ignored the comment and continued with her own string of thoughts. "I wonder if the other two staves would work if I tried to use them."

He continued looking through books. "They would. You have a very unique mana. It is not tied to any particular element."

"But I'm the earthy part of water," she said, half in protest. She looked out the window into the gray sky. "Both water and earth sorcery come to me naturally."

"Then building walls should be of little problem for you. If you notice, there, in the corner of this page," he pointed it out with a thick, calloused finger. "Is the symbol for earth. Protection is an earth sorcery."

She looked at the symbol, noting it looked much like a tree near a hill. "Perhaps that is the reason we were all protected from Seth's blate. Do you think all sorcerers have the ability to do almost anything?"

"Most of us are restricted to the strongest elements present in our mana. Yours, however, is what we call *benign*."

"Doesn't that mean 'not dangerous'?" Her eyes stood wide with question.

"On the contrary, it means you are balanced and able to work with all of the elements equally. For you, especially with the strength of your mana, sorcery is second nature in all of its forms."

The mere thought of being capable of such power sent a chill down her spine. "But I still have limitations…everyone has limitations. Don't they?"

"You will always be limited by your own mind, exhaustion, and the possibility that you could develop serious imbalances. Many of these things can be avoided, however. Through regular elemental balancing and using your mana responsibly, you could be a formidable sorceress indeed. You will never be infallible or god-like. And it's unlikely you can part oceans or move mountains. However, you could easily manipulate both in your own way." He leaned back in the chair and gazed at her.

"And I'm not immortal, as Priestess Caitlan pointed out before I left," she said thoughtfully.

A chuckle escaped his lips. "Well, that's true. None of us is immortal, but many of us often forget that. I do believe sorcerers live long enough."

"How old are you?" she asked.

"Around one hundred." He winked at her. "And you?"

"Nineteen."

"Hmm." His smile seemed even broader.

"What?"

"I expected you were a little older. Not by your looks, certainly, but by your wisdom."

"Ha. Wisdom? I'm really showing my inexperience, aren't I?"

"I don't look at it that way." He began going through the books again. "You are merely confirming, for me, that Natyis made the right decision in sending some of our own to assist you."

"Same thing. I couldn't possibly have done it alone," she said in almost a whisper.

"I found it." He pushed the other books aside, ignoring her previous comment. "It says here that you can numb another sorcerer's sense of presence by carrying Skariolon Root."

"Let me guess. You are fresh out and the only place it grows is along the Northern fortification walls of the city of Danaria? And it's probably good in teas?" She laughed, finding amusement in her own wit. It brought back fond memories of Kalath. He would have appreciated her jest.

Ronove lifted an eyebrow in confusion. "No. The plant grows in Southern Ryea. It is used as a spice by humans, but is poisonous to our kind if ingested or absorbed through the skin. We do not touch it. I believe there is a spice shop in the Eastern district that may carry enough for all of you to carry some with you. Though we might need to consult with Verrine for an herb that would render your bodies immune to the poison. It would make you quite ill otherwise, but it isn't deadly."

Tnasha rolled her eyes. "It's my luck, isn't it?"

"It seems to me you have much better luck than you realize." He smiled again. "Keep reading. I will consult with Verrine, find several men brave enough to throw blates at you, and when I get back we will go to the armory where you can practice blocking mana attacks."

He left the room immediately. Now alone, Tnasha put her full concentration in the book. What it said made sense, but it seemed more like all the things she already knew instinctively. With a deep sigh, she kept reading. Before long, she drifted to sleep.

In close proximity the staff sat propped against a wall. She floated to it. Aithian stood near a window, looking out over an ocean that appeared from nowhere. A palm tree. She faced Seth, at his feet another sorcerer knelt. She held the weapon. Ran with it toward the ocean. Aithian stopped her. She woke in a cold sweat and with labored breathing. The dreams were starting again. But this time, they were more terrifying.

CHAPTER 41

Ronove's mere presence woke her. "Sleeping when you should be studying?"

She lifted her head from the table, bleary-eyed. "How long have I slept?" She looked over to her right, noticing the Eagle's Talon and the Crow's Foot stood propped against the wall.

"We must go to the armory now. You will practice blocking. I have sent Verrine to gather the Skariolon Root needed to protect you, and the antidote for the poison. He will make a potion you must drink to keep the root's poison from absorbing into your body." Ronove motioned her to the door. "Shall we?"

She stood, wiping the sleep from her eyes. With a yawn, she followed him out of the library, through the corridors, and to their destination. Inside the armory was another room. Large and cold, the second room boasted rows of benches and high ceilings. "This is a practice room? Inside?"

"The weather can be much too cold to practice outside in an arena." He motioned her in.

On the wooden benches, five men sat waiting.

Ronove held out a hand in introduction. His tone since returning to the library to retrieve her had turned serious. "This is Flery. This is Berith, Agalia, Tchort, and finally Atan. This," he motioned toward her, "is Tnasha." He took her by the shoulders and led her at the far side of the room.

Flery leaned his head against the wall. "The rest of us should stay behind whoever is throwing the blate, yes?"

Ronove nodded. "For now. We may attempt to see if she can protect several of you, as well. But for now, we will test her ability to protect herself."

Tnasha felt a sense of anxiety overwhelm her. "I have no incantation."

"Then I suggest you create one, and quickly. Because in several moments I will have Atan throw a blate at you and you will have no choice."

A young, dark-haired woman carrying a satchel entered the room, interrupting him. "Verrine sent me just in case there are any injuries," she said in soft voice.

Ronove turned to her. "Ah, Verrier. Please, sit down. We may need you."

Tnasha's eyes went wide. She shook her head, wondering if she would indeed need medical attention.

Ronove's jovial mood returned and he laughed. "It is wise to take precaution. You will not intentionally be hurt. In all honesty I feared more for *their* well-being rather than yours."

She relaxed a little and took her stance, as if she wielded a sword. "I suppose I'm ready. Hit me."

Atan stood and took his own stance across from her. The room fell silent. Not even a breath or footfall echoed off the hollow walls and high ceilings. He lifted his hands, holding them inches apart. She could see his mana fold inward, running through his veins to his hands and pooling into a fiery ball of energy between his palms. It turned a fiery red, solid almost. He hurled it at her thrusting both palms toward her. In response, her own hands shot out, palms outward. She uttered one word, "Block!"

A wall of violet mana blocked the blate, absorbing it. Her knees trembled, giving way beneath her. With a thud, she fell to the floor light-headed and out of breath.

Verrier stood, lifting her white skirts ever so slightly, and hurried to Tnasha's side. She leaned down, placing her delicate hands on Tnasha's shoulders. "How do you feel?"

"Dizzy."

"That should pass in a few moments. Can you stand?" She helped Tnasha back to her feet then with some reluctance went back to the men and sat down. "Give her a few moments. She is expending large amounts of energy and isn't used to it."

Flery shook his dark head of hair. It was black with a red sheen, probably from his mana. Tnasha regained her footing and her head cleared. She looked at Flery. "You're next?"

He bit his lip and looked at Ronove with question. "If that exhausted her, how is she going to block a blate from the weapon?"

"She will be able to expend more energy without tiring so quickly as she becomes more experienced." His response seemed almost too calm, and too confident. He stood back. "Go ahead."

In the same fashion as Atan, he created his blate. But he built it more quickly. He transferred it to one hand, stepped back, and threw it like one might throw a knife. A jagged line of blood-red mana shot out at her like lightening. She blocked it, feeling it run through her mana and into her body, feeling her body thrown backward by its force. Her mana wall weakened, becoming thin and more translucent. It failed. He pulled the stream back just in time.

Ronove smiled. "Very good. There are different types of blates. I chose these sorcerers because they all have varying strengths, as well as technique for throwing blates. You should be very familiar with all of them."

She held up her hand. "Can I rest a moment?"

"You will not have opportunity to rest in the face of Seth," he said with a wary eye.

"All right, point taken." She righted herself and made sure she had solid footing. "I'm ready."

He nodded and motioned Berith to come forward.

Berith's blate came strong and fast, small spurts of mana energy flew at her like an explosion. Instead of being directed at one spot, they came at her in a wide spread, causing her to force her range of protection beyond the immediate space in front of her. The violet wall pulled back slightly, then flicked forward, throwing Berith's blates back at him. Atan grabbed Verrier with one arm and Ronove with the other, pulling them out of range.

The others dove off to the side, and Berith pulled his own blates back to him, absorbing them. He said nothing and sat back down.

"Why didn't he have to protect himself from his own blates?" Tnasha asked, surprised by the display.

With a sigh of relief, Ronove turned to her. "You do not need to protect yourself from your own mana once it has been released from you. It will merely absorb back into that which already surrounds you. It goes back from whence it came."

After successfully blocking the two other men's' blates, Ronove bade Berith to stand across from her again. He did as instructed. Ronove then sent two of the men to stand near Tnasha so she could protect them.

Tnasha yawned and took a deep breath. She felt as though she had not slept in weeks. The fatigue settled in her feet, calves, arms, and shoulders. But she pressed on, knowing that her ability to protect herself and others would play a vital role in retrieving the weapon from Seth. With a sigh she forced a half smile and looked at her charges, hoping she could protect them. "I'm ready…" she called across the room.

Atan and Flery stood beside her. Atan looked at her with curious black eyes. "If I end up imbalanced…"

She rolled her eyes. "Don't worry. I have no plan of letting anyone get hurt. Not intentionally anyway."

Once again, Berith let loose a wide spread of fast moving blates. She thrust her palms forward like she had several times before. "Block!"

Nothing happened.

CHAPTER 42

She awoke startled and tried to sit up. But the minute she moved, pain throbbed in her temples and behind her eyes. Falling backward, she opened her eyes ever so slightly. Aithian sat next to her. He placed a hand on her shoulder. "Relax."

"What happened?" she asked in a weak voice.

"You panicked." Ronove's voice seemed distant.

"Atan and Flery?"

"They were knocked unconscious as you were. Luckily Berith was able to stop the flow of mana quickly."

Nausea swept over her and her stomach churned. "I'm gonna be sick." She leaned over the side of the bed and heaved. Within moments, she faded back into the darkness of unconsciousness.

Natyis stepped forward from where he stood behind Aithian. "She was correct in that she needed help."

"There was a time she would have been too stubborn to ask for help," Oron said. Then added, "From what I've been told about her."

"Perhaps it would be unwise for us to send her at all." Natyis turned to him.

Oron shrugged. "She is the only one who can transport us to Zul using sorcery. Any other method of transportation could alert Seth to our arrival, and could give him more time to plan his attack against us."

Natyis nodded with reluctance. "We should let her rest."

In agreement, the room cleared. Aithian stayed behind. He took her small hand into his, wrapping his long fingers around it. "You must have strength," he said. "I do not want anything to happen to you."

He stood and left, knowing Tnasha had no interest in him. She wore blinders and focused only on one thing. Her task. Until the weapon was safely disposed of, she would not rest. Only then, he figured, would she realize his love for her. He intended to wait, no matter how long, or what it took. Eventually she would see that she loved him, too. She would be his.

●

Tnasha woke up from the deep, balancing sleep three days later. Upon opening her eyes to her blurry surroundings, she found herself alone in the room. She sat up and wiped her eyes. Things were clearer now, and her head was free of the fog and pain. A ray of sunlight slipped through the drapes on the window. She swung her legs over the side of the bed. When her feet hit the cool floor, she shivered and stood, then walked to the window, pulling back the heavy black drape. The room looked over a large courtyard. Below, a woman knelt near a bed of freshly turned soil planting flowers. She smiled, knowing it must be getting warmer outside. At least she would not have to endure the same cold she had felt since her legion left Danaria to save the warlord Kyran's daughter. The familiar longing for home overwhelmed her. She wanted to cry, but instead she frowned. Nothing would ever be the same.

Her clothing lay folded neatly on a chair near the window. She set about getting dressed. In the pit of her stomach, a sense of anxiety grew. Her patience waned. She wanted nothing more than to get this over with. Her failings as a sorceress and soldier weighed heavily on her shoulders. She wondered then if the Imperial Hierarchy had rethought their agreement to send Aithian and Lucas. After all, she had put two of their brethren in the infirmary. She remembered that. What would those sorcerers say when they awoke? Having assured them they would be fine, she ultimately failed them.

With a deep sigh, she sat and put on her boots. Finally, she stood, leaving the warmth of the room behind her. She moved down the hallway steadily, making her way to the dining hall. Once there, she peeked in. It stood empty save for one young woman. Tnasha cleared her throat. "Excuse me."

Annah turned to her. "Hello Tnasha."

Tnasha stepped into the room. "Do you know where everyone is?"

"Most everyone has gone out. It is a beautiful spring day. Are you hungry?"

"I am kind of hungry." She felt her stomach growl, and realized for the first time since she woke up just how hungry she was. "When will they be back?"

The woman, who was no older than Tnasha, smiled at her again. "They should be back this afternoon I would suppose. Let me get you something to eat."

"Can I help?"

"Oh no. Please, sit down. I will be right back." Annah left the room in a swirl of gray skirts leaving a faint trail of white mana behind her.

She returned almost immediately with a plate filled with cheese, bread, meat, an apple, and a cup filled with weak ale. Setting the plate and glass in front of Tnasha, she sat down across from her. "I wanted to thank you."

Tnasha began eating, feeling ravenous. "For what?" she asked with a mouthful of food.

Annah leaned toward her, her long ebony tresses falling in smooth, silky ringlets around her shoulders. "For believing in Morvack and lending him your trust."

"You must be Annah." Tnasha paused and took a sip of the ale. "Oron and his friend, and my friends, thought he was insane. Hearing voices and all of that."

"I had no other way to contact him." Her eyes lit up. "He really is a kind and gentle man."

"Ha. Who used to kill people as part of his spiritual practice."

Annah nodded thoughtfully. "Well, none of us is perfect. We have all done things we regret."

"Regret?" Tnasha let out a laugh. "Understatement. But in a way, you're right. We cannot always judge a man by his past. We must judge him by his present."

The petite sorceress tipped her head in thought. "Or perhaps we should not judge at all."

"Well that's not possible. It is in our nature to be judgmental based on our personal convictions, morals, and beliefs. All those things are based on our personal experiences."

"A valid observation." Annah sat up straight and smoothed her gray skirts, then looked up at Tnasha again. "I love him."

Tnasha felt her gag reflex respond unexpectedly. She coughed, putting her hand over her mouth so that the food did not spill out. "You barely know him."

"I know his mind and his heart."

She narrowed her eyes and leaned toward the young sorceress. "Just when did Morvack have a change of heart? The last time I met him he was dead set on killing my friends and I."

"He never *really* wanted to kill you. But Kolgern bruised his pride. His motivations would surprise you."

"They did. He wants a family. And peace."

"Yes. He told you?"

"I expected an explanation." She sat back and looked down at her plate. It stood empty. A look of surprise shot across her face.

Amused, Annah giggled. "You must have been starving after sleeping for three days. Would you like more?"

"No, thank you." She changed the subject back to Morvack quickly, embarrassed by her own lack of manners. "I knew Morvack did not want to kill *me*. It sounded contrived. But I do think he would have killed Kolgern given half a chance."

"He began doubting his faith and his brothers when he found out about the weapon. That is when I first contacted him."

"He seemed very disturbed about you." Tnasha smiled. "It was amusing. I would have loved to have seen the look on his face when he first heard you in his head. Or when he first met you in the flesh." She took another drink from the cup.

"I intend to make him my husband," she said matter-of-fact.

"What?" Tnasha choked on the ale. "Why are you telling me this?"

"I think it is important for you to see him through my eyes. So you can trust him." She smiled.

"Well, keep in mind he may not even survive this confrontation with Seth. At the pace I'm going, no one else will either."

Annah's expression turned toward reassurance. "He will survive. And so will you and everyone with you."

"How do you know? Are you a seeress?"

"I can see the present moment. I can see what is in your mind. Communicate with anyone I choose over a long distance through mind-speak. I was searching for my true love and I found him."

Tnasha stood, shook her head in disbelief, and wiped her mouth and hands with the cloth napkin. She threw it on the table. "Well, I suppose there really is someone for everyone. I need to find something to occupy me until the others return."

Annah stood, too, and held out a slender hand to Tnasha. "Let's go to the temple. We should meditate."

"On what?" Tnasha could not mask her signature puzzled look.

"You can do a rite to Liale."

A flush of red crept into her cheeks. "You know?"

"If it makes you feel strong, then you should do it. Follow your heart." Annah stepped in front of her, leading the way.

Tnasha followed. It blurted from her lips unbidden. "But the warrior's blood still runs red. Regardless, the ritual will never make me infallible."

"Perhaps not infallible," she said over her shoulder. "But stronger. That is all you can expect from yourself."

Once again, Tnasha's own expectations of herself filtered to the surface.

Annah stopped suddenly and turned to her with a thoughtful look. "Perhaps you should accept yourself for who you are and what you can do. Maybe then, and only then, will you stop fighting your own potential."

CHAPTER 43

"Where have you been?" Seth looked up, annoyed.

Alax kept his eyes cast downward in humble servitude. "I apologize, brother. I had a wedding to perform."

"Someone else could have attended to that. Is that what you've lowered yourself to? Marrying human slaves?"

"I promised…"

Seth waved his hand. "Well, you are here now and that's all that really matters. I have called you back to tell you something I fear will upset you." Seth paused for emphasis. "You and I are the only ones left in our bloodline."

Alax looked up at him, a look of shock made its way across his face. Unshaven, he boasted soft features. Like a woman. Seth sneered at him. "You look surprised, as well you should be. You know as well as I do that Gavgal was bound to get himself killed with all of the enemies he's made over the years. Morvack came to his end following Gavgal. He became a heathen at the last moment and the Unnamed punished him for it. Would you believe that?"

Alax's green eyes clearly displayed his disbelief. "Morvack, a heathen?"

"Morvack, a heathen?" Seth mimicked. He shook his head and picked up a flask of wine, putting it to his lips. When he finished, he wiped his mouth. "Yes, a heathen. He began doubting his faith and began plotting against us."

"You killed him?" Alax took a step back.

"No, though I should have. The sorceress killed him. The same sorceress who destroyed the temple while we were away. The staff I killed the sorceress with, killed Gavgal. He was looking at it... and..." He waived his hand pretentiously. "Well, you can imagine what happened when he pointed it at himself and looked into the stone, accidentally sending energy through it and killing himself. Hmm. He was never truly intelligent."

Alax lowered his eyes again. "What a sorrowful day this is."

"Good riddance. To both of them. They were punished by the Unnamed. Put to death. As the only living heirs, it is our right to rule the Kersian Empire in their place."

"We are hardly an empire, brother. We are but two men." Alax squinted slightly, expecting harsh retaliation.

Seth offered none. Instead, he stood with a smile. "Not yet an empire, Alax. But soon, with this weapon, I will rule as emperor and we will have everyone within the West Ocean Mainlands as our subjects."

"You mean to convert them as Gavgal sought to do?"

Seth rolled his eyes. "Uh, yes. I suppose it would be prudent to follow our brother's wishes and continue with what our god has asked of us. Would it not?" He narrowed his eyes, wondering if Alax would see through him.

Instead, this seemed to make sense to Alax. "Yes. It is what the Unnamed has ordained."

"Make yourself comfortable, Alax. Take your things to your room and settle in. Then join me for dinner?"

"Yes, Seth. I shall do that."

With a smug look of satisfaction, Seth watched his brother go then chuckled to himself. Alax would serve him so long as he believed Seth had the ordainment of an invisible god. The lie would be easy enough. After all, Gavgal had done it for years. How difficult could it be? A broad smile covered his lips. "As if I needed ordainment," he whispered to no one.

Later that night, after their evening meal, Alax joined Seth in the sitting room. A comfortable glow from the firelight danced over the walls, melting the shadows. In the flames that devoured the wood in the hearth, Seth saw his men. The ones who had died. They started back at him in pain and anguish. Begging him to save them. He shoved the bloody images from him mind and sat back with a goblet of wine.

Alax poured himself a glass of wine then looked at his brother expectantly. "I missed their funerals."

"You are too somber, brother. Our family is with the Unnamed now."

Alax noticed the cold tone to Seth's voice and his face hardened. "You sound almost as if you don't care."

Seth cocked his head to one side, leaning into the chair cushions. "I wear a strong expression on the outside, Alax. Inside, however, I am tortured with pain and loss. I merely hide it better. Our people must know our leadership is still strong. That we have not forsaken them in lieu of their beloved leader's death."

His younger brother nodded. It made sense. Alax looked up to all of his brothers. But he could not shrug off his sense of feeling alone. Seth always seemed so distant. They never developed a close relationship, and now, Seth was all he had. "When shall we continue Gavgal's plans?"

"Soon." Seth stared into the hearth pensively. "We do not want to act hastily. Patience will carry us further."

"Do you think the Arkeeronish or the Danarians, once they realize several of their own have been slain, will wage war upon us?"

Seth shook his head. "Possibly, but the more I consider it, the less likely that is. We have their ethics on our side. They will not use their sorcery against humans to get to us. Right now, we have thousands of humans between us." Seth's gaze went distant. "You are much like Morvack in that you worry too much, Alax. The Danarians will not discover their missing warriors for months. Even then, it is doubtful they will be able to put the puzzle together. It could take months, even years for them to figure it out. Or perhaps they will never know the truth at all. We need time to assemble our armies. We shall take the smaller kingdoms first. Cabalia and after that, Arkeereon."

"What about Sherok? Sherok would be an easy attainment if we..."

"No. Gavgal failed with Sherok the first time because Sherok is allied with Danaria. We do not want to wake Danaria until the very last. Once we take Cabalia and Arkeereon, we will take Sherok and Carinth at the same time with separate forces. *Then* we will move to take Danaria. It will be a swift attack."

"They have more sorcerers than we do."

"If we are careful in how we take Arkeereon that will not be so. We will force their sorcerer factions to fight with us or they will die. They will have no choice." Seth tapped his hand on the table.

"What will be our..." Alax paused, searching for the right word, "motivation for them to agree to help us?"

"Simple. If they do not, we will kill their women and children. They have a similar problem as we do. Their women and children are highly prized. Otherwise, their bloodlines die and are forgotten. A basic struggle for survival. It seems simple enough, doesn't it?"

"Yes."

"You would be surprised how quickly people change their minds when their preservation is at stake." Seth smiled knowingly and poured himself another goblet of wine. "Brother, I envision ruling a peaceful world. One in which the humans are subservient to the sorcerers, and the sorcerers have sworn their allegiance to me as their emperor. And you, you will stand at my side as the new High Priest to the Unnamed."

CHAPTER 44

In the temple, Tnasha found the soil waiting for her at the altar in the Northwest corner of the room. She sat down in front of it, turning to watch Annah approach the South altar. Carefully, she turned so that Annah could not see her. She did not want the mysteries of her self-created ritual to go noticed. But Annah knew already, she reminded herself. Otherwise, the soil and spoon would not be there, waiting for her. She tried to hide her thoughts with a prayer.

"In the name of Liale, of earth and steel, grant me strength and resolve to overcome the wicked actions of my enemies," she whispered. She lowered her head in prayer, feeling her mana move around her body like swirling water. She dipped the spoon into the soil, put it in her mouth, and allowed the granules to make their way down her throat. It seemed unfortunate she had no water to wash it down. The Arkeeronish soil was dry. She started to giggle.

Annah joined her. "I had not thought of that," she said from across the room. Within the small temple, the quiet turned to laughter.

A knock upon the door silenced them. "Who is it?" Annah called.

"Lord Eury. I have come to collect Tnasha. Lord Natyis would like to see her."

"How did he know I was here?"

Annah shrugged. "He probably sensed your mana and followed its trail until it became strong."

A thought came to Tnasha's mind. She said it aloud. "Natyis wants me to help him regain his sight."

"Yes," said Annah. "It's driving him mad."

Tnasha stood, bowing her head to Liale, and left the temple, following Eury back to Lord Natyis' personal study. All the while attempting to swallow the stray granules of dry soil in her mouth.

Once there, she sat down and watched Eury leave. She then turned her gaze to Natyis, who hid himself beneath the cowl hood of his dark robes. She noticed then that the room had no windows. "The light must bother you greatly.

"I do find it harsh at times. Would you like some tea?"

She practically jumped. "Yes, thank you." After she poured herself a cup, she sat back down. "You want me to help you see again."

"It's your mana that is blocking my sight."

"I am not sure what to do."

"Nor do I. But perhaps you could try." He reached out to her. "Take my hands"

She got up and kneeled before him, taking his hands into hers. "All right." Closing her eyes, she imagined the darkness lifting from him. Imagined he could see far and wide into the rest of the world.

"I see shadows instead of blackness," he said.

She tried harder, focusing on creating a white light around him that shunned the darkness. "Let him see," she whispered under her breath.

Natyis took a satisfied breath. "Ah. That's much better."

Upon pulling her own mana back, she noticed a stronger white light emanating from him. She opened her eyes and looked up at Natyis. He squinted his eyes closed, as though he searched for something. She closed her eyes again, concentrating on unveiling his sight. Then the blackness came back, pushing her mind backward. She opened her eyes feeling fatigued. Natyis was looking at her.

He sat back heavy in his chair. "The Kersians have no intention of attacking right away. There is still time for you to continue learning what you need to learn."

A strange feeling, a sense of something not right overwhelmed her. "I would really like to get this over with as soon as possible."

Natyis smiled at her like a father would smile at his child. "I understand. It is difficult to be so far from home for so long. But as long as you are here, you are welcome to make Arkeereon your home."

She stood and went back to the chair, returning the smile gratefully. "Thank you."

"You *are* welcome. Thank you for allowing me to see again, though I noticed it required quite an effort on your part."

"I don't understand why my mana hindered your sight to begin with."

Picking up his teacup, he took a drink. "Perhaps you hide how you truly feel, and as a result hide more than you mean to. But that no longer matters. My sight is restored, which gives me peace now that I can watch over the things I cannot be present for."

She knew he was talking about her mission. Standing, she placed her teacup back on the tray. "Thank you for the tea. I should go. I have a few things I would like to do."

He nodded, said nothing, and watched her leave.

Tnasha soon found herself back at the temple. She knocked first, then entered, only to find Annah waiting for her. "Something isn't right. When I was helping Lord Natyis regain his sight, I felt something. I can't explain it. Like something isn't right!"

"Perhaps you feel you are in the presence of forces that were once meant to betray you."

She narrowed her eyes and sat down on the ground next to Annah. "Who? Morvack?"

With a look of confusion, Annah shook her head. "No. The Angorans. You must not worry about that any more. They mean you no harm."

"What do you mean?"

"All you need to know is that everything that has happened and will happen was supposed to happen. You will be thankful it did."

"If I survive it."

Annah placed a reassuring hand on Tnasha's shoulder. "I told you. You will."

Tnasha gave her a wry smile. "Let what happens happen?"

The sorceress stood. "Oh, I know. It sounds so simple. But you will do what's right. As will everyone else. Now you must meditate longer for strength and resolve. I will leave you, for Morvack has returned and I wish to be near him."

She shook her head and tried not to share her thoughts even though she knew Annah already knew. How a woman like Annah could love a man like Morvack baffled her. With a shrug and a sigh, she went back to meditation in hopes that Annah's observations and foresight were correct.

The following day Tnasha practiced protecting others until she nearly fell from exhaustion.

Ronove hurried up to her, helping her to her feet. "You must rest. Here, take the staves and get a feeling for them. Tomorrow you will learn to use these. All of you shall. That way we will know who has the ability to use them."

She took the Eagle's Talon. A vision, clear as day, of Seth and Alax sitting inside a room, came to her. She opened and closed her eyes a few times. "This staff really is a seer's staff. Perhaps we should give it to Lord Natyis. Maybe then he will never have the misfortune of losing his sight when someone like me comes along."

Unannounced, Natyis entered the room. It was anyone's guess how long he'd been standing there. His voice came at her from doorway. "While it is tempting, I think it best you take it with you. *You* may need more help than you know."

"But..." Tnasha hated not knowing what he obviously knew.

"Don't argue with me, child. You will take it with you. The matter is settled."

Her eyes followed him from the room. She turned back to the others in disbelief. "Does he know something we don't?"

The question was met with a dozen nods and several shrugs. She realized then she had asked a stupid question. Of course Natyis knew. Just like Kalath had always known. Male seers, though rare, were quite powerful. She took the staff and retreated to her room. Wanting nothing more than rest, she got into bed and fell quickly to sleep. The dreams came more clearly.

She stood, overlooking the cliff. Soldiers came, wearing their battle garb, with great broad swords affixed at their sides. They were Sirus. Oron stood next to her, looking out over the water.

"This is too soon," he said.

Suddenly, she felt her body thrust back into a vortex and all that surrounded her vanished into a blur. She felt as though she were falling- backward into an abyss. The grey blur around her turned black. She found herself standing on a beach. Palm trees rose high above her. Looking around, she saw Zul. It looked distant and far away. She ran toward the city. It moved away from her, and suddenly, she stood at the entrance to the palace. It loomed high above her and glowed a deep red. The sky, varying shades of black, swirled above her. Whipping winds rushed around her. She was nude. Covering herself, she ran into the palace. Before her stood a maze. A deep crimson light emerged from one of the hidden passages and Seth appeared, with another sorcerer at his side. He held the staff. Tnasha reached for it. As she felt her arm and hand stretch as far as they could, she heard a sharp snap and a blate of mana ripped into her like a bolt of lightening. She bolted upright, feeling the sweat pouring down her face. Fighting to catch her breath she stared into the dark room around her. "Help me," she gasped. Her own voice sounded distant, yet she knew she was screaming because the door opened and Oron and Arick, both shirtless, entered. They hurried to her side.

Oron put his hand on her knee. "Are you all right? We heard you screaming."

"I was having a nightmare." She turned to him, wiping the sweat from her neck. "I was screaming?"

"And thrashing about," Arick said with genuine concern.

She took several more deep breaths and settled back into the bed. "It was just a nightmare. I'm sure it was nothing." Looking over she saw the staff. The black stone crowning it glowed gray.

Both men's gaze followed hers, finally settling on the staff. "What?" Oron asked.

"The stone was glowing gray, as if there was a white light inside it."

"You need to rest. It is very important you are alert when we leave." Oron pulled the blanket up over her shoulders, wrapping it around her and tucking it in.

She laughed. "I cannot believe you just tucked me into my bed."

He smiled and laughed. "I'm sorry."

Arick shook his head. "He has a daughter a few years younger than you."

"You don't tuck her into bed, do you?" A wide grin spread over her lips. She closed her eyes.

"I cannot help myself. I feel the need to stand watch over you."

"To protect me?"

He and Arick stepped out into the hallway. "Yes, to protect you," he said, closing the door.

The following morning she woke to breakfast brought to her room, and afterward, she made her way to the armory to use the staves. She sat against the wall, allowing the others to use the Crow's Foot while she studied the Eagle's Talon. The wood of the staff was smooth and lacquered with a substance that gave it a shine. The talon itself was cast of high polished silver that did not seem to tarnish. And finally, the stone, Black Onyx, was polished so highly she could have used it as a mirror if she wanted to. When she held the staff, the visions came. At first she fought them back, but finally gave into them and allowed them to surface. The minute she saw anything clearly she fought the visions back again. They were always frightening.

She closed her eyes and held it. The same visions from her dream the night before returned to her. She pulled them back and forced her eyes open. Once again, the stone glowed eerily with the gray light. Aithian approached her. "Can I see it?"

With a shrug, she handed it over, watching his face as he held it. He pulled back a little. "You see it too, then?" she asked.

"I had a flash of something. People." He handed it back to her and shook his head. "A little uncomfortable, I think."

"You have to shove back the staff's power and direct your thoughts. Then let the vision come to you," she said, rubbing the stone.

"Shove it back?"

"It will show you what it wants to show you unless you direct it," she tried to explain.

"Oh." He clearly didn't understand.

She motioned toward Ronove. "I think it is your turn with the Crow's Foot."

She watched him. Berith threw a blate at him. Aithian merely held the staff in front of him and the blate missed him completely, fizzling to nothing in mere seconds.

Ronove grinned. "It looks like one or two of you could carry this and you would be protected. Which means her range of protection only needs to spread out far enough to protect the rest of you."

Tnasha yawned. For as much sleep as she had the past week, she did not think she should be as tired. "That is still bound to make me tired."

"Our hope is you can hold Seth off long enough so we can disarm him. We will throw blates at him in rapid succession. The Raven's Claw cannot project mana as broadly. Its focus will be specific." Ronove lifted an eyebrow. "Hopefully it will be aimed at you."

"How is everyone else doing at protecting themselves?" she asked. She hoped at least one of them was able to protect himself.

"They can each protect themselves from small blasts of mana. But not a concentrated attack."

She sighed heavily. "I just hope I can live up to my expectations."

Lucas snickered. "I hope you can live up to ours."

"That's not fair, is it?" Aithian asked angrily. His expression softened when he turned to her. "Don't worry, Tnasha. I'll try to help myself as long as I can."

"Thank you. See?" she asked Lucas. "Chivalry is not dead."

He rolled his eyes. "So who gets the Crow's Foot?"

Ronove left the staff in Aithian's hand. "Aithian seems to have the widest range with it. He will most likely be able to protect himself and possibly several of you. Let's test it."

While they tested the Crow's Foot, Tnasha put her attention back on the Talon. She found it amusing the Crow's Foot, when held, could protect them from blates. What were the chances that with the weapon sat a literal good luck charm. While the second staff, when she touched it, gave her visions. She thought about it. A weapon, a protection, and a seer stone. The perfect magical defense against a sorcerer's war. Whoever made the items had made them to be used with one another. Not against one another. It was doubtful she would have use for the seer stone unless she wanted to find out where Seth was hiding once they arrived on Zul. That fact alone made the staff she held invaluable.

Ronove approached her. "Well it works. Now what does this one do again?"

"I'm really surprised your people left them in Ramathra. They were a complete defensive set. They were never meant to be used against one another."

"Well, now they will be."

"I know. The only thing this does is help one see, and it's supposed to help project mana further, but I think that has to do with seeing, too. The more mana I put through it, the stronger the visions are. Evidently, I have a gift for it because I have been able to manipulate its powers. With it I will be able to find the exact location of Seth when we arrive on Zul."

"May I?"

She handed it to him. "Feel free."

Sitting back, she lost herself in thought while the others worked with the staves.

Her attention fell back on them.

"It's like a flash of something then nothing," Aithian said.

"It is settled then. Tnasha will use the Eagle's Talon. She seems most adept at *seeing* with it."

CHAPTER 45

Alax settled in to the room he once occupied as a child. Mourning loss was not something he felt comfortable with. A sorrowful sigh emerged from his lips and hung in the air in front of him. Poor Morvack and Gavgal, he thought. A sudden smile played on his lips as he imagined his brothers in the realm of the Unnamed. They were with *Him* now, most likely serving Him still, for all eternity.

Now, he and Seth were the only survivors of their family line. Seth was much stronger. Though not as wise as Gavgal, and certainly not as empathetic as Morvack, he decided. He wondered then how Seth would manage to make his plan work. After all, there were only two of them. Both Arkeereon and Danaria boasted a larger population of sorcerers. Even with the Arkeeronish on their side, converted against their will, they would still be outnumbered. What if the Arkeeronish rebelled at the last moment? He shuddered at the thought.

These were concerns he would bring to Seth in the morning. Now, he was too tired to do much of anything. He fell into bed, exhausted, and quickly fell to sleep.

Morning came too soon. He found himself waiting for the morning meal with Seth in the sitting room. Too many questions were left unanswered. "I was thinking last night," he started carefully. He did not wish to anger Seth.

"Do not strain yourself, brother."

Sibling rivalry first thing in the morning did nothing to calm his growing fear that Seth was in a bad mood as usual. "If the Arkeeronish, once we convert them I mean, decide to rebel when we attack Sherok or Danaria…"

"Not if we have their women and children as our assurance that they will cooperate. They will comply with our demands or we will kill their precious children first." Seth looked out the window with angry, seething eyes. Then added with a sneer, "In front of their mothers."

Alax's eyes went wide with horror. "That seems harsh."

"But necessary. Do you know what your problem is, Alax? You're just like Morvack. Too faint-hearted and weak. That is why *I* will be the one to do the planning."

"If they feel they have nothing to lose they may not care. And we would still be outnumbered."

"Are you trying to be the voice of reason?" Seth sat down. "What you don't seem to understand is the Arkeeronish bloodlines are much older. Do you know what that means?"

Alax shook his head. He did not.

"It means they are more adept. They could help us fool Danaria in some way. Cause the Danarians to falter. Then we will take Danaria's sorceresses and children, bending them to our will. Blood. Blood is the bind that ties them together. Even warriors who have killed thousands in cold blood have families."

Alax nodded in agreement, knowing his brother did not have a perfect plan. But he held his tongue because he knew if he said anything, Seth would become enraged.

Seth's expression softened. "Besides. We have the staff. The weapon. Not even their anomalous fifth generation sorceress. Their *strongest* sorceress. Not even *she* could withstand my attack. The weapon increases the power of my blates. What makes you think the others could withstand it any better?"

Alax did not answer.

"Let us discuss something else. I tire of this subject. There will be plenty of time to plan. They have no knowledge of what we intend to do." He looked at his brother with a forced smile. "How are things going in Exavia? Have the remaining heathens been driven out?"

"Yes."

"And how is the king?"

"Concerned. Though I believe I have eased his mind about his faith and our alliance. When things did not go as planned in Sherok, and he lost his son, Hermond, his faith faltered."

Seth scowled as he poured himself a glass of wine. "You handled that well."

"I thought so," said Alax. Little did Seth know that Alax's mind was not on Exavia. Instead, he tried to make sense of his brother's plan in hopes he could find a more reasonable way to make it work.

The uncomfortable silence seemed to make Seth nervous. He began fidgeting with the seam of his tunic. "You seem upset."

Alax let out an exasperated sigh, which he quickly tried to hide as a yawn. With his hand to his mouth he said, "I'm thinking."

"About what?"

Alax's hand dropped to his lap and he lifted his eyes warily. "I can convince people the sky is always black if I wish to. Perhaps we could convince the Arkeeronish that the Danarian's wish to wage war on them. Bring them to our side somehow. We don't want to destroy them if we don't have to, right? Sorcerers above humans, and you above sorcerers?"

Much to his surprise Seth did not fly into the violent rage he expected. Instead, his brother lifted an eyebrow and nodded slowly. "Exactly. Don't forget your place beside me in our new world, Alax. Your plan might actually work. I'll keep it in mind."

Threatening to push his good fortune, Alax continued. "Or perhaps we could convince them…"

Seth held up a hand to stop him. "The first suggestion was a good one. Let us leave it at that for the day."

Alax nodded. "I suppose you're right. I worry too much. Perhaps we should go to the dining hall for the morning meal." He smiled at his brother.

Seth nodded in agreement. Together, they left the room.

CHAPTER 46

The passage of another week led them to that morning. Verrine, a calmly man with dark hair, a thin crooked nose and brown eyes, handed each of them a vial containing an herbal mixture. The thick, syrup-like liquid inside shined a brilliant green. "Drink this first," he said.

Tnasha scrunched her nose in disgust. "It looks unpleasant."

Oron coughed. She noted the empty vial in his hand. "You think it looks unpleasant, you should taste it."

"I admit it's not the best flavored concoction, but it is highly effective," Verrine assured them with a smile. The remaining sorcerers emptied the vials with bitter looks of contempt. With the vials now empty, Verrine reached into the bag of roots, handing one to each of them. "Place these in your clothing."

When he handed Tnasha the root, she examined it. It looked like a dog dropping. She frowned and stuck it into a pocket in her tunic. Pulling it out partway and gathering the other's attention she said, "I have dog droppings in my pocket!"

A wave of laughter rose and fell. Verrine shook his head. "The root should greatly impair another sorcerer's senses. Including your own. You will have to be alert so you do not mistake one another as the enemy."

Tnasha nodded, still choking on the sharp medicinal taste of the potion. She smacked her lips together, realizing

Verrine was right. Feeling uneasy, she realized she was not aware of their mana, something most sorcerers must take for granted. It was, after all, one of the simplest ways for a sorcerer to identify a stranger or friend. "How can I transport all of us if I have no feel for them?" Her eyes went directly to Ronove.

"I suppose you will have to use your imagination and visualize all of them."

With a heavy sigh, she turned to Natyis who handed her both staves. She passed the Crow's Foot on to Aithian and gripped the Eagle's Talon tightly. Her eyes traveled over the sorcerers. She closed her eyes. Natyis' face flashed in front of her. Her eyes flew open. "This isn't going to work. I can't concentrate."

"Close your eyes," Ronove said.

She did as she was told.

"Now ignore us. Repeat the incantation several times to focus yourself and then force your will into it."

With eyes closed, she repeated the incantation beneath her breath. Her delicate features trembled slightly, her breathing sounded louder. She could hear her heart beating in her chest. The incantation fell faster from her lips as she dove into Morvack's mind where he concentrated on a secluded spot on the Island of Zul. She did not see what he saw, but she could feel what he concentrated on. An impression of a place. The impression coursed through her body with feelings of safety and contentment. Isolation. When she felt comfortable enough in her own concentration, she forced her will, extending the violet light of her mana around them. As if they were mere impressions themselves, she and her companions vanished in a fizzle of rainbow colored light.

Upon opening her eyes, Tnasha looked around. She counted heads. The dark forms of Aithian and Lucas stood to her left, while Morvack, Oron, and Arick stood at her right. They were indoors, that much was clear. A heavy thump, followed by a loud crash indicated that one of them knocked up against something, sending it plummeting to the floor.

"By Natyis!" she whispered through clenched teeth. "Where are we?"

"Sorry," Morvack said quietly. She heard him draw in a deep breath. "I think we are in my quarters within the palace."

"You idiot," came Oron's voice through the darkness.

She heard a slap. Morvack responded quickly. "It was an accident, I'm sorry."

"Stop bickering, *now!*" Her voice emerged scolding, like a mother. She listened to the silence.

"Seth should be in a nearby room," Morvack finally said.

She held her hand upright in front of her, closed her eyes and imagined a cool fire burning in the center of her palm. An orb of violet light appeared, casting little light on anything except the faces of the men around her. "Is there a lantern in here?"

Morvack hurried to the bedside, took a lantern from the table and brought it to her. She lit it with a spark of violet mana. The room lit up, and it was not as large as she imagined. They stood crammed next to one another. Directly in front of them stood the bed, and she could see clearly the table that one of the men had knocked over. She looked at Morvack hopelessly.

"I'm sorry," he said again.

She looked toward the door behind him, listening for some noise beyond it. Hearing nothing, she turned her attention back to him. "We're in the heart of enemy territory. What do we do now?"

He shrugged.

"He did it on purpose!" Oron said with narrowed eyes. "We should never have agreed to bring him with us."

"I did no such thing. My mind must have wandered." Morvack's eyes pled with them to believe him.

"Wandered into a trap?"

"Will you two stop? Right now." Tnasha could not believe her ears. They were in danger and Oron wanted to argue. "I believe it was an honest mistake. My mind can wander just as easily."

Oron set his jaw.

She continued on, her eyes threatening retaliation if they started to argue again. "Two of you will need to stay here to keep watch while the rest of us venture outside the room."

"Leave Morvack here," Oron said with distaste.

"No. We need him so we can navigate the palace."

"Let's leave Aithian and Arick here," Lucas suggested.

She thought about it for a moment. "We cannot leave Aithian here; he has the staff to protect all of you."

"We can protect ourselves. It's when we get back, that Aithian can use the staff to make sure we get away."

She thought about it quickly and made the decision in haste. "All right. Oron, Morvack and Lucas will come with me. Aithian and Arick can stay here, take up the rear if need be and help us escape. We don't know if that table crashing to the floor drew any attention or not."

Morvack shook his head. "If it did, someone would have been here by now."

"How are the guards usually placed?"

"Outside the palace in the courtyards usually. Gavgal only allowed a few trusted guards in the palace. Seth however... being a soldier, he's likely better prepared."

"Where would Seth be sleeping."

"Probably in Gavgal's quarters. It's the largest sleeping chamber in the palace."

"What is your impression of large?" Lucas asked, looking around the small room.

"Three times the size of this room."

He snorted. "That's not large. That's a proper room."

Oron said nothing. Instead, he continued to glare at Morvack.

Tnasha tried to cut the tension with another practical question. "Which side of the palace is that room on?"

"Another corridor entirely. But it isn't more than several hundred foots lengths down this corridor."

"Would anyone else be here, in this hallway?"

"The only other rooms in this corridor are empty. Unless he has company."

"Like Alax?" Oron asked.

"Possibly. But I don't see why..."

Tnasha took hold of the Eagle's Talon. "Instead of assuming, perhaps I should use this. We did bring them, after all."

The men quieted, watching her. She held the staff to her chest and closed her eyes. The images passed quickly. She willed them to slow down and tried to force direction on the corridor to find out if anyone else might be present. In her mind a vision formed. A man lay sleeping only rooms away. "He sleeps heavily. It is a sorcerer."

"See? That's why I asked," Oron said. He rolled his eyes at Morvack.

Tnasha opened her eyes as the stone lost its gray light and dimmed back into black. "Look, if you two cannot get along, I'm going to leave both of you in here and the rest of us will go."

"If I recall correctly, no one here is in charge. This is an effort we *chose* to help you with." Oron's tone was arrogant.

She felt the anger swell in the pit of her stomach. Oron was pulling rank. She decided to pull some leverage of her own and met his tone. "I'm in charge here. You knew that when you agreed to come."

"Then perhaps you do not need our help at all."

Arick shook his head. "Oron, just stop it."

"This is not the time to be bickering. I realize you came here voluntarily, but by Natyis, I will not put up with the snide comments and bickering. If we can't get along then we can't stand together. And if we don't stand together, we *will* fail."

Lucas sighed and opened the door carefully. "She's right. Let's go. We don't have time for this."

With reluctance, Oron followed them through the doorway and into the corridor, closing the door to Morvack's room behind them.

Tnasha held the staff in front of her, making every effort to keep her boots from making noise on the marble floors. She wished the corridor had carpets. As she approached the third door on the left she stopped and motioned them forward. "In here."

"We cannot attack Alax," Morvack whispered. Horror filled his voice.

"Why not? He is just as guilty."

Tnasha shook her head. "No, he's right."

"He always is."

"That's not what I'm saying. I'm saying we are here to get the weapon back. That's all. We assumed we would have a confrontation. We may and we may not. Lord Natyis' idea to come here at night was perfect. We can get the weapon and get out."

She searched their eyes for agreement, but found none. Even she doubted they would have such fortune. Nonetheless, they continued past Alax's room, further down the corridor and down another corridor on their right. When they finally reached the door, they stopped. In silence, they listened for footfalls coming from either direction, relieved in hearing none. Tnasha used the staff again. This time to look beyond the door and into the room where Seth was. She was not happy with what she saw. While Seth slept, he was restless. The staff lay beside him on the bed, beneath the blankets so that no one could take it without disturbing him. She lowered the staff and opened her eyes.

"What is it?" Oron's mistrust of Morvack seemed to vanish.

"He sleeps with the staff, and he does not sleep heavily," she said in defeat.

Morvack took a step toward the door. "It's my fault he has it. So I will be the one to go in and get it."

"That's a stupid idea." Tnasha said abruptly. "He'll have it out and poised at you in seconds. You would not survive."

"You could protect me."

A sinking feeling engulfed her. Something was not right. She felt it. "He's awake."

She motioned them for silence. It was too late and she knew it. For Seth had been standing at the door, staff in hand, listening. So it did not surprise her when the door flew open. At first, a look of shock adorned his face, but soon after his mouth contorted into a vile grimace.

"I should have made sure you were all dead." Seth eyed Morvack. "And much to my dismay, I was right that my brother had become a heathen."

"You tried to kill me. What choice did I have?" Morvack's voice turned to a growl. "Give me the staff."

Seth narrowed his eyes. "Alax!" he called down the corridor.

"We killed him," Tnasha lied.

Seth saw right through her attempt. "Nonsense. You aren't a good liar. But it is possible I have use for you."

Much to their chagrin, Alax came around the corner half dressed, wild eyed and surprised.

"Summon soldiers," he ordered.

Alax held his hand to one side of his mouth. "Guards!"

The echo of footfalls resounded through the corridor and Alax started toward them. When he saw Morvack, he looked at Seth, confused.

"He has switched sides. I did not have the heart to tell you," Seth said in a voice that seethed with anger.

Alax's expression turned sour. A look of betrayal fell over his face.

"Great plan," Oron whispered in her ear.

"Don't start," she said through clenched teeth. Once again her eyes met Seth's. "Are you going to kill us?"

He narrowed his eyes. "No. Alax gave me an idea earlier. I believe I have other plans for you. All of you."

Tnasha's mind raced back to her training. Nothing in it had prepared her for a situation like this. She truly had no idea what they were going to do.

It was then that Seth noticed the staff she held. "You were planning to switch them while I was sleeping." He let out a laugh, cold and void of emotion. "How cunning."

Morvack stepped forward, only inches from Seth's face. "There are four of us, and two of you."

"I have the staff, Morvack. Stand down before I use it on you."

He continued his challenge. "We survived your first blate."

"I've had practice since then. Besides, if I recall correctly, it knocked all of you unconscious the first time. Which means that I could easily kill you with the second blate."

With a sudden jerk, Morvack threw his weight forward, knocking Seth into the door. It flew open, sending both men to the floor. As they struggled, Oron grabbed Alax and shoved him up against the wall, placing a dagger to his throat. Tnasha hurried into the room, trying to pull the staff from Seth's grasp, without losing hold of the Eagle's Talon. He did not loosen his grasp. Instead, he held on tightly, shoving her away and knocking her off balance. She fell to the floor. Lucas drew his sword.

An onrush of guards hurried through the corridor with swords drawn causing Oron to lose his grasp. In his own desperation, he threw a blate and the guards fell, like rocks, to the floor. Alax freed himself, and threw a weak blate at Tnasha and Lucas knocking them back. Seth stood victorious.

"I do not want to attack you with sorcery, Seth. Give me the weapon," she said. She heard her voice quiver, noticing her legs followed suit.

"I hear the fear in your voice." He lifted the staff to eye level.

She could feel it building in him. A strong blate of deep orange mana. She closed her eyes. Just as the blate emerged from the crown of the staff, it met the wall, knocking the wind from her nonetheless. She staggered back, gasping for air.

From the ground, Morvack pulled himself up, throwing a blate from behind Seth at close range. Alax sent a blate at Morvack. Not strong, but strong enough to make Morvack pause. Tnasha did not realize they would be fighting in such close quarters. None of them did.

Seth tried again. He built the blate more quickly this time. Just before it came forth from the now orange stone, Tnasha had an idea. She closed her eyes focusing on her friends, and the staff. She uttered the incantation. The sound of the blate surfacing from the stone hit her ears. Just as it stretched out far enough to reach them, the staff, and four heathen sorcerers, vanished in front of the Kersian Sorcerer's eyes leaving behind a trail of brilliant color that dissipated into nothing.

Seth stood beyond rage now. His eyes glowed deep orange with mere black slits for pupils. "Find them!"

The beastly sound of his voice sent a stinging chill up Alax's spine.

Tnasha opened her eyes and saw the blate still coming toward her. She pushed her will forward, blocking it, then fell exhausted in a heap on the floor. Her breath became shallow and she felt Aithian kneeling beside her.

"We have to get out of here, quick!" Oron locked the latch on the door.

"She needs a moment to recover," Aithian said. His voice seemed distant.

Arick bent down and picked up the staff, handing it to Lucas who immediately put his foot on the crown for leverage. The wood shaft of the staff split with a crack. With a few twists, he separated the staff from the crown, handing the wooden shaft to Arick. "I will take this part, you take the other."

Voices came at them from down the corridor. "I can feel him," Seth snarled. "Morvack!"

Tnasha stood, leaning on Aithian for balance. Aithian held the Crow's Foot in front of him, ready to block any final blates. "How can they feel us?" she whispered.

Morvack's quickly patted himself down. "I lost the root, probably when I fell. He can sense *me*."

"What are you worried about, we have the staff..." Oron's voice trailed off when he noticed Arick holding the staff, and Lucas grasping the claw and stone in one hand. "Never mind."

"I can only send several of us at a time," she said, still fighting to calm her labored breath. With an outstretched arm, she pulled Morvack near Aithian and Lucas. She closed her eyes.

"Tnasha, no," Aithian said. A sense of sadness and hurt filled his voice.

She imagined the great hall in Arkeereon and focused on them. Before Aithian could stop her, they vanished into thin air. She intended to send them back to Arkeereon as well. But as she concentrated, what she wanted more than anything came into her mind. Home.

The door broke open; splinters of wood flew at them. Oron and Arick huddled close to her.

Seth breathed in, his mana seething violently, moving quickly around his body. He threw the blate. As they vanished, she felt the blate hit her in the chest. She held onto the Eagle's Talon, feeling her nails bite into the smooth wood. A vision entered her mind. It was Graneck.

When she opened her eyes for that brief moment, many startled faces stood over her. Oron and Arick were with her. The darkness dragged her down into its depths and everything went black except the pain in her chest that seethed an orange glow and shot pain down her spine. Then she went numb, succumbing to the darkness closing in on her.

CHAPTER 47

"**I**'m concerned." Luithian paced Natyis' chambers wringing his hands. "Aithian is not eating."

"Did Berith and Flery destroy the claw?" Natyis' vision had returned completely now, and was even stronger than it had ever been. He knew they had.

"It was dropped in the middle of the West Ocean as you instructed." He stopped in front of Natyis, barely aware that Eury stood in the doorway. "What about my son?"

"He has a broken heart. What do you expect?"

Luithian shook his head. "She took his heart and stomped on it."

"She was preoccupied with the task given her." Natyis looked up at him and smiled. "He will not die from a broken heart, Luithian."

"Our son's are lonely. They will never know love. Never have families." Luithian could not mask the trace of bitterness in his voice.

"What can we do?"

"We can talk to the Danarians and negotiate a peace treaty with their daughters as assurance," Eury said from the doorway.

Natyis knew it wouldn't work. "They would never agree to it. They do not need peace from us. We have left them alone."

"Then what do you suggest?" Natyis asked, perplexed.

"We could kidnap her. Her power would be useful in defending our city."

Eury entered the room. "We cannot do such a thing. We would risk waging war with a kingdom of warriors. I realize you have Aithian's best interest at heart. Perhaps what we should allow is Aithian to travel to Danaria to seek her out in the proper manner."

Luithian narrowed his eyes and gazed into the fire.

"Let it be, Luithian. If it was meant to be, it shall be. We cannot force fate to our will."

Luithian nodded and strode from the room. He knew Natyis was right.

"Should we be concerned?" Eury asked.

Natyis shook his head. "No."

Eury grew quiet, watching Natyis. It seemed to him Natyis always knew more about their future than he cared to divulge. It bothered Eury, and at the same time, comforted him. Natyis always knew when to take action, and in that alone, Eury had faith. He left the room quietly, shutting the door carefully behind him, leaving Natyis to see.

•

Aithian stared into the courtyard outside his chamber window. His thoughts had not left her. But hers had left him. He had to face it. She did not feel the same way he did. Just then, he felt Lucas come up behind him.

"You can't keep on like this, Aithian. You'll kill yourself."

"She sent me away knowing exactly what she was doing."

"To protect you."

"Out of fear."

"To protect you," Lucas repeated, annunciating every word. "You cannot dwell on it. Let her go."

"I can't. You don't understand because you have never been in love. I need her."

Lucas backed up, noting the strange look in Aithian's eyes and the underlying pain in his voice. A state of Aithian's emotions he had never seen before. "You're starting to scare me. You have lost your grasp on reality."

Aithian stood and looked him straight in the eye, and in the practical tone Lucas heard him use so many times he said, "She and I will be together..." His voice trailed off. "Some day. Would you like to place a wager?"

As if nothing had happened at all, and without another word, he stepped past Lucas and left the room. Lucas watched him leave, speechless and agape.

●

Morvack and Annah sat in the garden holding hands. "Do you think they will kill me now?" he asked.

Beautiful laughter emerged softly from her throat. "You amuse me, Morvack. Why would you think such things?"

He leaned in close to her, putting his arms around her. "I want to marry you. I love you."

She smiled up at him, returning his embrace and resting her soft head of black hair on his shoulder. "I love you, too. I want to marry you. But I fear you must ask my father's permission."

He pulled back and looked into her eyes. "What do you think he will say?"

Again, that beautiful laughter emerged. "I don't know. But if you ask, perhaps you will find out."

Morvack smiled. For the first time in his life, he truly knew what it meant to love and be loved.

CHAPTER 48

"**W**e have searched the entire island, My Holy Liege." The guard bowed deeply, and stepped back with downcast eyes.

Seth growled and looked over at Alax, who stayed a pace behind his brother. "We have lost everything because of you," he snarled.

Alax hung his head in shame. "Please forgive me, Seth."

Seth whirled around, shoving him in the chest. "Walk with me."

Following, Alax remained a pace behind.

"If you had not slept so deeply you would have realized they had broken in!"

"I, I did not sense them," he stammered, recoiling in case his brother shoved him again.

Seth turned to him, sensing Alax's fear. The growing knowledge that his allies were already thin forced him to calm himself. "I'm sorry I became angry. Of course you did not sense them; they used sorcery to hide themselves from you."

A deep sigh of relief escaped him. "But we lost the weapon," he said in a small voice.

A light went off in Seth's dull eyes. "It can be replaced. Another sorcerer made the weapon, and there is no reason we cannot make our own. In the meantime, I believe you and I should take wives."

A look of confusion washed over Alax's face. "There are no sorceresses…"

"There are plenty of sorceresses." He put his hand over Alax's shoulders, leading him into the sitting room to a table with a waiting bottle of wine. "You know what I think we need around here, Alax?"

He shook his head, still confused.

"The laughter of children." He took the stopper from the bottle and poured two glasses of wine. "And two beautiful women. You are the one who can make this happen. Get your things packed and be ready to leave next week. You are taking a trip."

"Where?" he asked. His stomach tangled into a mass of knots.

Seth handed one goblet of wine to his brother. "To the Onyx Mountains, of course. You are going to find two sorceresses and convert them. It is your greatest skill, after all."

CHAPTER 49

After the physicians took Tnasha away, Graneck pulled Oron and Arick away from the crowd of curious onlookers. Tnasha and her two companions caused quite a stir appearing in front of the altar in the Temple Dagon during the annual spring Rite to Aithian.

When he was sure they were alone, he glared at them. "Did you receive my message? Please tell me you did not kill her!"

They met his inquiry with looks of confusion.

Oron leaned in toward him. "She was struck in the chest with a blate from the Kersian Sorcerer Seth."

Arick shook his head. "We decided to use our own judgment about the sorceress' disposal. We decided it was not necessary."

A deep sigh of relief poured over Graneck. "Thank the gods."

"I must admit. I am disgusted we agreed to do it in the first place," Oron said. "It is a sad day when the Angoran people resort to such things just to feed and clothe our families."

Arick nodded in agreement.

Graneck narrowed his dark eyes. "I expect you will not tell anyone."

Caitlan's voice toned cold and angry from behind him. "I know. And now half of Danaria knows. You bastard."

He turned to her, holding out his hands to stop her. "You don't understand. It was not *them*." He forced a smile, hoping her anger would be redirected. "It was the Kersian Sorcerer."

A low growl escaped her throat and her attention turned to the Angoran sorcerers. "Is this true?"

"Yes, High Priestess." Oron bowed his head politely.

"I am going to see her." She looked down at what Arick held in his hands.

"May we go?" Arick asked. "We have to know how she is."

She furrowed her brow and pointed at the staves. "What are those?"

"The Eagle's Talon was given to her by the Arkeeronish. The other," he said, lifting the broken staff. "Is the remaining piece of the Raven's Claw. It is my task to bury it where no one can find it."

"Come then," she said, eyeing both suspiciously.

As they left, Graneck called after them, "Does she know?"

Caitlan turned to him with an angry glare. "Instead of wondering whether she knew of your plan to destroy her, perhaps you should contemplate our marriage."

●

The presence of mana woke her. She choked and tried to open her eyes. From afar, Caitlan's voice came to her. "Don't try to move, Tnasha. You have been injured badly."

She tried to speak. "Oron and Arick." Her breath rasped from her throat.

"Shhhh. They're here and they're fine. See? You're safe now." Caitlan brushed away the strands of auburn hair back from Tnasha's eyes.

"Will I die?" she asked in a small voice, using every ounce of will just to move her eyes to see them all.

A tear rolled down Caitlan's cheek. "You have a severe elemental imbalance. The physicians are hoping your body will heal itself. You must rest."

"The staff," she whispered.

Arick knelt beside her, putting the Eagle's Talon in her hand and closing her fingers around it. "Here is the Eagle's Talon. The Raven's Claw has been destroyed. I will bury the staff where no one will find it. Lucas took the claw and stone to drop in the ocean."

She tried to smile, but her face would not move. She was too weak.

Caitlan patted her hand gently. Her voice drifted further and further away. "You should rest. Your body needs strength to heal."

Once again, the blackness surrounded her. Her last conscious thought took her into her dreams. In them, she and Aithian sat upon a beach bathed in full moonlight. He wrapped his arms around her and kissed her gently on the forehead. "Don't leave me," he whispered.

She looked into his deep blue eyes and smiled. "I won't." ■

www.ingramcontent.com/pod-product-compliance
Lightning Source LLC
Chambersburg PA
CBHW071250250626
47163CB00002B/400

* 9 7 8 0 9 6 6 9 7 8 8 9 6 *